THE RED GHOST AND A CHOCOLATE BUNNY

Mark D. Trollinger

Published by Myths and Malts Productions Chandler, AZ

The book is a work of fiction. The author drew the characters, incidents, and dialogue from his imagination and did not construe them as real. Some events from the original cryptid sightings have been retold, modernized, and at times, fictionalized.

This book includes the use of trademarks for realism. Product names, logos, brands, and other trademarks featured or referred to within this manuscript are the property of their respective trademark holders.

These trademark holders are not affiliated with the author or any of the author's representatives. They do not sponsor or endorse the contents, materials, or processes discussed within this book.

Drink responsibly and do not drink and drive

If you or a loved one need help with an alcohol problem, please reach out to SAMHSA's National Helpline: 1-800-662-HELP (4357).

The author will donate 15% of the sales from this book to the Phoenix Indian Center in Phoenix, AZ. I will make donations quarterly. See the Field Notes section at the back of the book for more details.

Cover by Nyssa Iniguez
Library of Congress Control Number: 2023907945
First Edition, first printing

Printed in the United States of America

ISBN: 9798988082828

also by Mark Trollinger

Texans Investigating Mysterious Entities Series:

The Chupacabra and the Bat Rastard

Champ and a Bit of Sunshine

The Red Ghost and a Chocolate Bunny

The Loveland Frog and the Narrow Path

Tegan Stone and the Gibson County Beast

The Ringdocus and a Guy on a Buffalo

Other Books:
Corrè

TABLE OF CONTENTS

DEDICATION

To my family: My lovely wife Susana, and kids: Karmina and Jorge, and my mother-in-law, Lydia. My mom, Dr. Linda Burcham, my late father, Doug Trollinger. My grandparents: Ray & Ginny Burcham and Mary Lou & Marvin Trollinger.

I also want to dedicate this book to Scott, Mekala, & Jason from Freetail Brewing for being the first to have me come out for a book signing. To Loren Coleman of the International Cryptozoology Museum in Portland, Maine, for being the first to plant the idea of a book tour in my head. In addition, to Derek Hayes for including me in the August 2018 Cryptid Crate box.

To Tim Brehm and Aaron Kauffman for the encouragement and discussions (and criticism), Ronda Keys and Marsha Cole for the continued support. I am glad the Traveling Trio rode again for a brief weekend in Palm Springs. To David Landau for the marketing discussions, ideas, inspiration, and later, in your memory, my return to running. Rest in Peace, David.

ACCOLADES

The Red Ghost and a Chocolate Bunny won Honorable Mention in the category of Fiction > Supernatural - Supernatural Creatures & Beings at The BookFest Awards Spring 2023

CHAPTER 1

NIGHTFALL IN GOLDFIELD

Thursday, March 10, 2016

Sunset. Every town has one, but few can match the majestic palette of Phoenix. It is one of the most magical moments of the day. A time where the strongest words aren't enough to describe the collection of colors melting together: deep pink, brilliant orange, vibrant yellow, noble purple, and a variety of blues all swirling together, melting over the burning, bouncing ball of orange fire as it sinks into the dark cool water of the night.

It was 6:35 p.m. and the Goldfield Ghost Town once again was deserted. Once a bustling town that had struck gold in 1892, an initial strike believed to have been worth as much as three million dollars, Goldfield emerged on the map of the Old West, drawing prospectors to the area. Subsequent strikes continued to support a vibrant population growing to over four thousand people, even threatening to outshine and outgrow nearby Mesa, as the fifty mines within its district appeared to have a lasting promise of wealth. Luck can be a fickle lady. As quickly as the town rose, it declined because of a break in the gold vein. Without the promise of wealth, the town's population rapidly declined and within five years, Goldfield went dark. There were multiple attempts to reopen the town from 1910 to 1926, but because the mines never returned to life, they were unsuccessful.

Today, travelers to the area visit to get a feel for its old western past as a commercial Ghost Town brought back to life, complete with recreated buildings, period characters, a mine tour, and tales of a lost treasure in the Superstition Mountains. However, this time of night, the tourists were gone, the stores closed, and even the saloon and workers at Lu Lu's Bordello had called it a night.

Low-beam headlights disrupted the quiet darkness of the uninhabited village and the slow crunching of tires on gravel as a lone vehicle pulled into the deserted parking lot. A car door closed, and from the parking lot a figure emerged walking the dusty, dirt road through the makeshift town.

Leland Swacker, a man small in stature with white hair on the sides, and a messy brown cut on top, stopped and scouted the scene. He had a broad face with a sharp and long chin, adorned with a bushy mustache of mostly gray, but holding on to some last remnants of brown. Tired from a busy day working at Carter Brothers Manufacturing, an ornamental and architectural metal products manufacturing company, he started trudging up the hill toward the old church.

He landed two large job contracts this week, putting him in the running for Employee of the Month just two weeks into March, but he couldn't take time to celebrate his recent successes. He had to work on this week's project for his digital photography class from Mesa Community College. His instructor frequently praised his work for its creativity and artistic beauty. Leland hoped that a degree in digital arts would help make his future retirement from Carter Brothers a little easier. Besides, he enjoyed taking photos, especially of the beautiful Arizona landscape. The old 19th century church at sunset with the backdrop of the Superstition Mountains would be the perfect subject for this week's assignment.

Leland's mind pondered the possibilities of being a hired photographer, maybe one day being lucky enough to get a contributing job at Arizona Highways magazine. Even though retirement was about ten years away, it was an enjoyable thought. He prepared, as best he could, through contributions to his 401K plan and supplemental payroll deductions direct to an extra savings account that might one day replace his above-average salary at Carter Brother's Manufacturing. The photography would keep some money coming in, but its main purpose would be to ease boredom and keep his mind active. It was a pleasant thought that helped keep him going when work was slow, contracts fell through, and the boss was in one of his frequent unpleasant moods.

Even at his slow pace, his tired feet kicked up dust and occasionally small rocks from the dry road that hadn't seen rain in months. The night was peaceful as he approached the old church; a quiet evening with perfect temperatures, a slight breeze, and the beauty of Mother Nature as the sun was now almost completely below the skyline. He smiled, watching the colors changed minute-to-minute as the sun continued its journey. He walked a little further around the hill to capture the old wooden wagon next to the church, and then back toward the eastern side where he captured the front of the church from different angles; the metal bell from its steeple glowing as the remaining light bounced from its curved edges.

Satisfied with his efforts, Leland began walking down the hill toward the car before it became too dark to see. He paused in the middle of the main area of the little town and then took a couple of quick photos of the bordello and saloon while there was still an opportunity to capture the last of the sunset's rays.

It was a reconstructed town, but it was still an enjoyable and a highly recommended stop for any visitors spending more than a day in Phoenix. Basking in the town's beauty for a moment, he closed his eyes and tried to imagine what it might have been like living here during the town's heyday in the late 1800s. The smell of the wildflowers, the warmth of a spring evening, and the gentle breeze took his mind away from the busyness of the earlier day. He soaked in the sensations and embraced the comfort of the waning light and peaceful silence of the ghost town.

He snapped back to the present and began walking toward the car, the muffled grind of his shoes against the gravel being the only sound in the small village. The saloon was the furthest building in the back of the town. He walked past the bank, the bordello, an old jail, and stopped across from the water tower marking the entrance to the town center. As he plunged his right hand into the pocket of his jeans to retrieve his keys, he heard a noise. It sounded like a distant rattling, like metal buckets falling and clanging together. He jerked his head to one side, trying to make out the source of the noise. Uncertain, he turned, as the sound appeared to be coming from behind him. The rattling grew louder, into a thunder followed by a loud bellow and several rumbling roars. The hairs in his mustache tingled, a feeling he frequently had when something wasn't quite right. Recognizing the sensation, he stopped and turned around as the feeling of nervousness and a small dash of panic alerted him to nearby danger.

Almost immediately, the source of the sound was upon him. It was a creature, but he didn't have time to make out what it was. With its speed and proximity, he could only determine it was a gigantic beast. With the limited light, he thought he glimpsed red fur, but it was only a blur. He raised his arms and wildly snapped several reactionary photos in the general direction of the charging creature.

He gasped loudly, perhaps even emitting a near-yell as the culprit leaped past him. The rear hooves grazed him and kicked up a cloud of dust as it disappeared into the distance. Leland stopped in his tracks, his mouth wide-open in shock, and his mind discovering it an impossible task to interpret the sudden blur of motion that just occurred before his eyes. Even though the event only lasted mere seconds, it was enough to cause his forehead to dampen and his heart to race. As he tried to shake off the fright and resume his journey to the car, his breathing labored, and he placed his right hand over his heart. He felt its pace quicken and the muscle tighten. He bent over, his hands resting on his knees like a gassed linebacker. His left arm tingled, and he found it difficult to catch his breath. Suddenly, he dropped to his knees in the dusty street of the Old West mining town. Seconds later, he collapsed on his back.

He had one last thought as he laid in the street, looking up at the stars now beginning to appear in the dark sky, back to the days when the town was a booming mining town. He wondered how many others had laid on this dusty trail awaiting their last gasp. The current town had reenactments of gunfights, but in the old days, those events were regular occurrences, and they were real. His mind floated to the chorus of Bon Jovi's Blaze of Glory. Unlike the song, it wasn't a gunshot that caused him to meet his demise. His was less glamorous, even though he didn't know what the exact cause was. He didn't get a good look at it because it was too close, but he knew it was a creature. Something living, and something big and fast.

Like the evening sky just an hour before, the light dimmed in Leland's eyes. He took in a breath, then remembering the words of Metallica, looked to the sky just before he died. It was the last time he did.

Early the next morning, there was a positive energy in the offices of Carter Brothers Manufacturing. The sales department was off to a great start this month and on pace to beat last month's sales record, thanks to solid performances from the entire staff, but especially Leland Swacker's two new long-term contracts. Leland and the client signed the paperwork on Tuesday, and the owner, Jeff Carter, reviewed and approved the deal yesterday.

Jeff wanted to show his appreciation to the team for their hard work and stopped on his way to the office to purchase a few boxes of celebratory donuts to welcome Friday and the upcoming weekend. After several months of struggle, it appeared as though the recession was over and construction jobs were increasing in Phoenix, and that was great news for his company. During the deepest part of the recession, Jeff faced several unwelcomed dilemmas. Problems whose solutions seemed to increase the likelihood the company may face closure, ending a dream started in 1955 by his father, Jefferson Carter. He had to lay off a few workers, temporarily freeze merit pay increases, and put expansion plans on hold for a couple of years, but now things were looking brighter.

He was proud to see the hard work Leland had been putting in was finally paying off. Not only for his personal success, but also in creating an example for his fellow employees. Leland's strong ethical background, always listening to the customer's wants, and his knowledge of the company's product line represented characteristics Jeff wanted all of his staff to possess. Leland's good natured and caring approach earned him the trust of the client, and he ensured that after the sale he would always be available to answer questions or help with any follow-up the customer needed.

Jeff considered making Leland a Team Lead, an official mentor for newer reps. He was certain Leland would appreciate the modest increase in salary that would come with the title. He planned to make it official today in the office after coffee and donuts. Besides the donuts, it was casual Friday and payday. It was shaping up to be a great day.

Arriving at the office just before 8:30 a.m., Jeff pulled into his reserved parking spot and walked to the front door. The staff turned to greet him and their eyes lit up, seeing the boxes of donuts in his hands. Regardless of a person's age or socioeconomic level, a box of donuts brings smiles and motivation to an otherwise mundane daily grind. Especially on Friday.

Jeff placed the boxes on an empty table in the break room and one-by-one employees filed in to greet him and claim their donut. Some took two rather than wait, just in case donut demand exceeded their expectations. Soon, the entire department was in the break room. Jeff made small talk with some of the earlier entrants. He planned to say a few words, thanking everyone for their hard work and to congratulate them on the success. He knew the company's performance was because of the employees and acknowledging that publicly would show his appreciation.

He scanned the crowd as he continued to talk and noticed Leland was not present. He became slightly distracted in his conversation as he continued scanning the break room. It wasn't like Leland to be absent from work or to arrive late. In fact, Jeff couldn't recall the last time Leland called in sick or took a vacation. He finished his conversation with one of the newer sales reps and turned to address the crowd.

"Good morning," he began, as the break room murmur subsided. "I ran the weekly and monthly numbers yesterday, and I just wanted to thank everyone for their hard work over the past few weeks. It's still early in the year, but so far, we have experienced some of the best months in the company's history. January was a big month for us. Better than any month in 2015. We topped that in February by posting the highest monthly revenue total. We're only two weeks into March, but we are on pace to surpass last month's sales. I appreciate everyone's dedication."

He paused and scanned the crowd as a light smattering of applause grew into a more fulsome praise.

"I wanted to single out someone for their recent efforts. We received long-term commitments from two major customers just last week. Those contracts will ensure steady production needs throughout this year and next."

The group's applause grew in intensity.

"Where–where is Leland Swacker?" he asked, searching the crowd and peering through the break room glass wall and into the office sales floor.

Employees turned toward each other, mumbling in quiet conversations, asking each other if they had seen Leland today. A woman from the middle of the group spoke up.

"Um–I haven't seen him today," said Jessica Wheeler, a six-year employee who sat next to Leland.

"Really? That's unusual," said Jeff. "Has anyone heard from him? Maybe he had car trouble this morning and is running late?"

Heads shook as no one in the break room had information on the whereabouts of Leland Swacker.

"It's okay. I will catch up with him later. Someone let me know if he calls or comes in. Please stay and enjoy the donuts," Jeff said as he made his way through the clapping crowd and exited the break room, heading for his office.

For some reason, Jeff had an uneasy feeling about Leland. It wasn't like him to be late for work. He returned to his office, closed the door, and sat down in the leather office chair behind his desk, his thumb and pointer finger stroking his chin, as he attempted to search his memory for details about Leland. He knew Leland was single and lived alone. He never really mentioned family or friends when they talked. It was always about work, except on the rare occasion when he talked about photography.

He elected to try another route and clicked a button on his desktop, awakening the computer. After typing in his password, the computer was ready for use. He looked at the unorganized collection of files and folders on his desktop, then located and clicked a program containing human resource records. Typing in Leland's name, he found the contact information he was looking for: home address, cell phone number, and home phone.

He glanced at the demographic fields and confirmed his memory that Leland was single. Looking over other information on file, he found the data to be limited. He wasn't sure why he had a bad feeling in his stomach as he thought about his long-time employee, but there was no denying he felt it, and it was intensifying. He clicked on the benefits tab on the website, but it was equally ineffective. It showed Leland had not selected supplementary life insurance or disability coverage offered by the company. Jeff had hoped he could find a beneficiary's name. Someone he could contact to check in on Leland, but there was no information.

Jeff's mind turned to relationships within the office. Who was Leland close to at work? He didn't want to be the one to call him, thinking it looked bad if the boss were calling to check in if he were only running late, or worse if Leland had mentioned a personal appointment previously that perhaps Jeff forgot to write on the company calendar. A call coming from a friend from work would be better, he thought.

However, while Leland was friendly with everyone, Jeff couldn't recall anyone that he was close to outside of work. He thought for a minute and called Jessica Wheeler's desk.

"Yes, sir," she answered, seeing the owner's name on the caller ID display. "Oh, and thank you for the donuts. It was a nice way to start the day," she added.

"You're welcome. I appreciate the hard work, and it is a good way to lead into the weekend. Say, anything more on Leland this morning?"

"No, nothing, sir."

"I'm getting a little worried. Are you close to him? Do you have his phone number?" he asked.

"I don't think so, sir. He is my Facebook friend, but we rarely communicate online, and I have never called him, but he might have the number listed on his profile," she suggested optimistically.

"I have his phone number, but I thought it might be better for someone from the office to call him. You know, instead of the owner."

"I understand. If you give me the number, I can call it," she said.

"Thank you, and thanks for mentioning Facebook. I completely forgot about that. Maybe I could see if there is any activity on his page to show where he might be," Jeff replied. "Here're the numbers."

"Thank you, sir. I will call each right now," she said as she wrote the numbers down on the stack of yellow Post-It notes on her desk.

As he hung up the phone, he typed in the URL address for Facebook and searched for Leland's profile. Jeff found the profile, but again, there was minimal. Less than one hundred friends, and most of them were from a photography group. He had friends outside of the hobby, but the profile did not contain any recent conversations. The only activity was a photo uploaded last night of the church in Goldfield just before the sunset. A caption read *Beautiful evening in Goldfield. Working on a project for class.* The image had eight likes and one comment simply reading, *Beautiful!*

At least we know where he was last night, Jeff thought to himself.

The ringing phone interrupted his thought process. It was Jessica calling him back.

"Sir? I called both numbers, but got no answer. I left a message on each for him to call me back. I will let you know when I hear something," she said.

"Thank you," Jeff said as he hit the button on the speakerphone, ending the call.

His mind raced to hospitals and police officers, but he dismissed it as being too soon. He elected to give some time for Leland to hopefully either come in or return Jessica's calls.

The day continued, but without the positive energy from the early morning. By mid-afternoon, with no word from his employee, Jeff phoned the non-emergency number of the Mesa Police Department.

"Good afternoon. Officer Ryan Downing speaking, how may I help you?"

"Yes, officer. My name is Jeff Carter, and I am the owner of Carter Brothers Manufacturing over on Country Club Drive. I don't know if there is an issue, but one of my employees did not report for work this morning and it does not fit his nature. Another employee called all the numbers we have on file, but there was no answer. I don't know if it has been long enough for a missing person report or not, but I didn't know where else to check. For some reason, I have an uncomfortable feeling. Like I said, it's not like him to miss work," reported Jeff.

"Thank you for contacting us, Mr. Carter. There are many misconceptions about these types of investigations. For instance, people believe they must wait a certain length of time to report a disappearance. This isn't true. There's no time limit. Often quick reporting leads to finding the individual in most cases," replied Officer Downing. "You should exercise common sense and exhaust other means before filing a report. By that, I mean first contact with family and friends of the missing person to ensure there was not a miscommunication, traffic delay, or other reason for the disappearance. Check hospitals and the local jails. And make every attempt to contact and locate the missing person before filing a report," the officer stated.

"Yes, we attempted to reach out. Our records show no known family members, and he doesn't seem to have many friends. I have not called the hospitals yet, and I didn't think about jails. I looked at his Facebook activity, but there is minimal information. The last thing I saw was a photo of a church he took last night out at the Goldfield ghost town," responded Jeff.

"Goldfield is out in Apache Junction," replied Officer Downing. "Call the PD over there and see if they have anything. Maybe if he was out there after dark, they picked him up for trespassing or something," suggested Officer Downing.

"That's a possibility I had not thought of," said Jeff. "He's a really exemplary employee and I have been unproductive today thinking about him. Hopefully, you can locate him, or he turns up and returns our call," said Jeff.

"Right. That's the hope. Since Goldfield is the last information you have, I suggest you call them and file the report. Give them his name, description, and any information you have on him. Do you know what type of car he drives? We can look up the registration and get the details," said Officer Downing. "Since there is concern, you should file a report. Any search for a missing person must begin where the person was last seen as law enforcement jurisdiction responsible for that area is best suited to conduct any search. If foul play is involved in the person's disappearance, then the jurisdiction where they disappeared will probably handle the subsequent criminal investigation," he concluded.

"Foul play? God, I hadn't thought of that! I will call over to them and file the report now, but I don't think I am going to get anything accomplished in the office today, so I will probably leave soon," Jeff said.

As soon as he ended the call, he typed Apache Junction Police Department into an internet search and located the number to file the missing person report.

Later that evening, two Apache Junction police cars pulled into Goldfield's gravel driveway to investigate the last known location of Leland Swacker for any clues. Officers Mickelson and Gomez exited their vehicles and walked toward the town's entrance. Arriving at the scene, they spotted a light gold 2004 Kia Rio alone in the parking lot. Cautiously approaching the vehicle with flashlights in hand, they looked through the vehicle's windows, but did not see a body or any signs of suspicious activity.

"Let's call this in and get forensics to come out and dust for prints," suggested Officer Gomez.

Officer Sarah Gomez continued walking toward the ghost town as Officer Tony Mickelson called dispatch with the information on the parked Kia. Officer Gomez did not have far to walk until she spotted the body of Leland Swacker.

"Tony, we have a body," she called out to her fellow officer.

Officer Michelson updated dispatch with the finding and requested contact with the medical examiner's office.

While awaiting forensics, Officer Gomez walked around the body, searching for evidence. The trail was dusty, making it difficult to look for footprints. Officer Gomez noted the deceased man had a camera. Perhaps the camera contained clues of an altercation. Forensics would photograph and document the scene and collect the evidence upon arrival.

When the forensic team arrived, Jonathan Daniels approached Officer Gomez.

"Some mess you've got out here," Jonathan said.

"Yeah, not how I thought the evening would go," replied Officer Gomez.

"We're going to run a Hexagon OBTI test. It's simple to use and we can get results in about three minutes. At least that will tell us if the blood sample is human or animal," Jonathan replied.

"Animal?" asked Officer Gomez.

"Well, since you found the body, you can never be sure what happened before you arrived. Might be coyotes or something out here," replied Jonathan.

The forensic team completed the incident scene search using a circular approach. They discovered hair and fiber samples on Leland's jacket, located his camera, and found some blood from scratches likely incurred during the altercation. Fifteen minutes later, Johnathan walked back to Officer Gomez.

"Well, the results are interesting," he said.

"Some of the man's blood is present. Looks like it is from a cut that he suffered during the attack. However, we found some animal blood too. Unsure what kind of animal it is so far, but we can narrow it down back at the lab. We found his camera at the scene. We will have the boys at the lab check that out, too. Perhaps we will get lucky and discover the old man captured his attacker in a couple photos. Even if they are blurry images, we might make out some details that can point us in the right direction," replied Jonathon.

Concluding their investigation of the scene, the examiners dropped a white blanket over the deceased man.

"Let's bag him up and get him to examination back at the lab," ordered Officer Daniels.

CHAPTER 2

QUINCE

Friday, March 11, 2016

The music from inside the recently renovated Pearl's Banquet Hall escaped into the stillness of the night as late-arriving guests opened the door and entered the building. Other guests stirred in the lobby, snapping pictures in the rented photo booth and talking with friends away from the energy and loudness of the main reception area. Inside the hall, dozens of guests enjoyed the quinceañera, or *fiesta de quince años*, the cultural celebration of a Latin American girl's transition from childhood to young womanhood.

Following the Catholic tradition, the Mass portion of the celebration occurred earlier in the day at a local church in Chandler where the parents, godparents, and court of honor accompanied the Quinceañera. The quinceañera was the party, and the Quinceañera was the girl.

They devoted this portion of the day to the celebratory reception where the events to honor the young woman take place, beginning about an hour prior when the family introduced to her the guests in a grand entrance in the first part of a traditional six-part reception. She wore elegant jewelry, makeup, and wore a formal evening dress, a traditionally long, elegant ball gown in pink and black chosen by the girl and her mother. The second part of the reception was the formal toast to the birthday girl by family and guests. The third part was the first dance, which traditionally represented the young woman's first public dance, a waltz with her father. After dancing with the father, the family dance included a waltz involving only the immediate relatives, the boys in the Quinceañera court - or *chambelanes* as they are called, godparents, and the closest friends of the girl.

The surprise dance was the next component in the reception; a dance rehearsed for several weeks by the Quinceañera and her chambelanes to be unveiled during the party. Finally, the formalities concluded with the general dance open for anyone in attendance.

Other celebration included many traditional ceremonial components. Among them, the ceremony of the Change of Shoes, in which the father presented the Quinceañera with her first pair of high heel shoes and *la ceremonia de la ultima muñeca,* or ceremony of the last doll, during which the father presented her with a doll wearing a dress similar to the one she wore.

Afterwards, the Quinceañera and her chambelanes enjoyed dinner while a hired DJ played music. After finishing her meal, the chambelanes escorted her to a chair on the main floor where a mariachi serenaded her. Some people danced to cumbias played by Banda La Finikera while other people visited a table containing *dulces* and *chucherías* made by the Quinceañera's mother.

The band played *Viva Tepupa*, their final number in the first part of the set. The band members, wearing black pants and a black dress shirt, danced and played their instruments while the lights reflected off their sequined blazers. After the energetic song, the lead singer announced they would take a brief break before finishing their time.

The Banda members left their instruments on stage and walked out of the back door into the alley behind the building. A couple of members smoked cigarettes while discussing the party and going over the songs they would play after the break, while others enjoyed the break to take in some fresh night air.

Two young musicians walked further down the dark blacktopped alley, a narrow path barely wide enough for a single car.

"Great turnout tonight," said accordionist Octavio Arias.

"Yes, bigger than last weekend's show and they are really enjoying the music," said Charlie Muñez, a recent addition to the band's trumpet section.

"We have about another thirty minutes and will start with *Besos y Cerezas* when we return," said Octavio. "How do you like playing in the band so far?"

"It's been a great few months," Charlie said positively. "I'm finally getting settled in my apartment and more familiar with Phoenix. So much to explore and the weather is perfect," he said.

"Don't let it fool you. It will warm up, but nine months of the year, it is great. However, those couple of months in the summer the temperatures are unreal. When I first moved here and someone told me it had been over one-twenty the prior year, I thought he made that up. But no, it happens. There isn't the humidity we had back in Texas, but that also climbs during monsoon season," replied Octavio.

They continued to walk behind Pearl's until they came to the concrete retaining wall with a large black metal door.

"What do you think is back there?" asked Octavio inquisitively.

Walking closer to the gate, Octavio lifted the latch, and the door swung open.

"Looks like a small park," Octavio replied as he sauntered through the gate, with Charlie following behind him.

The park was an open, grassy area mostly covered in darkness, except for a streetlight on the northeast corner of the park. The men could see there was a small rim surrounding the park. Octavio recognized it as a stormwater retention basin, one of three hundred and seventy acres of open parks and basins maintained by the city of Mesa. The men heard a rustling noise on the far side of the park and turned their attention, peering into the darkness to find the source.

It surprised them to see what appeared to be an enormous creature grazing on the sparse grass in the park. The men stared and struggled to make out details.

"Is that a horse?" asked Charlie. "It looks like a horse."

"I don't think so," responded Octavio. "I don't know what it is. Does it look like it is kinda glowing to you?" he asked.

"Now that you mention it, it seems to have a faint glow," suggested Charlie. "Kind of like a haze or something, almost like a red aura."

"Yes, and the eyes look like they are glowing. Like embers from a fire," Octavio said in an uncertain tone.

The gate closed with a suppressed but audible *Clang!* causing both men to turn and look behind them. The sound caused the animal to stop what it was doing, raise its head, and look at the visitors. It stared at the men, and the men at the creature. Charlie squinted his eyes and tried to get a better look at the strange animal.

"It looks like, how do you call it? *Un camello*?" asked Charlie.

"Yeah, a camel. However, there are no camels here. There are wild horses around the Salt River and down around Wild Horse Pass, and wild donkeys at Lake Pleasant, but no camels," said Octavio bewilderedly.

"Unless the circus is in town or something. Maybe one escaped?" questioned Charlie. "But it has that weird glow and it looks like something is on its back. What the heck is it? It looks like it has glowing eyes, too. Yellow ones. Is it a man?"

Before they could make out any details to answer their questions, the animal turned around and leaped off into the darkness. The men looked at each other, trying to decide if they should stay near the assumed safety of the metal gate or try to identify the creature by giving chase and getting a better look. They rushed to the sidewalk at the basin's edge where maybe a streetlight could cast enough light to get a solid description. By the time they made it to the street, the animal was gone. They peered into the now quiet darkness of the neighborhood, trying to locate the animal once again. Just then, the band's manager called them to come back to the party, breaking the night's silence.

Octavio and Charlie rejoined the group and walked back in to resume playing the last songs of the night, but their minds were elsewhere. Despite the performance, neither man could forget the thing they saw during the break. After the band wrapped up for the evening, they exited to a small room in the back of the reception hall to return the instruments to their cases and talk about other scheduled events over the upcoming weekend.

Walking through the parking lot back to their car, the two men tried to piece together what they saw earlier, the brief encounter still stuck in their minds. It was uncommon, but not unheard of, to encounter horses in parts of Phoenix. There were farms around town, and even a few houses in Chandler, known to keep horses in the yard. They were certain it wasn't a horse. When the animal looked at them after the gate closed, they could see it had an elongated neck, which is why Charlie thought it was a camel, but that would be unheard of in Phoenix, and he didn't know anyone who rode camels. Not here anyway.

"I have no answers for what we saw," said Octavio. "It was certainly something unusual - a mysterious beast."

"A beast... It was definitely an animal, right? We're not making that up?" asked Charlie.

"Yes, I don't know what it was, but it was an animal. However, it was glowing - and that thing on its back was glowing. I don't know what that was. Some kind of entity?" pondered Octavio.

"A mysterious entity - that's what kind of entity," said Charlie.

He paused, his mind racing through answers while reflecting on their conversation.

"Mysterious entities," continued Charlie. "We may not be familiar with mysterious entities or can say what that thing was, but I think I know someone who might," he said optimistically.

"You do? Who?" questioned Octavio.

"This guy from Texas. Mysterious entities. That's what he does… Well, it's a hobby of his. He was my physical therapist when I lived in Austin. That's how I met him," revealed Charlie.

"Physical therapist? What happened?"

"I used to play tight end for the Huston–Tillotson University Rams. I suffered a knee injury in the last game in 2015 against Bacone College Warriors from Muskogee, Oklahoma. They were one of our biggest rivals. They would leave the Red River Athletic Conference after that season. That game also turned out to be the end of my playing career. I was a junior, but the surgery prevented me from playing my senior season. I had weekly physical therapy sessions with Kareem for several months. We talked about football, college, and just general life things. He also talked about something he had started with a group of friends. He invited me to like a page on Facebook where they started calling themselves *Texans Investigating Mysterious Entities* toward the end of the year," Charlie recalled. "That definitely fits, don't you think? I know I have seen nothing like it, but maybe he has, you know, because he's put himself out there to look for those types of things," suggested Charlie.

"Um, yeah, I guess, but how would you even explain it? We do not know what we saw," asked Octavio.

"I don't know. But maybe just talking through it he will identify it," Charlie pondered. "We stayed in touch online for a while after I stopped with the sessions. He's still on my friend list, but we haven't talked or messaged since I moved here."

Charlie removed the cell phone from his jacket pocket and scrolled through the contact list.

"Yes! Kareem Ortiz. I do still have his number," he said, looking at the phone's screen. "What do you say? Let's see if he's available," he said, looking up at Octavio as he hit the *Call* button on the contact card. "Daylight savings time starts on Sunday, so right now he should be just an hour ahead of us now and hopefully still awake," he said as the phone rang.

"I forget about the time change since Arizona doesn't observe it," said Octavio.

"I am still getting used to not changing the clocks. I will have to remember my family and friends in Texas will have a two-hour time difference after the weekend," replied Charlie.

After three rings, a voice answered.

"Hello? Charlie?" answered Kareem, looking at the caller ID after hitting the accept button.

"Yes, it's me! How have you been, Kareem?"

"Doing well. Just about to leave the office," replied Kareem.

"Office? They got you working this late at the clinic now?" asked Charlie.

"No, actually I have cut my hours back with the practice. I still see the occasional patient, but things have been picking up with something that started as a side project last year," Kareem said.

"Side project? Is that the creature thing you told me about?" asked Charlie.

"Yes, it's been just about nine months, but man, you wouldn't believe how many calls we get to investigate things. I started out last June just thinking we were going to have a fun weekend getaway, drink some beer, and relax, but it didn't turn out that way at all. The things people are seeing are real, mostly. We went to San Antonio in June, Burlington in October, and have had a few calls around central Texas. We get more calls than we can investigate. Some turn out to be bogus, but a lot are real," Kareem replied. "So, what's new with you? How's the knee? Did you graduate?"

"Yes, I graduated in December and the knee is doing fine. Good as new, I think. I don't really test it out much except on the treadmill and a few trail runs. Got a job in Phoenix and moved out here after graduation. I picked up a side gig making extra money in a Banda. We actually just finished playing a quinceañera last night," Charlie reported.

"Banda? That's great! I'm glad to see you recovered from the injury and enjoying the life and culture in Phoenix. I haven't been there in a long time," replied Kareem. "What instrument do you play?"

"Trumpet - finally putting those middle school music classes to use!" he said. "So hey, speaking of phone calls and people seeing things," he paused, "that's why I am calling… One of my bandmates and I were walking around during our break tonight and we saw something. Well, to be honest, we don't know what we saw. But it was unusual, and I remember you talking about going out with your friends down to San Antonio."

"Unusual? What did you see?" asked Kareem.

"Well, it was dark, and it was at a bit of a distance. Across a small park. Whatever it was, it was large. At first, we thought it was a horse. It was close to that size and it looked like it had a guy riding it," started Charlie.

"So an animal? A horse wouldn't be too unusual in Phoenix. I remember seeing some of them the last time I was there. I actually met a guy riding one down those canals they have there while I was out running one morning," replied Kareem.

"That's what we thought at first, but it wasn't a horse. There was a little light from a streetlamp and we made some noise, which caught its attention. The animal looked at us and something really stood out… it had a long neck. Not like a horse, but more like… a camel," added Charlie.

"A camel? That is strange. I don't know of any camels in Phoenix," said Kareem.

"We didn't either. That wasn't the weird thing. The animal glowed. Like an aura around it, and it also had glowing eyes.

You know in sci-fi movies where there is some volatile molecule, and it's radiating and glowing? Kind of like that. Whatever was on top of the animal looked like a rider, and it had yellow eyes that radiated, too," said Charlie.

"Wow, that's…" Kareem's voice trailed off. "I don't know what you saw, but that's a wild description. I have heard nothing like it. You said you were at a party. Any drinking? Maybe sleep deprivation?" asked Kareem.

"No, not really. A couple of Bud Lights, but not enough to even get a buzz," said Charlie.

"Man, I have no clue, but I am intrigued by the description. I know you and trust you. I just don't have an answer for you, but let me search online. See if there are similar sightings in the area and run it by my friends. Did it seem dangerous?" asked Kareem.

"I don't know. It was just eating grass and didn't even notice us until the gate closed and made noise. Then it raised up, and the three of us, or four of us, just looked at each other for a while before it finally ran off. It didn't attack us, so I don't know how dangerous it is. Like most animals, maybe it was just scared of humans and ran off," he said.

"This rider. Did he say or do anything while it was watching? Maybe he told it to go?"

Charlie looked at Octavio and asked him if he saw or heard anything. Octavio shook his head.

"No, we heard nothing and didn't see him move or command the animal," reported Charlie. "But like I said, it was dark."

"I don't know. But I will check it out for you and follow up in a couple of days," said Kareem.

"Thanks, man. I knew you've seen more than me, so I thought you might know. As you said, just wondered what it was. But it was great talking to you, and if you are ever out in Phoenix, call me and we can get together for some drinks or something," invited Charlie.

"Yes, that would definitely be nice. I hear Phoenix is really coming up in the craft beer scene. I would love to check it out someday," said Kareem.

"Definitely! There are a lot of places and some excellent beers out here. I will introduce you!"

"Sounds good. Talk to you soon," said Kareem as he clicked the *End* button.

Mid-Saturday morning in Austin, Kareem was still thinking about Friday night's conversation with Charlie. Walking in the door of Friends & Allies Brewing Company, he sat in the corner at one of the wooden tables in the taproom and reflected on the conversation. As he sat down, the bartender automatically poured a pint of Noisy Cricket session IPA, a recent favorite new discovery of Kareem's since stopping by the brewery the past few weeks. He walked it over to Kareem.

"How's the rock climbing?" asked Jaxson.

"Oh man. I know I've only been going to the Austin Bouldering Project for two weeks, but that rock climbing kicks my ass. I definitely need to hit the weights and build up more body strength, especially in my legs," Kareem admitted.

"I have only been once or twice, but it was pretty cool. I need to go more often. It is the largest bouldering gym in North America and it's right down the street. No excuses, really," Jaxson replied.

"If nothing else, it works up a powerful thirst, and this Noisy Cricket does the job of satisfying it," responded Kareem as he took an initial sip.

It was a lightly hopped IPA with a hint of fruit and a clean, dry finish. It was a nice cap to an afternoon of physical challenge. Still struggling to learn the basics, Kareem found the climbing classes were a good mix of instruction, fun, hard work, success, failure, laughter, and maybe the occasional cuss word. And it was next door to a brewery? That was a pleasant addition to his normal workout activities and allowed him to see some minimal gains in a short time. He always enjoyed challenging himself to learn new things, and he was glad his friend Miguel talked him into trying it.

As he took a sip, his mind pondered the creature that Charlie saw. He turned to his phone and Googled strange sightings in Phoenix. It returned many results ranging from aliens, unexplained lights in the sky, a winged humanoid, the token Bigfoot sighting or Mogollon Monster up closer to the Grand Canyon, a giant turtle man creature, and a recent report of a giant bird-like creature named the Santanimal that chased a poor local author.

"Nothing about unusual camels," said Kareem. "It doesn't look like the circus is in town," he said, looking at the events calendar.

Wild horses were the only thing that he could reconcile with the description of the animal. He knew they existed in

Phoenix, and that might explain the lack of sightings online. Unless it was just too early yet. Charlie called him just hours after it happened. What if that was the first sighting and there is more to come? His impression of Charlie, having spent so much time with him, was that he was an honest kid. If he said he saw something, then he saw something. But what? A horse wouldn't be unusual, but it might be unexpected for him. One wouldn't expect to see one in the city, especially someone who was new to the city and not familiar with wild horses. However, something prevented him from simply writing it off as a horse in a park. He felt it was time to close his tab and return home, where he could research a little more deeply and comfortably. He motioned to Jaxson for the check.

CHAPTER 3

NANANANANA (BATMAN)

Saturday, March 12, 2016

The sun set on a wonderful spring Austin evening as Carson Quinn walked to a table with a beer in hand. It was a pint of Electric Jellyfish IPA for him and a twenty-two-ounce bottle of Commissar with an accompanying pint glass for his friend, Tyson Carr. Still in the upper sixties, it was perfect patio weather to watch the sunset and attempt to get a glimpse of the bats from the nearby Congress Street Bridge. With the beer delivery complete, Carson turned his attention to the Via 313 food truck in the parking lot. He ordered a Gorgonzola and fig preserve Detroit-style pizza called The Cadillac to share with Ty.

They could get a closer look at the bats from the observation center on the other side of the river, or even better, one of the riverboat or kayak bat watching tours, but they usually saved that for the tourists. Craft Pride offered the best of everything: a nice patio, close to the office, delicious pizza, and cold craft beer. Usually on Saturday night, live music played until midnight. The new T.I.M.E. office at 603 Davis Street was a short walk to Rainey Street. Since moving in, Craft Pride had become a regular after work happy hour spot for the team of cryptid investigators.

Fifteen minutes later, Descendants of Erdrick took the wooden stage behind the building. Pizza in hand, Carson rejoined his friend. He pulled out a wooden chair with his right foot and sat down to enjoy the music and the evening.

"Sorry about coming into the office today. I know it sucks on a Saturday," Carson said.

"It's cool. We've had a lot of calls recently," Ty responded.

Carson took a sip of his beer. "This might be the best IPA in Austin," said Carson.

"It's hard to beat a beer-and-pizza combo after a day of working in the office," replied Ty. "The new office is in a great location and the new assistant is working out so far. Business is busy. Just having someone to answer the phones and keep us organized is a tremendous help. Who knew things would take off this quickly? Not even a year after we went to San Antonio and we are presenting at conferences, speaking at colleges, writing articles, and investigating cases."

"Yes, Jourdyn has been great. We are lucky to have her. Mysterious and unknown animals might scare a lot of other people off, but she's a trooper and gets along with everyone on the team," replied Carson.

"I am sure she didn't expect the things she hears about when she answered the ad. It's not every day you come face-to-face with things that you may have thought were only urban legends," said Ty.

"She's jumped up to speed in just the one month that she's been on board. Running the phones can be tricky because there are so many prank calls. She has a pretty good bullshit detector when people call in with stories," said Carson. "Can you imagine how much more we would have to look at if everything got through?"

"I don't even want to think about that," Ty said with a chuckle as he poured a little more of the Blanco, TX-based Imperial Stout from the bottle and into his glass. "But our personal social media sites are still getting bombarded. At least mine is."

"I thought you were going to delete Tinder," Carson snarkily replied.

"Not that site. That's blowing up on a whole 'nother level," Ty shot back. "But I wish I could get people to stop sending me stories about ghosts. I tell them that's not what we do, but I still have to run through them," he said.

"Definitely not our field. I get some ghost stories too, and I had one story sent to me about a mermaid. I don't think I am going to read that one either," replied Carson. "But there are some good eyewitness reports out there. I got one from Ohio and I heard Tegan say she was checking out a story around Mount St. Helens. Who knows what else is out there that people are seeing?" asked Carson rhetorically.

Carson's phone rang. "Oh, hey, it's Kareem. Maybe he can join us?" he stated as he hit the answer button.

"What's up, buddy? Where you at?" Carson asked.

"I am just leaving the house. I've been doing some research all morning after a call I received yesterday. Where are you? I was thinking of taking a break and grabbing a cold one," Kareem said.

"Ty and I are down at Craft Pride just having a pizza and a couple of beers ourselves. You mentioned a call, anything wrong?" he asked.

"No, nothing like that. It was a call from a former patient of mine. He moved to Phoenix a few months ago. He and a buddy play in a band and he said they saw something last night that they couldn't identify. They were a little shaken from the experience. You guys mind if I join up with you? I can explain it more when I get there."

"Come on out. We'll be here a while. Have you heard from Tegan? Maybe get her over here and we can make it a party," replied Carson.

"I haven't talked to her today. I will call and see what she's doing. If she's available, I will pick her up. See you soon," he said as he hung up.

"That's intriguing," said Carson. "Apparently Kareem received a call with a lead. He seemed excited about it and already started researching it. He's picking up Tegan and coming here to tell us about it. Stay tuned for more on that, I guess," Carson said into the glass as he raised it for a drink.

By the time Kareem and Tegan arrived, Ty finished the bottle of Commissar, Carson was ending his second Electric Jellyfish, and looking over the menu for more options, because the pizza was a distant memory.

"Hey, guys," said Tegan excitedly as she and Kareem pulled up two chairs. "What's up?" she asked, greeting each man with a hug.

"Oh, Carson and I were just talking about WrestleMania 32. It's in a couple weeks up in Arlington. We were thinking about going and making a long weekend out of it," said Ty.

"Yep. I love AT&T Stadium and April 3rd is just around the corner. I think we need to check it out. I mean, it's WrestleMania!" said Carson.

"Tickets are probably expensive, but I would go," said Kareem.

"You could always watch it on the giant television if you're in the nosebleeds," replied Tegan. She thought about it for a second. "What the hell. I'm in too," Tegan said as she stood back up and headed to the bar.

"I will check on the tickets tomorrow," said Ty. "There's an expo for the two days prior, then the NXT event on Saturday, and smaller independent events scattered around town all weekend. I have already seen a few ads showing up on my timeline," he continued.

Tegan returned with a can of Real Ale Brewing Company's Phoenix Winter Ale for her and a Celis White for Kareem.

"Nice choice," said Kareem. "This Celis White follows Pierre Celis' original recipe from 1965 when he revived the witbier style back in his father's barn in Belgium," he added.

"I was thinking this Phoenix winter ale won't be around much longer, so I better get it while I can," said Tegan.

"What's this call you were talking about, Kareem?" asked Carson.

"Funny you mention Phoenix," he said, pointing at Tegan's drink with a lazy single finger gun. "I had a call from a kid who was a patient of mine last year. I told Carson on the phone that he and a friend were walking through the back alley behind a building in Phoenix and they saw something unknown. At least to them it was unknown," he said, filling Tegan and Ty in one the preliminary information he provided Carson an hour ago.

"Something unknown covers a lot of things. We established that over the past year. Any description to narrow it down?" asked Tegan.

"That's where it gets weird. He and his friend thought it was a camel. I thought maybe a wild horse, but the wild horses are over ten miles away from that part of town," replied Kareem.

"What about a domesticated horse?" suggested Carson. "Phoenix is an Old West town like much of Texas, and I've seen guys here ride horses up to a drive thru before," he continued.

"There are places where people have horses in Phoenix. Some outskirts perhaps, but not usually where they saw this animal," said Kareem.

"He said it was dark and from across the park. At a distance and in those conditions, it might be hard to tell the difference between a horse and a camel, but I don't recall hearing stories of any camels in the United States. Not wild ones, at least. Oh, and get this, he said they also thought it was glowing, like a red aura," added Kareem.

"Glowing? Now, come on. Are you sure this guy is credible?" asked Ty.

"I've known him for a couple of years, and I have had no reason to doubt him or question something he said." Said Kareem.

"Okay, so a glowing camel in the desert?" questioned Tegan.

"Oh, and it had a rider too," Kareem updated. "I looked online to see if there were any reports, but so far, nothing."

"When did this sighting happen?" asked Ty.

"Just last night," said Kareem.

"So this might be the first reported sighting, and just yesterday means that maybe this creature is still in the area. I am pretty sure that it is just a horse, but if you believe this guy, then it could be something that is a new discovery," said Carson.

"Plus, it is spring training. We could catch a game while we're out there," added Ty.

"Good call on that," added Carson.

"I like the idea that this is so fresh. We might get some good evidence if it is something unknown. It doesn't get much fresher than this," said Tegan.

"I agree. Since you have a history with this guy and know his character, it's worth the trip to check it out. What do you think, Ty?" asked Carson.

"I'm on board. Kareem, since it's your friend, can you take the lead and make the call to set it up? See when we can meet and I will get with Jourdyn to help get the travel arrangements booked," Ty replied.

"Yes, I will call him first thing in the morning," replied Kareem.

"Looks like we are off to Phoenix for another adventure. I am interested to see what this creature is. I haven't heard of a cryptid that resembles a camel, which leads me to believe it is something known, but was just unexpected to him. You said he was new to the area. Maybe that's why others haven't reported it yet. Others have seen it before, but maybe your friend just hasn't yet," said Carson. "Either way, we'll check it out."

CHAPTER 4

IT'S A DRY HEAT

Monday, March 14, 2016

The sun was still high overhead and the heat rising from the brown Sonoran Desert as Southwest Flight 1767, a non-stop flight from Austin to Phoenix arrived on the runway around 3:55 p.m. Carson, Ty, Tegan, and Kareem stood up and stretched after the two hour and seventeen-minute flight from Austin Bergstrom airport.

"I love these non-stop flights," said Ty. "I used to love to fly, but anymore it is too much of a hassle."

"I am glad we're here. I'm eager to meet up with Charlie and investigate this mysterious camel of the desert," said Kareem. "It has been several years since I have been to Phoenix, so I am also excited to see how the city has changed. Did you see that landscape coming in? I love the mountains here. It is a pretty landscape, although a different pretty - not a lot of green. Kind of desert khaki everywhere and everything is so dry," he added.

"I saw some trees and a few spots of water flying in, but only a few. Lots of swimming pools,' said Tegan.

"Arizona is a cool state though," said Carson as the group disembarked the plane and headed toward baggage claim. "It's the only state in the entire country that's home to one of the Seven Wonders of the World. The northern region has beautiful areas with Monument Valley, Antelope Canyon, Horseshoe Bend, and Canyon de Chelly. You have Havasu Falls, the Petrified Forest, Sedona, and Kartchner Caverns around the state. Not to mention, it's only been a state since 1912. Hard to imagine, but The Old West and history such as Wyatt Earp and the OK Corral in Tombstone were just in the 1880s. Arizona also has the world's best-preserved meteorite impact site in the world and the world's oldest rodeo, dating back to 1888."

"I love a good rodeo," replied Kareem.

"Definitely a lot of things to do outdoors. But those summers!" said Tegan.

"Summer is certainly hot, often between 110 to one 120, but that lasts only a few months. The rest of the year, the weather makes up for it. Not much rain except during the monsoon season, which makes it a great location for golf, baseball, and hiking. Maybe we can get some hiking in while we are here?" suggest Carson.

"Charlie said the beer scene is really booming with some excellent breweries out here. I am definitely looking forward to that!" added Kareem.

When they arrived at Baggage Claim, their luggage was already there. Picking up the bags, they headed outside to catch the airport shuttle to the rental car station. While waiting on the shuttle, Kareem opened his carry-on backpack and removed a small piece of aluminum foil where he unwrapped a donut. He closed his eyes as he took a bite, but was aware that the others were watching him.

"What? I stopped by Voodoo Donut late this morning. They don't have a location out here, and I thought I might be hungry by the time we landed. Just a small snack," he said.

"I'm surprised you put those donuts in your satchel," said Tegan. "Crumbs might fall out and dirty up the bag."

"I wrapped them individually in foil and double bagged them in Ziplocs," retorted Kareem. "Want one?" he offered rhetorically.

He finished the donut just as the bus pulled up along the sidewalk. Once they arrived, Carson led them to the Alamo car rental parking lot where they could skip the counter and go straight to a new-model Alien 2 Green Kia Soul.

"This should be fine," said Carson.

"I texted Charlie when we landed, and he just sent me directions to a place where we can meet up. I told him we were a little hungry and very thirsty," said Kareem.

"Sounds good. Where are we meeting?" asked Carson.

"A place in Mesa, not too far from his apartment. You might like this. It's called the Beer Research Institute," replied Kareem.

"I like the sound of that research," Carson replied.

As Carson drove the fifteen miles from the airport to South Stapley Drive, it amazed the group how beautiful the city looked. The colorful art displayed along the highway frontage roads added an artistic touch that blended with the natural landscape of the area. Each underpass showed a different depiction, telling a story of the local neighborhood, not only beautifying the city but also making each segment unique.

Tempe Town Lake, a man-made reservoir running along the Loop 202 that appeared to be a mirage in an otherwise dry landscape, equally impressed the group of visitors. The journey continued to the 101 Loop, giving a view of the newly constructed Sloan Park, spring training home to the Chicago Cubs.

"Hey, we might have to check out that ballpark," suggested Ty. "I saw online that it just opened two seasons ago and. It looks amazing."

"I'd love to hit up some ballgames while we are here," said Carson. "That's a bucket list item for me."

"For me as well," added Ty.

"I just love how flat it is here in town, but you can see the mountains surrounding the city," said Tegan.

Carson pulled into the Mesa Grand Shopping Center, where in the back near the movie theater and House of Sushi sat the Beer Research Institute. A black iron fence created a small patio large enough to accommodate a few guests outside. The temperature was in the mid-seventies, which was pleasant with the passing clouds and twenty-six percent humidity.

"There is enough seating outside for us, and it's a nice evening to sit and watch the beautiful sunset, but let's see if Charlie is inside," suggested Kareem.

Inside, the brewpub was busy for a Monday night. The seats at the bar were full, as were most of the booths. Three long community tables occupied the middle of the brewery. The first two were not full, but there were enough people to make it difficult to sit as a group. Ty spotted a hand waving from the back table.

"Looks like that's our guy at the back table and he's saved us seats," said Ty.

Kareem led the way and smiled as he saw his former client. The two men vigorously embraced and exchanged pleasantries while the others watched and awaited introduction.

"It's good to see you again, Charlie. These are my friends... Tegan..."

She smiled and extended a hand. "How do you do?" she asked.

"Ty," continued Kareem. "What's up?" he said, shaking hands with Charlie.

"And Carson," concluded Kareem. "Pleasure," he said with a handshake. "Thanks for calling us out here. Kareem filled us in on your encounter. It really caught our interest," replied Carson.

"Thanks for coming. Great meeting you all," said Charlie as they all took a seat at the table. "Yeah, that creature was definitely unexpected. We were taking a break from playing at the party and just stepped outside to get some fresh air. You don't really expect to see something like that."

"No doubt. Any more reports on it from the local news?" asked Tegan.

"I heard something odd on the news yesterday morning, but I didn't get to hear all of it. I rushed out to grab some lunch and meet up with friends, so I was in a bit of a hurry," said Charlie.

"What was the story? Was it about the animal you saw Friday?" asked Ty.

"Can't say for sure. It was a story about the body of a man found in Goldfield. It's a recreated ghost town outside of Apache Junction that people like to visit. Gives them a feel for the Old West. It gets some good traffic on the weekends, but they said they found this guy Thursday night," said Charlie.

"So I take it not as much traffic during the week? Do they suspect foul play?" asked Carson.

"No, apparently the man died of a heart attack. However, the weird thing is that they say some large animal may have trampled him. There were long strands of red hair on his jacket and large cloven footprints bigger than a horse around the area," added Charlie.

"That sounds unusual. Cloven footprints would suggest a horse, but you said the prints were larger than a horse... Cows? Kareem said there are cattle yards here. And a cow would be unexpected," suggested Carson.

"I don't know about the guy, but what we saw was definitely not a cow. Being from Texas, cows are definitely familiar to me," said Charlie.

"What about a donkey?" asked Kareem. "There are wild donkeys in Arizona."

"No, the creature we saw was large. Much taller than a donkey. Not a sheep. Not a pig. I keep coming back to camel. But it makes little sense," Charlie said.

"You said they found this guy in Goldfield on Thursday, and your encounter was Friday. Might be the same animal," suggested Tegan.

A young man approached the table.

"How's it going? I'm Delton. Here are a few menus. We have some great burgers. I also highly recommend the meat candy," he said.

"What is meat candy?" asked Tegan.

"Very addictive," Delton replied with a chuckle. "It's candied bacon with sriracha."

"That sounds amazing," said Carson, looking up from his menu. "And you have poutine? That's unexpected."

"It's a southwest poutine. We take fries and cover them with cheese, gravy, and machaca."

"That's one of my favorites," added Charlie. "I will have that."

"Speaking of machaca, the Green Chile mac and cheese with machaca sounds excellent," said Kareem.

"I'm thinking this meat candy meatloaf, mashed potatoes, and asparagus doesn't sound half bad either," added Ty.

"Put me down for a BBQ pineapple bacon burger," said Tegan. "Can I get a side of meat candy?"

"The loaded cheese crisp, that's like a Mexican pizza?" asked Carson.

"Yes, it's a tortilla and we load it down with cheese, tomatoes, onions, jalapenos, beans, and machaca," said Delton.

"Sounds good to me," replied Carson.

"And did you look at the drinks?" Delton asked.

"Definitely a flight for me," said Carson.

"The flights here are cool," said Charlie. "They come in a holder that resembles brass knuckles, and they serve them in little beaker glasses."

"That sounds cool," said Tegan. Looking over the menu, she attempted to select four beers.

"Since I have red hair, let's go with the Fire Squirrel Red Ale, the 480G IPA, the War Paint Red IPA. I don't think I have had a red IPA before and… oh, the Sticky Morning Sex. That just sounds good," she said with a flirtatious smile.

"That one is pretty good," said Delton. "It's a smooth, sweet milk stout."

"One of my favorites right now is the Dark Side Till I Die," said Charlie. "I will have a pint of that."

Ty also selected a flight. "That Dark Side sounds good, and the 480G, the Street Cred Black IPA, and what's this? #dontfuckinworryaboutit?"

"Yes, that's the Belgian Tickler, a collaboration we did with College Street Brewing. It's a brown ale with a Belgian yeast," added Delton, laughing.

Kareem ordered the 480G, Sticky Morning Sex, Belgian Tickler, and Dark Side in a flight as well.

"I think I definitely need the Dark Side and the Belgian Tickler, and add a 480G and a Dirty Jesus Brown Ale," said Carson.

"Nice. I have everything. Your drinks will be up in a minute, and I will bring the food when it's ready."

"Sounds good," said Ty. "Thanks!"

"So, I did some research after Kareem first mentioned you thought it was a camel," said Carson. "In prehistoric days there was an extinct genus of a camel called the protylopus. It was a type of camel, but about the size of a rabbit. Later camelops, large North American camels appeared, but then they migrated into Asia and beyond, leaving no camels in North America, other than those brought here for other purposes. Something I came across in my research that I found interesting to this case was that camels have been right here in Mesa," reported Carson.

"Really, here?" asked Charlie.

"Yes, in 2007, construction workers at the Mesa Walmart found two camel skeletons. Both of them were young, one just a baby. Although scientists attempted to evaluate the Walmart camels, tests were inconclusive. They estimate that those camels may have lived here around ten thousand years ago," reported Carson.

"We're in Mesa now, and isn't there a Walmart at the other end of this plaza?" asked Ty.

"Yes, but it wasn't this Walmart. This one was at Lindsay Road near McKellips Road," replied Carson.

"That's only about seven miles from here," said Charlie.

"And in 2008 there were findings of other camel bones at the construction of the San Tan Vista Drinking Water Treatment Plant on Recker and Ocotillo Roads," added Carson.

"That's probably about twenty miles from here, on the other side of the 202, past Chandler and out toward the Power Ranch community," said Charlie.

"Okay, so there were camels here, but those are all thousands of years ago. Not around here today," said Tegan.

"I think one thing going in our favor is that the sighting happened just a couple of days ago. Maybe if we head back to the sighting area and check for clues, we might have an excellent shot. It doesn't rain here often, so the tracks may still be present," said Ty.

"You're right. I think we have to explore the area and see what else is out there. Talk to some people and see if they've seen anything unusual. We should also hit up that Goldfield area. What else is around there?" asked Carson.

"Not much. Out there you are looking at the Usery Mountains, the Salt River, Superstition Mountains...," started Charlie.

"Superstition Mountains? Isn't that where the legend of the Lost Dutchman's mine takes place?" interrupted Kareem.

"Yes, that's a cool spot where you can find ancient cliff dwellings and caves from some of the Native Americans that first settled this area. As the legend goes, in the 1840s the Peralta family of northern Mexico developed a few rich gold mines in the Superstitions. They regularly dug the gold and carried it back to their ranch in Mexico. Their last expedition occurred in 1848 when Apaches ambushed the party. During the battle, everyone died except for one or two Peralta family members who escaped. They call that area Massacre Grounds today," said Charlie.

"I heard about the legend of the mines, but didn't know the story behind them. I saw a show on television where people were going to search for the Lost Dutchman's gold," replied Carson.

"A few people were supposed to have known the mine's location and even worked it. They found several maps over the years supposedly showing the location, but somehow they became lost whenever interested parties pressed for facts. Men who claimed to have found the Peralta mine could not return to it or some disaster occurred before they could file a claim, of course adding to the lore of a lost mine," Charlie continued.

"Who was this Dutchman?" asked Tegan. "You said the mines were from some guys from Mexico.

"In the 1870s a guy named Jacob Waltz, nicknamed The Dutchman because he was from Deutschland, what they called Germany then. Legend said he located the mine through the aid of one of the Peralta ancestors. Waltz and his partner, Jacob Weiser, worked the mine and allegedly hid one or more large caches of gold in the Superstitions. Most stories place the gold near a well-known landmark called Weaver's Needle. Someone killed Weiser soon after that. Some say Apaches and others say Waltz himself."

"When his health grew worse, Jacob Waltz moved to town and died about twenty years later. He supposedly described the mine's location to his neighbor, Julia. She took care of him prior to his death. However, neither she nor dozens who sought the location in the years following his death could find the Lost Dutchman's mine. Even today, people continue searching for it. Some of those searchers have met with foul play or, in some other way, died. That contributed to the superstition and legend that surround these mountains," reported Charlie.

"No one has ever found the gold?" asked Ty.

"Not that I know. At least I've heard about it on the news. People still go looking for it. Those mountains are expansive, and it gets hot out here. Even in the spring and fall, when it isn't over 115, it can create exhaustion and dehydration spending time in the mountains. Many people don't come back from looking for it," added Charlie.

"You mentioned this animal you saw had cloven hooves. Just thinking about some other animals like alpacas, sheep, deer, antelopes, and goats, especially mountain goats. These are animals that live in mountain areas. So maybe this animal lives in the mountains and wandered a little farther into the city?" pondered Carson.

"It is a bit of a distance, but who knows? Maybe with the canal system, it could follow water and end up in Mesa. The canal isn't far from where I saw it," responded Charlie. "I know there are some bighorn sheep out near Saguaro Lake."

"Even if it is a camel, water is still something it would need. We learned that by narrowing down the search area for the chupacabra. Is the Salt River far from these mountains?" asked Ty.

"No. There's the Salt River Pima-Maricopa Indian Community out there and the river runs through it. Goldfield is at the edge, but leads into the mountains," said Charlie.

"Charlie, do you or your friends have any camping equipment? I think we should check out this park where you saw the animal, but tonight we should camp out near that river," Carson suggested.

"That's a great idea. There's some beautiful land and excellent trails out there. My roommate and I go nearly every weekend. You'll need a pass to camp in the area because it is part of the Tonto National Forest, but I can pick that up for you," he said.

"How about we go check out the small park where you encountered the animal while you pick up the pass, then we'll all meet back at your apartment? After that, we can head out to Goldfield, then to the Salt River to set up camp for the night," suggested Kareem.

"That works for me. The park where I saw it is behind a plaza across the street from my apartment," said Charlie.

Ty looked down at his watch.

"We better get to bustin' a move. It's already dark and if we're going to check out the park and Goldfield, it might be a late night before we hit the sack."

"It's best to park at Pearl's Banquet Hall and walk behind the building. Just pull out of this parking lot, turn right, and you will see the shopping center with Pearl's just passed the highway, not even a mile from here," said Charlie.

"Sounds like a plan. We'll see you in a few minutes," said Carson.

About six minutes later, Tegan pulled into the parking lot where Pearl's Banquet Hall is located.

"Check it out," said Ty, pointing to a neighboring business in the shopping center. "Laser Tag!"

"I used to be great at that back in the day," bragged Kareem.

"Maybe we should see if you've still got it," suggested Tegan.

"I think those days have passed. It's been a long time since 1988," said Kareem.

The group walked toward Pearl's and made their way around the back of the building and into the alley. They followed the road until they came to the concrete retaining wall with the gate Charlie mentioned he and his friend Octavio had entered just days ago.

"This looks like the spot," said Kareem.

Carson walked to the gate and opened the latch. The gate swung open and allowed them to look inside at the dark and empty small park.

"No signs of mysterious entities tonight," said Ty as he and the rest of the group walked through the gate and surveyed the area.

"Charlie said the creature was on the opposite side of the park. Likely over there," said Tegan, pointing to a flickering streetlight in the back corner of the basin.

"He said it had a glow. Maybe from that streetlight?" suggested Ty.

"Let's walk over and scope the area," suggested Carson.

The grass and dirt underneath were dry as they walked across the basin. Carson removed his cell phone and swept the ground with the flashlight app as they made their way toward the intended search site.

"The ground is hard and dry here. I hope we can find some tracks. That's what we need to tell the story of what happened out here. The earth is a manuscript, being written and unwritten every day. After an animal makes a track, that track wears down through the forces of natural erosion and gravity. Gravity ultimately wants everything to be at the same level. A track is the earth's reaction to something passing over it," said Carson.

"I know little about tracking animals, other than what I've seen going out with you guys," admitted Kareem. "But I would expect a camel, being a large, heavy animal, would leave a footprint."

"It takes time getting started," said Carson. "The more time you spend, the better your skills become and eventually it gets easier. Study the ground closely. Get down on your hands and knees. Note the size of the track and determine if it shows signs of claw marks. Now, in this case, we know what we are looking for doesn't have claws. We are looking for hooves," said Carson.

"If you lose the trail, search in a circle around the track until you pick up the trail again," suggested Ty.

"We want to witness the track for ourselves and attempt to put the story together of the line of events. If we see footprints here, then later if we see similar tracks, we can tie them together," replied Carson.

"We will probably find dog tracks here. I imagine people in the neighborhood walk their dogs in this grass. Even if you haven't tracked an animal before, you likely know a dog print when you see it. As you said, this animal is obviously bigger and should be heavier. The track, even on this hard ground, will be deep. Charlie said it was a cloven animal, which means we are looking for a hoof. A small animal might be an antelope. Larger examples like a horse, donkey, or camel, which is what he thought it was. A camel would have two broad toes on each foot with undivided soles that can spread widely as an adaptation to walking on sand," said Ty.

"Even I know what a camel toe looks like," replied Kareem in a snarky tone.

"Hey, guys. Over here," called out Tegan. "Seems to be something large. Not deep, but it could be because of the dry ground," said Tegan.

The guys joined her in the basin's corner and reviewed her discovery.

"Nice find. You can see the grass here is shorter than in the middle of the basin. Charlie said it was eating grass, which could explain the lower height here," said Carson. He bent down and felt the ground and track. "Yes, I think this belongs to the animal. Look at this print and note the features. A horse's hoof capsule is usually an even thickness all the way around, while a donkey's hoof is thicker at the toe. The horse print cuts in almost a V-shape at the front of the hoof. A camel print is more rounded, with a split between two symmetrical halves," responded Carson.

"Based on that, it looks like a camel, even though one in town still stumps me," replied Ty.

"Charlie said it ran off when it saw him. It probably walked in, which means the tracks going in will be closer together, but the quicker retreat will place them further apart on the exit," suggested Carson.

He turned in a circle, looking for the next print, and eventually stumbled onto additional tracks.

"Here we go. These appear to be from the animal as it was leaving the scene," he said, turning toward the street.

He walked toward the road, following the path of the tracks. Against one tree in the northeast corner of the basin, Carson found a patch of coarse auburn hair.

"Look here! It appears the creature passed here between the tree and the wall when escaping. This patch of hair appears to be like the coarse guard hair of a camel. Based on the footprints, it likely belongs to the same animal," said Carson.

The group gathered around to look at the clues.

"It has a reddish tint to it," said Ty, holding the hair closer to his eye. "Maybe under the streetlight it would give it that glowing appearance Charlie described."

"I think it's one thing to put a camel on the list of suspects given the fur and the footprints, but I don't know that we can yet conclude that's what Charlie saw. As you said, there aren't camels around here. And if we connect the story from Goldfield to this, camels are friendly, aren't they?" asked Tegan.

"We don't know yet if the Goldfield story relates to this. Charlie just said it was a weird story on the news, but we are going there next, so we'll find out more. They domesticated camels in parts of the world, but they can be dangerous. Do you remember the story last January at Camel Kisses Farm in Wichita Falls? Camels trampled two people," said Carson. "Certainly incidents related to aggression from heat, traffic incidents, and injuries from camels are higher in parts of the world where they are more prevalent, but anything could happen. They are animals and something could spook them or cause them to perceive danger and injure someone."

Ty looked around the basin and the quiet neighborhood. "Not much traffic out here. You would think others would have seen or heard something unusual. It's not every day you see a camel walking through a suburban neighborhood like this one. And if it was running on its exit, the hooves on the road should have made a loud and unusual noise," Ty said.

"We've probably seen everything there is to see here. Let's head over to Charlie's and pick up the park pass, and then get over to Goldfield before it gets too late," suggested Carson.

After getting back into the car and driving across the street to Indigo Springs Apartments, they walked down the sidewalk between the orange and beige buildings until they arrived at Apartment 2067. The terracotta iron stairs led to a small patio where Charlie's apartment was located. After a quick knock, the door opened, and a young man greeted them.

"Hey guys, I'm Octavio. Charlie's roommate. He's in the kitchen loading up."

"Loading up what?" inquired Kareem.

"The best part of a camping trip," said Octavio.

"The cooler!" rejoiced the gang.

"Ha-ha. I see you've been camping before!" responded Octavio.

"A time or two," said Tegan.

Octavio flashed a smile at the redhead.

"I love it. Charlie and me, we go camping or hiking a lot. Maybe we can hit some trails while you all are out here?"

"That would be sweet," said Ty. "I love the outdoors and this weather just begs to be enjoyed."

"We struggle for a few months in the summer, but the rest of the year makes up for it," replied Octavio.

Charlie entered the room, lugging the cooler filled with ice and beer.

"Couldn't let you guys go away empty-handed. Just a few cans of some local Phoenix suds to keep you company out in the woods," said Charlie. "I mean, I was at the gas station getting the pass anyway, right?"

"Right! Sounds like a winner to me," said Carson. "Let me help you with that," he said as Charlie handed the cooler off to him.

"Here's the parking pass," Charlie said as he handed it to Ty. "Just hook that around the rear-view mirror and you'll be good."

Octavio entered the room with the camping equipment.

"Don't forget these. The tent, a couple of sleeping bags, and I've got a box of camping equipment like a small stove and cooking tools in the closet if you want it."

"Maybe you better take the parking pass," Ty said, handing it off to Tegan. "Kareem and I will get the equipment."

"No complaints here," said Tegan.

She opened the door for the boys, and they began making their way down the stairs and to the car.

"We will see you tomorrow," said Tegan to Charlie and Octavio as she turned to leave.

It was about 10:30 p.m. when the group pulled up at Goldfield.

"Man, check out this place," Ty said, peering through the dusty windshield from the passenger's seat. "It looks like the wild west!"

"A little spooky at night, if you ask me," admitted Kareem.

"Yeah, but I bet it's sweet during the day," Carson said, opening the door and stepping into the night air. "It is like a whole town. There's the church over there. Looks like a brothel up ahead. I'm sure there's a saloon here too," he said.

The others joined him outside the vehicle and began walking toward the buildings.

"Even though it's only been a few days, I bet this place sees a lot of foot traffic on the weekend. I didn't hear if they closed it down after the discovery of the body to preserve the scene or not. If they didn't, the tracks will get lost in the weekend's traffic," said Carson.

"I'm sure they did," suggested Tegan. "Since they found the man's body here, it is likely an active investigation site. We must be careful not to disturb anything and contaminate the area."

The group began walking up the dusty street that ran through the middle of the old mining town. They searched the ground with their cell phone flashlights as they sauntered up the small hill.

"Yes, everything here is just dust, some gravel, and an orgy of footprints," said Carson.

"That's probably the common foot traffic path. Off to the side is where there will be less action," suggested Ty. "Like this right here," he said, shining his cell phone down on a large footprint by the side of the Coffee Cantina. "Few people walk against the side of the building, and it looks like something large came right through here."

Carson, Tegan, and Kareem joined him.

"You're right, Ty. That print looks like the one we saw in the park in Mesa. And here's another!" said Carson. He looked ahead, trying to shine his light in the distance.

"I can't see much, but it looks like a field or some clearing just up ahead. I can see a mountain back there in the moonlight. Maybe that's where it came from?" he suggested.

"Could be," said Kareem as he turned and looked behind him. "If that is open desert back there and leads into the town, it would be just down that hill and into the parking lot. Driving in here, it looked like there isn't much around. This little town is probably the only thing that was in its path."

"If that's true, sucks for the guy on the news. Wrong place, wrong time," said Tegan.

"Certainly seems to be an unusual incident," said Carson. "If it was on the news that means someone saw it. Or at least saw the body. That means there is a police report. Let's call tomorrow and see if we can find out anything from the local authorities. Maybe they have more clues about what went down Thursday night in Goldfield!"

CHAPTER 5

TENTS ON SALT RIVER

Monday, March 14, 2016 (PM)

The city lights disappeared as the road changed from North Power Road into North Bush Highway. The sky was dark except for the light of the moon and stars. The headlights occasionally fell upon a *Horse Xing* sign, reminding the passengers wild horses still exist and roam this area. Tegan drove with caution, looking for any occurrence of eye shine off the side of the road that may belong to the advertised horses. She also searched for the road into the Granite Reef Recreation Area. It was a near hidden turnoff the GPS promised was a short distance away.

Turn left in five hundred feet, the female GPS voice announced.

Tegan slowed until finally she spotted the driveway. It was a narrow and windy road through the entrance of the recreational site. Dense covering from trees made the group almost unaware a river lay just a few hundred feet away. There were five parking spaces near the front of the recreation area, and all were empty.

"Looks like we picked a good evening," suggested Carson.

"I'm sure they don't have many campers on a Monday night in March," said Kareem.

Looking down at his watch, Ty stated, "Actually, it's Tuesday morning now. Well, almost. Give it ten more minutes."

"Either way, I'm beat. Let's set this camp up and get some rest. It's been a long day," Kareem said.

"Hard to believe we were in Austin this morning and we're still awake," said Tegan.

"Let's give the area a quick scout to see where we can set up. I don't want to carry everything while we are searching," suggested Carson.

"It looks like there is a path to the left that heads off through the trees and likely out toward the river," said Ty. "Or, how about right here? There's a lot of tree cover to keep us hidden from the road, and there is a nice wide clearance here. Not too far from the car. The facilities are just over there, and we are close to the riverbank."

"Works for me. Let's get the stuff," suggested Kareem.

Carson and Ty found level ground under the trees a safe distance from a fire ring and cooking area, then worked on setting up the tent and establishing the campground.

Meanwhile, Tegan carried the sleeping bags, and Kareem brought the cooler.

"You boys are pretty good at setting up a campsite," said Kareem.

"Old Boy Scout habit," answered Carson. "I put up quite a few in my day. How about you?" he asked Ty.

"I was in the Scouts too. Plus, my family liked to camp, so I got plenty of practice growing up."

The two men continued working on the campsite construction. Within fifteen minutes, the team erected the tent and Tegan laid out the sleeping bags. Kareem sat the cooler outside of the tent and found a large, flat rock to set on.

"Should we build a fire?" Kareem asked.

"Probably not," said Carson. "I don't plan on being awake too long. Maybe check out the cooler and unwind while planning for tomorrow morning, then it's hit the hay for this ole boy," he said.

"Everything's ready inside," said Tegan, joining the guys outside of the tent. "Let's check out this cooler."

Kareem opened the lid. "Charlie purchased some beer at the gas station, but also had beer left over from a recent get-together. About a dozen local beers," said Kareem as he plunged his hand into the icy water and pulled out a wet can. "Borderlands Noche Dulce Vanilla Porter. That sounds good and in a nice, tall sixteen ounce can. These guys are out of Tucson, it says," Kareem read from the can.

He opened the can and tried to get a sniff from the can's opening. "It smells like a hint of vanilla, but even more like roasted coffee and chocolate." He took a sip and enjoyed the smooth taste, with a little bite and an easy finish. "Man, that's smooth. Tastes just like it smells: layers of espresso, cocoa, and a little vanilla," he said.

Tegan stood up and walked over to the cooler. "Let's see what I come out with," she said as she drove her hand blindly into the ice-water bath, and then removed a dark brown can. "This is like bobbing for apples," she said with a chuckle as she turned the can to read it. "Achocolypse from Prescott Brewing. Isn't that up north?" she asked.

"Yes, about two hours north of Phoenix. Some pretty country up there with lots of trees. Not too far from Sedona and Flagstaff, on the way to the Grand Canyon," replied Carson.

"People think of Arizona and visualize a desert, but there's a diverse landscape throughout the state," said Ty. "Up there in that part you have Ponderosa forests and Pinyon-Juniper woodlands along the Mogollon Rim. If you're lucky, maybe you spot the Mogollon Monster."

"What is the Mogollon Monster?" asked Tegan.

"It's a bipedal creature spotted in central and eastern Arizona along the Mogollon Rim and similar to Bigfoot," said Carson. "Most reports put it around seven feet tall, with a body covered in long black or reddish-brown hair."

"Sounds like an opportunity for another investigation," said Kareem.

"Maybe after we find this mysterious camel," Tegan suggested as she took a sip from her beer. "This would be a great dessert beer. Smooth, sweet, and chocolatey!"

“Speaking of those characteristics… it’s my turn,” said Ty, stepping up to the cooler. He reached in and removed a can of Four Peaks Scottish-Style Amber, Kilt Lifter.

“Sweet, I’ve heard of this beer, but have never tried it,” Ty said. “Four Peaks is one of the O.G.’s of the city. They’ve been around over twenty years and helped put Phoenix on the craft beer map,” Ty continued. “Kilt Lifter has become not only the brewery's flagship ale, but one of Phoenix’s most popular beers,” Ty said.

“Looks like I am next,” said Carson. He reached in and pulled out an icy green and orange can.

“Speaking of O.G.’s, San Tan Brewing is another one of the early founders of the Phoenix market,” he said, looking over the can of HopShock. “This IPA won gold at the US Open Beer Championship last year. Although they’ve been around a while, that win put it on my radar. Glad I get the chance to try it out! You’ve heard of New England IPAs. Obviously we enjoyed quite a few last fall up in Burlington. Now there’s the West Coast IPA. They call this one a Southwestern IPA, which is a new term for me.”

“So then tomorrow morning we scout out this area for clues?” asked Tegan.

“Right. We know the creature was in Mesa on Friday and it appears Goldfield Thursday night. Many canals run throughout Phoenix that could allow the animal to travel with limited risk of people seeing it. Every day, hundreds of thousands of Phoenicians drive over canals that cut through the city, with many likely not realizing they've crossed flowing water. Water is precious in the desert and this town grew around canals built by the Hohokam Indians. That was their way to bring in irrigation and establish an agriculture system. Phoenix modernized the canals in the 1860s and they continue to serve the town today. Many people now use them as running or biking paths. That water could also attract the animal because there isn't a lot of open water in this part of the country," said Carson.

"The river that runs here near the campsite could be another big attraction for the animal. It runs through the mountain range. If that's its primary home, this could be a regular travel route, which is what we are hoping to find," suggested Ty.

"If it is a camel, it would eat dried leaves, seeds, and whatever desert plants it can find. This area along the river should provide a lot of that food," suggested Carson.

"I think I will have one more and call it a night," suggested Kareem. "There is a lot of ground to cover, and it will be difficult to find the creature in all of this open land." He returned to the cooler and pulled out a red can from Phoenix Ale Brewery. "Watermelon Ale. A fruit flavored wheat ale under five percent," said Kareem.

"Toss me one?" asked Tegan.

Kareem returned his hand to the cooler and, in a soft underhand motion, tossed Her a can.

"White Chocolate Ale from Sonoran Brewing Company? That sounds refreshing. It's also a wheat ale under five percent," she added.

"Wheat beers are big out here. The summers are even hotter than we get in Texas and with even less rain. The wheat beers are light and clean on those dry summer days," said Ty as he finished his beer. "Looks like you're the dealer, Kareem. Hit me."

This time Kareem reached in, pulled out a can from Huss Brewing, and tossed it to Ty.

"Magic in the Ivy. A pale ale named in honor of the Chicago Cubs. We saw their spring training field on our drive in," said Ty.

"We need to check the Baseball schedule so we can get in that game," replied Carson.

"Hell yeah! I told you earlier that's on my bucket list. I've been thinking about the chance since we were watching the playoffs on our way back from New England last fall," said Ty.

"That's right. Strange how those things work out!" replied Carson.

"Just a few choices left in the cooler," said Kareem. "Whatcha want, Carson?"

"What's left in there?" Carson asked.

Kareem shined his cell phone flashlight into the cooler. "Looks like a Parched Pooch Hefeweizen from Sleepy Dog, a bottle of Dark Knight Porter from Old World Brewery, and a couple IPAs: Mother Road Tower Station and Lumberyard's Flagstaff IPA," replied Kareem.

"Toss me the Lumberyard. That's another award winner I've wanted to try. That one took the 2009 Silver at Great American Beer Fest and the 2010 Bronze at the World Beer Cup," responded Carson.

Carson raised his beer in the air. "To our first day in Phoenix. I hope that we have another successful investigation! It will be a busy few days searching this town for clues and trying to solve this mystery, but I'm confident about our team. Here's to a good and restful night's sleep!"

Ty, Kareem, and Tegan stood and clanged their beers together, signaling their agreement. They finished the beer, tossed the empties back in the cooler, and entered the tent, ready to sleep. It wasn't long before the day's journey caught up with them and they were asleep.

Hours later, with the group in a deep slumber, the faint sound of a distant thunder grew increasingly louder. A lone brown rabbit exited the brambles and chewed on a leaf several feet behind the group's tent. It watched as the thunderous sound grew even louder. The source of the sound revealed itself to be hooves from a large, dark animal galloping at full stride along the dusty path. The creature did not see, or perhaps did not care, that a tent impeded its route along the trail. The beast continued on its course through the campground, striking the tent and causing it to come smashing down on the heads of the group, jarring them awake.

They heard a loud scream and the sound of pounding hooves as they frantically fought with the tent to locate its opening and escape outside. Carson and Ty were the first to escape, but in the darkness, caught only the outline of what appeared to be an impossibly tall horse as it disappeared off into the brush.

"What the hell was that?" asked Carson. "Did you see it?"

"Looked like a horse, but bigger than any I've ever seen," said Ty.

"The wild horses live in this area and are seen in the river, but you're right, that looks larger," added Carson.

Kareem emerged, rubbed his head, and attempted to awaken.

"That thing destroyed the tent. I was not expecting that!" he said.

"There's no way we can catch it," said Tegan. "We'll have to wait until morning and scour the area to search for clues."

"That should only be a couple of hours until daybreak, but it jacked this tent. I don't think we can put it back up. Maybe we should pack it up and try to sleep in the car until morning," suggested Carson.

"I'm down for sleeping in the car, but we should leave the tent here so we can inspect it in the sunlight," said Ty.

They returned to the car where they attempted, mostly unsuccessfully, to get a couple more hours' sleep.

The group stirred around 6 a.m. By 6:36 a.m. sunrise was already underway, and they saw the aftermath of what once was their campsite.

The ground around the campsite was dry and sandy, but they could make out huge hoof prints throughout the camp.

"The animal was running down this dusty path along the edge here, from northeast toward southwest," said Carson.

The group followed Carson up the northeast trail and scanned the ground.

"This path runs along the rec site and continues along the river. That's where he came from," continued Carson. "When we were in Goldfield last night, that's almost exactly due East from here. This could be a regular route for the creature."

"Yes, our tent was right along the path and he trampled it while running to… wherever he goes," added Kareem.

"Right!" replied Carson.

"Looks like just hoof prints around here. Check out the size of those things! Definitely not a horse. Unique shape and much larger," added Ty.

Tegan walked back to the tent and examined it for clues. She began moving the poles and tent canvas. "Not much here. A lot of damage to Charlie's tent, though. He won't like that. Looks like a hoof tore a hole through part of it," she said.

The guys continued southwest past the tent. "Look, the trail that way bends through this… what used to be a gate," said Ty, looking at the small wire fence that lay collapsed on the ground. "Not strong enough to stop that creature!"

"You can't stop him, you can only hope to contain him," replied Carson, quoting his favorite Stuart Scott *SportsCenter* catch phrase.

"Check it out though," Ty said as he bent down to get a closer look. "Looks like that gate caught some hair as the animal crashed through it." Ty reached down and pulled a patch of long red hairs from the fence. "I don't know where we can put this. We really need to come prepared for sample collections so we don't have evidence contamination when we go on these trips," suggested Ty.

They followed the path along the bed of the river, finding more prints of the huge hooves. "It appears he went down here to the river to get water," said Tegan, looking at sunken prints in the mud.

"Yes, then up here it looks like it went through this tall grass," said Kareem, looking through the brush leading uphill to a trail that an obviously large animal had broken.

"And even though it seems we're way out in the wilderness, remember the town is only a couple miles southwest from here. It wouldn't take long for it to get in town and follow the canal over to where the guys spotted it at Pearl's," suggested Carson.

"I don't think it will do us any good to follow the path further. We saw it was an animal bigger than a horse. The hooves and clumps of red hair appear to support the theory of a camel, but why would it be here in Phoenix? Where would it have come from?"

"And remember, Charlie said it seemed to have something on its back. What could that be?" asked Tegan.

"All good questions. We will have to do more exploring and research. Let's check back in with Charlie and let him know what we've found after we clean up the campsite," suggested Carson.

CHAPTER 6

TAKE A HIKE

Tuesday, March 15, 2016 (AM)

The gang arrived at Charlie's apartment about forty-five minutes after cleaning up the campsite. Charlie answered the door, eager to hear about their overnight adventures.

"How'd it go last night?" Charlie asked.

"There's good news and bad news," said Kareem.

"What's the bad news?" asked Charlie.

"Bad news is it trashed your tent. The poles are bent, there's a hole in the top, and… yeah…," replied Kareem.

"It's cool. I have a backup and that one was getting old. I was planning on getting a new one anyway," Charlie stated.

"Good news is we are pretty confident we saw the

creature," said Kareem.

"That is good news! So I am not crazy!" said Charlie excitedly.

"Pretty sure not. We were sleeping when it trounced through the campsite. We woke up after it ran over the tent and everything collapsed on us," said Kareem.

"By the time we could make it out of the tent, it was too far away, and in the dark we couldn't see many details. It could have been a wild horse, but it looked taller," said Ty.

"We found large hoof prints that do not look like a horse, and we also found some hair from a fence it ran over," said Ty. "We saw nothing on top of it, like a rider, but like I said, it was a good distance away when we finally realized what was happening," replied Ty.

"We talked about it, and we think it is a camel based on the glimpse we saw plus the collected evidence. We do not know why it's here, and we didn't get confirmation of a rider," responded Carson.

"So, what's the next step?" asked Charlie.

"I'm not sure yet. We need more research and more investigation based on what we've seen so far at the three sites we've visited," said Carson.

"You've seen a lot in just a day. What do you say you take a step back to reflect and let's do something this morning?" asked Charlie.

"What did you have in mind?" questioned Kareem

"The weather is glorious. It is supposed to be only eighty-four degrees and partly cloudy today. What do you say we hike some of our amazing trails and get a marvelous view of the city?" suggested Charlie.

"Hiking? I'm down," replied Tegan.

"Do you do a lot of hiking in Texas?" Charlie asked.

"I do some. I enjoy going to Longhorn Caverns, Mount Bonnell, and a lot of trails around Lady Bird Lake and along the Greenbelt," said Kareem.

"This one is an above average hike in difficulty, but it's a great Arizona hike, and offers some excellent views of the city," stated Charlie.

"Sounds good to me," added Ty.

"It's called Camelback Mountain, so maybe it will offer some inspiration for your search," Charlie added.

"They say to get high when searching for something, and if it is a camel we are after, we might as well climb one," said Carson.

"There are two main trails to Camelback. I won't lie, both are difficult. When you see the mountain from town, it looks like a giant camel sitting down. The trail up the nose of the camel is very difficult. That is Echo Canyon Trail, probably one of the most intense and hardcore hiking experiences in Phoenix. I hike it sometimes, but for your first time and just getting to the top of the mountain, I wouldn't recommend it. It's definitely a strenuous workout," reported Charlie. "Instead, we will take the Cholla Trail. It's also one of the most popular hikes in Phoenix, and about two and a half miles long," added Charlie.

"Two and a half? That's not bad," said Carson.

"No, not too far distance-wise, but it is still difficult and will require good conditioning and a strong will to finish. My first attempt to climb it saw me make it only maybe a little more than halfway. Then I called it quits," Charlie said.

"Must be a tough climb," asked Tegan.

"About twelve hundred feet and the terrain changes during the hike," said Charlie.

"How long will it take us?" asked Kareem.

"I would plan on three hours. I recommend good shoes, some water in a backpack, and some sunscreen, even in March. I have the sunscreen here, and we can stop at a gas station for water. We should bring at least thirty-two ounces, but I recommend a couple of bottles," Charlie added, looking down at his watch. "And we should probably head out now. With Camelback, it is best to get there early because the temperatures do climb later in the day, and with it being so popular, it gets crowded. Sometimes you see people running up and back down the trail. Not me though. I am afraid of slipping on the rocks and falling down. That would be embarrassing. A bit of warning: if you don't feel you can make it, we can always stop and turn back. They have to air lift people out of there frequently. Maybe they get lost, injured, too tired, or dehydrated to continue."

"How about some celebratory beers for the summit?" asked Ty.

"Throw them in the bag," said Charlie.

"A toast on the top might make a good team photo," suggested Carson.

"Before we stop at the gas station for water, we need to hit up Dutch Bros. and grab some coffee. That's a good kick starter for the hike," suggested Charlie.

"We are all coffee fans, so there won't be any arguments from us," said Tegan.

"Cool. There's one right up the Sixty and Alma School. We can stop there and get coffee, hit the gas station, and head to the mountain," Charlie outlined.

Less than four miles later, they arrived at Dutch Bros., a small blue hut reminiscent of the 1970s Fotomat stores. It had a drive thru on one side and a walk-up service window on the other. A large line of cars extended from the window bay, past the menu, and around to the street. A young man with an electronic order pad stood in the drive thru lane taking orders from cars in line.

"Here," said Charlie, handing Kareem his phone. "Look at the menu because he will take our order before we get to the menu board. The vibe is laid back and chill here. The line is long, but it's fun. Looking online at the menu helps because they also have a secret menu," he said.

"I love the secret menu. We actually have a few locations in Austin!" said Tegan.

"It has a nice kick, and it is awesomely delicious. One thing about it is they don't have a brewed coffee option. They make their standard coffee like an Americano with espresso shots. For their twelve and their sixteen-ounce drinks, they used a double shot of espresso. For the twenty ounces, it's two double shots. I like one classic, the Double Torture Mocha. It's vanilla with added shots," revealed Charlie.

"The Black Forest Mocha with dark chocolate and cherry

is one of my regular selections," said Tegan.

"I want the caramel, white chocolate, cinnamon horchata latte, hot," added Kareem.

"A large vanilla, caramel with caramel drizzle, Golden Eagle Breve," said Carson.

"After last night, you better give me the ER-911," ordered Ty.

"That's a good one. I love the Irish cream, but it's one of the extreme coffees with six shots of three-bean Irish cream espresso in the blend. You're basically looking at an ounce and a half shot of espresso containing roughly seventy-seven milligrams of caffeine, so that's about four hundred sixty-two milligrams of caffeine in a twenty-ounce cup of ER-911," warned Charlie.

"Sounds like just the pick me up I need," replied Ty.

Eventually, they made it to the friendly young man in the lane, taking orders. He had an abundance of peppy energy for this early in the morning. Charlie placed the order and handed the man his debit card.

"Thanks, you're all set," said the young man after swiping the card in the portable machine.

It was another few minutes before they made it to the window. Another young, perky employee confirmed the order and asked how their day was going so far, what they had planned for the rest of the day, and other small talk while several other employees inside the hut prepared the orders.

"We are going to climb Camelback Mountain," said Charlie, handing the woman his punch card. After several stamps of the loyalty card, she returned it to Charlie.

"Look at that. Just this trip alone and my card is nearly full. Tenth drink is free!" he said excitedly.

"Here you go, hun," she said, handing a tray of drinks to Charlie. "You got it?"

"Yes, I'm good," Charlie said.

"Enjoy the mountain. See you next time," she said.

Charlie handed the tray to Carson, who distributed the drinks to everyone.

"How do they fit so many people in that tiny booth? And how are they so energetic already?" asked Carson.

"They are much younger than us," replied Ty. "We used to have energy like that. Remember back in college?"

"In my mind, it doesn't seem like that long ago," Carson responded. "But my body tells a different story."

"Let's hit the road. It's about twenty-five or thirty minutes to the mountain. We'll park by the west side of the road next to the fence for the Phoenician Golf Course around 64th Street and walk about a quarter mile to the trailhead."

After arriving, they exited the vehicle, grabbed their backpacks, and began walking toward the trailhead. Parking was already becoming difficult to find. Another benefit of early arrival. As they walked along the private city street, Charlie warned them to be aware of their surroundings.

"There is loose gravel on parts of the trail and the hiking gets intense near the top. Also, there are a lot of animals to be seen along the way: Harris antelope squirrels, quail, roadrunners, hawks, chuckwallas, but also the potential for rattlesnakes, who are waking up this time of year," Charlie informed the group.

As they neared the trailhead, Carson looked up at the mountain ahead.

"This is a great urban peak, right here… where are we, Scottsdale? You don't normally think of a rigorous mountain hike in the middle of a downtown area. This is cool," Carson said.

"This part of town is called Paradise Valley," replied Charlie. "Lots of expensive homes in this area blended into the landscape and even some built into the mountain."

They arrived at the trailhead and began their ascension. The trail started flat with several switchbacks and bends on the trail. Large, fabricated stairs helped them ascend up the early part of the mountain. The path was wide, which allowed hikers and the occasional runner to pass each other up the path.

As they continued along the Cholla Trail, Charlie pointed out the expansive views of the Phoenician Resort and surrounding area as the path continued to bend and curve, gradually getting steeper. The trail varied in width but remained a clear dirt path that was easy to follow, despite the increased incline. After about a quarter mile, the group spoke up.

"This starts off nice, but I can feel it already in my legs," said Tegan.

"Yes, it seems like it will be an easy hike because it's downtown and the beginning of the path isn't too difficult. Just wait, there's more," replied Charlie.

The middle portion of the trail diverged to the north side of the mountain and continued to increase in steepness. The steady incline lasted for about a mile until they reached the saddle. They stopped to catch their breath, while Charlie pointed out the helipad that has been a landing spot used many times by rescue teams to help injured or lost hikers. Up to this point, the trail had been moderate; a relatively flat path with a steady incline.

"Hopefully we won't need their services today," said Ty, looking at the flat helipad as they continued. "But I'm not gonna lie, I'm feeling it."

"Ready to kick it up a notch? We've made it one mile. We're approximately to the saddle, but get ready. The last twenty percent of the trail is the strenuous part," warned Charlie.

"More strenuous than we have had? I'm already out of breath," said a beleaguered Carson. "It's been an awesome workout so far, but it's totally kicking my butt!"

"We're doing great so far, but the last leg is a stinker. I would say to make it all the way to the top, expect close to another hour of very steep climbing. With some assents ahead, the rock is almost completely smooth, and you have to pull yourself up using arm strength," advised Charlie.

"Damn, I guess those rock climbing classes back in Austin will come in handy now," replied Kareem.

"Shall we continue?" asked Charlie

All four guests continued to catch their breath and ponder the decision to continue or head back by trying to glimpse the trail ahead. Ultimately, they agreed to push on. From there, the trail transitioned into a rocky and uneven surface involving many sections requiring the hikers to resort to some scrambling.

"This is where many hikers complain that this part of the trail is their least favorite because of the need to climb certain portions," said Charlie. "But I think it gives the hike great versatility and provides a challenging finish before reaching the summit. No pain, no gain, right?" quipped Charlie.

There was a slanted rock located right along the edge of the trail that they needed to scramble up. Small notches along the right-hand side of the path allowed fingertip placement to help pull themselves up.

"This is literally up the side of the mountain, with lots of climbing on and around rocks," said a breathy Tegan. "It may be a shorter portion of the trail, but my God, this is tough. Probably the toughest hike I have attempted," she said.

The group looked ahead, and the mountain seemed to rise steeply for an eternity. This section of the trail allowed them to hike directly along portions of the ridgeline of the mountain. The path was wide and the danger of falling was minimal, but they still felt completely out in the open air with no protections along the side of the trail.

"Are we there yet?" called out Ty.

"Not yet. Getting closer," replied Charlie.

"I think I can see the top from here," said a nearly drained Kareem.

"Yes, it's that peak up ahead, but don't be fooled. It levels out just over our eye line here and then goes back up. It's a little further than it appears from here," said Charlie.

As they continued to climb, the path narrowed to a scramble up section, allowing only a single hiker to go at a time. As Charlie described, the trail did once again find somewhat level ground. As they got closer, they could see the summit and other hikers celebrating their victory at the top. From here, the hard part of the assent was over and they could follow the path up towards the top. With a final push, they did it. They arrived at the summit!

"Let's find a spot to sit, relax, and take in that view! We literally are on top of Phoenix!" said Charlie.

"Wow! Check it out," said Ty. "The view is worth the hike. You get that three-sixty view of the entire valley," he said, mesmerized, as he turned in a circle.

Carson was bent over, hands on his knees, and attempting to catch his breath.

"Let's crack those beers and get a photo and then get back to relaxing and enjoying that view," suggested Carson, still winded.

Kareem sat his backpack down and reached inside. "They're still cold," Kareem said, feeling the cans inside the bag.

He pulled out the cans blindly and handed them to each hiker. "Devil's Ale from San Tan Brewery?" He handed it to Carson. "Another one from San Tan, Sex Panther, is a chocolate porter."

"That's all me," said Ty.

"Wapiti Amber Ale from Mogollon Brewing Company for Charlie. Strawberry Blonde from THAT Brewery for Tegan. And that leaves this Koffee Kölsch from Huss for me," said Kareem.

Carson took his cell phone out and looked around for someone at the top to take some photos. "Ready, guys? Great job getting up to the top of this beautiful mountain. Let's toast!" said Carson.

They all stood in a circle and hoisted their cans together.

Together they yelled, "*Cheers!*" as a young woman snapped multiple photos before handing the phone back to Kareem.

"And a selfie for me," he said, posing in the phone's front-facing camera.

They walked around the summit and looked at the sprawling city below. From the highest point in Phoenix, they could see everything in the city. Besides the beautiful views, they saw several butterflies fluttering at the top of the peak.

"This is a splendid view. You get a good appreciation for how large the city is. Being able to see the downtown, the suburbs, and the mountains that surround the city. This is sweet. I am glad we got to do it," replied Ty.

"I never really thought of a desert as a place to visit, especially with all the stories of weird things out here in Phoenix," replied Tegan. "But the Sonoran Desert setting holds its own mystique. The surrounding mountains add to the overall appeal, creating a scenic environment, and I can't get enough of these pristine desert views and the glorious sunsets in the Valley," she said.

After a twenty-minute rest at the top, Charlie suggested it was time to continue. "You ready to start back yet?" asked Charlie.

"The strenuous climb worked up an appetite," replied Carson.

"We're going to hike down the way we came up. There's a sign for the Cholla Trail if you forgot where we entered the summit," said Charlie. "I think the scramble down is a little more difficult, at least at the beginning. I usually sit and scoot down the mountain, but overall it is easier because you can see the path, unlike the uncertainty if we were on the right trail coming up."

"Some drops are a little steep. I definitely will sit and take my time getting down to the next level," added Tegan.

"Once we make it back to the saddle, it isn't bad the rest of the way down to the car," added Charlie.

Along the two-and-a-half-mile trek return trip down the mountain, they spotted nearly a dozen lizards and a few scampering chipmunks, but to their relief, no rattlesnakes. When they made it back to the street, the group began rumbling about hunger.

"That's quite a hike. I barely made it," said Carson.

"I know a place not too far from here where we can grab a good burger for lunch, if you're into that," replied Charlie.

"I am always down for a good burger," stated Tegan.

"Carlsbad Tavern is one of the top spots in the valley," responded Charlie.

"Carlsbad Tavern?" asked Ty.

"Yes, Tavern. It's a play on Carlsbad Cavern and New Mexican themed, including bats," added Charlie.

"We know caves and bats in Austin," replied Carson.

"That's one reason I thought you would like this place," said Charlie. "That, and it has won many awards since it opened in 1995."

"What awards are we talking about?" asked Ty.

"*Best Burger in Phoenix* by *Leisure Magazine* in 2011, and the habañero cheeseburger, which is the one I recommend trying, won *Best Burger in Arizona* by *Food Network Magazine* in 2009. Plus, the patio has won awards for *Best Patio Dining in Phoenix* by *New Times Magazine*, and *Phoenix Magazine* named it one of its top eighty-five restaurants in 2011," Charlie revealed.

"I am down to try a habañero cheeseburger," said Tegan.

"The bat cave theme is really cool. Since they have been at this location, they have stepped it up. There is a water canal through the patio that they have named the *Guano Canal* and a waterfall on the patio and main dining room looks like a bat cave with a fountain inside," said Charlie.

"I do like the sound of dining in a bat cave, but this weather is awesome. Maybe we should try the patio when we get there?" replied Ty.

"Definitely. It shouldn't be busy yet, and the patio is large, so there should be plenty of seating. Plus, they have their own beer. A pale ale called Bat Brew," replied Charlie.

"Sounds like we don't even need to see a menu. Sign me up for the habañero burger and bat beer!" said Carson.

Five miles later, they pulled into a parking lot with a beige and brown building and terracotta accents. As they exited the vehicle, they walked toward the restaurant and under a large arch with a black reading *New Mexican Grub* across its chest.

They walked across a wooden planked bridge spanning the Guano Canal and into the bat cave, where a hostess awaited their arrival.

"How many today?" she asked.

"Five," said Carson. "Can we sit outside on the patio?"

"Of course. Right this way," she said as she turned and exited through a door inside the bat cave.

The group viewed the dimly lit interior with movie posters, bats, and all things from New Mexico as they walked past the water fountain and followed the host to the outside patio.

"Wow, this *is* a great patio," said Tegan.

"Yes, and this time of year, patio dining is wonderful in Phoenix. Next month it will get too warm during the afternoon, but nighttime will still be an option. Another month after that and it will be too hot even then. It's a good time to take advantage of it now," the host said.

"We picked a wonderful week to visit Phoenix," said Ty.

"Oh? Where are you visiting from?" the hostess asked.

"Charlie here is now local, but the rest of us are from Austin," replied Ty.

"Austin? I've never been. I used to watch *Austin City Limits* as a kid and I've always wanted to go to South by Southwest," she replied.

"Definitely a big attraction. It shows awesome things Austin offers and brings a lot of money into the community," said Ty. "But it's also a love-hate relationship for locals. A lot of traffic making it difficult to get around town."

"Yeah, parking is already difficult downtown when South by Southwest isn't underway. Then you add thousands upon thousands of visitors that are congregating around the convention center, the parking becomes non-existent," added Carson.

"Usually the locals lie low and avoid the scene. About seventy-five percent of the people that come out are music lovers and can be really chill, but the other twenty-five percent abuse it and just ask for free drinks," added Tegan.

"It makes it more difficult for us to get drinks and enjoy a beer after work. The visitors come in and take over the city for the week," added Kareem.

"I would still love to experience it," added the hostess.

"For sure, for someone from out of town, I would say it's a must-do at least once," said Carson.

"I will be back with some water and give you time to look over the menu," the hostess stated.

"Actually, we were talking about it on the way over. I think we already know what to get," said Carson.

"Sounds good. What'll it be?" the hostess asked.

"Five habañero burgers and five bat brews," replied Charlie.

"Easy enough. I'll be right back with the beers," she responded.

"Say, Charlie. Just down the street on the way here. Was that a baseball stadium?" asked Ty.

"That's Scottsdale Stadium, where the San Francisco Giants play in the spring. We're lucky the Giants are off tonight. Otherwise, the traffic would make driving difficult around here," said Charlie.

"We need to take in a game while we are here," said Carson.

"I love to go to the spring training games and the fall league games. I don't really get out to the ballpark much during the season," replied Charlie. "Of course it's a dome. You can't play in Arizona in the summer without a dome, but I like the smaller stadiums and natural open-air of the spring and fall games. In addition, you get closer to the players. Like old-school baseball."

Minutes later, the hostess returned with the round of pale ales.

"Enjoy. Your burgers should be out in just a few minutes. A little warning, these are spicy. You order it, you own it," warned the host. "Since you didn't look at the menu, you missed the medical warnings that stated this burger may cause temporary blindness or loss of hearing."

"I had to build up to it when I first started coming here," added Charlie. "My first time, two bites in and I tapped out. I love spice, but holy crap, it was insane."

"Do you like it?" Carson asked the host.

"It's one of our most popular dishes, but I can't do it, and I have a pretty high heat tolerance. I like habañero hot sauces, and I love fresh chilies on my food, but I balk at what looks like a food challenge item," she said.

"Oh, now I am intrigued. Can't wait," said Ty.

The host returned to the bat cave to check on the status of the food. Soon, she returned with the burgers, each served with fries and salad.

"Wow, I can smell it from here," Tegan said as the gentle breeze wafted the aroma toward the table.

The burgers, each containing freshly ground habañero chile, mixed with lean ground beef, grilled, and topped with melted jalapeño jack cheese, caused their mouths to water upon the first solid glimpse of the massive sandwich. Optional lettuce, tomatoes, pickle, and onions were available, and ketchup and mustard were waiting on the table.

"Damn, this looks like a feast," said Kareem. "I can smell the heat of the pepper from here!"

"It is well-earned after you all survived your hike up Camelback," said Charlie.

"I am sore now, but I imagine tomorrow will be miserable," followed Ty.

"I know I was my first time. There are seven stages of emotions climbing Camelback. It always sounds like a good time for the first time. There are hundreds of peaks to climb in the Phoenix area and you think if you can climb them, why not attempt Camelback? First came the shock. Once you pull into the parking lot and see the height of the mountain from the base, you realize what you've gotten yourself into. Seeing the gear is also a bit of a shock. The first time I went I had converse and khakis, and seeing people come down in hiking boots and backpacks, I realized I might have screwed up. Then comes denial. As you make your way up the dirt path, you doubt yourself and the mountain itself. There's no way that it's two and a half miles long. There's no way people have needed rescue from this hike. There's no way that individuals have actually made it to the peak," said Charlie.

"I definitely experienced that, especially the self-doubt part," said Kareem. "Without those rock climbing classes, I don't think I would have finished."

"Next stage is anger. Just as you think you get the hang of the hike and manage a balanced pace, you turn the corner and realize that you're not even a quarter of the way done. To get through it, I bargained, willing to risk everything just to quit the hike and turn around to stop my legs from going numb and to stop the flood of sweat dripping down my body because of the sun blazing on the back of my neck. Then depression as you've been crying for the past twenty minutes and your will to live has drastically dropped. You realize there's still a quarter mile left to the top, but you feel you've been at it for hours. When you discover the end is the hardest part, it doesn't seem fair. Especially mentally, when you feel you can't go any further," Charlie continued.

"You warned us it would be tough. I have to admit I was considering giving up and waiting for you guys to come back down," admitted Carson. "It was grueling in places."

"I agree. I still find it tough, even though I have made it to the top before. Once you finally catch your breath and take in the view, you realize how high you've gotten and that maybe reaching the top will be worth it. I felt I tested my limits, and it wasn't working. I thought about turning back and trying again when I'm in better shape. Finally, I accepted it and pushed through. Once you are standing at the peak of Camelback Mountain, it is truly such an amazing feeling. You look back and see that all the hard work truly paid off. Usually there is a pleasant breeze at the top, but you also get to sit down and take in the beauty of Phoenix from the top of the world. Plus, it's always a little nicer if you've brought some good friends along and some refreshing beers," concluded Charlie.

"I don't think I would have made it without the others. If I was on my own, I would have said screw it a long time ago," admitted Carson.

"It's not the first time you have worked through some difficult obstacles and pushed through to enjoy the view on the other side," Tegan reminded Carson.

"Indeed," replied Carson. "Thanks to some good friends."

"And some refreshing beers," added Ty.

"You're about to have another test and enormous obstacles with this burger," admitted Charlie. "My suggestion is to go slow, but steady. Do not stop. I cut it in half and go to one side, then immediately attack the second," advised Charlie. "I would jump right in and don't look back. That first bite will be hot, but you will get used to it. The only downside is that the fresh chopped habañero is not very much fun a few hours later when it's on its way out, if you know what I mean."

Carson grabbed the burger with two hands, the juice already running down the sides. He brought it to his mouth and paused as he was about to take a bite out of it. All the toppings and sauces mixed to create a perfect smell. He took a deep breath, exhaled, and moved in for a big first bite. The seasoning on and within the meat was the perfect blend of flavor. The burger, the cheese, the pepper, lettuce, tomato, onion - all the components work together. The heat hit, instantly warming his mouth. His eyes widened as the initial encounter was a little more than he expected, but it was enjoyable, and he took a second bite. He attempted to utter a couple of words, but the burger muffled the sound. He continued bite after bite until he finished the half. His eyes closed as he savored the flavor and the good ratio of burger to bun in each bite. After he consumed the first half, he finally came up for air and paused shortly before starting the second half. He briefly forgot he was around other people, as he was deeply lost in the burger.

"Damn, this is flavorful," replied Ty, only slightly behind Carson in burger completion rate. "I can see why it won so many awards. For me, it has a good heat that gives a kick, but not too hot to enjoy."

"The Congress burger at Second Bar + Kitchen near the office is one of my absolute favorite burgers in Austin, or anywhere," said Kareem. "This is right up there. The peppers really give it that something extra. I think the burger would be phenomenal without it and just a regular cheeseburger, but this is the next level."

The guys looked over at Tegan, who had been quiet during their evaluation of the burger. To their surprise, she had continued forging through the beast and was putting away the last bite.

"What?" she said with her mouth full. "You guys are busy talking. I'm busy eating."

She wiped her mouth, threw the napkin on the table, and took a drink of the Bat Brew, cementing herself as the legendary eater on the team.

The host returned to check on everyone. The guys were still stunned that Tegan finished first. They slowly and silently returned to their burgers as if they had just been scolded.

"Is there a dessert menu?" asked Tegan.

The boys remained silent, pensively eating the second half of their burger.

"We do. We have a basket of sopapillas that comes with powdered sugar and honey. You can add a butterscotch sauce to that for $1.25. We also have a dulce de leche fried ice cream, a chocolate bread pudding also with butterscotch sauce, a caramel flan with optional prickly pear drizzle, or a chocolate Grand Marnier flan. All of them are excellent. You can't go wrong with any of them," the host said.

Tegan looked over at the guys, who were slowing down as they neared the end of their burger.

"I should wait and see if they left any room for dessert," Tegan said with a smile.

Ty threw down the napkin and rubbed his stomach.

"None for me. I was hungry after that mountain, but I went from zero to a hundred real quick," he replied.

Tegan smiled at the host. "I guess we're finished. Just the check," she replied.

"Thanks for bringing us here, Charlie," said Carson. "This was an excellent find."

"If you don't have room for dessert, hopefully you left room for beer," Charlie responded.

"There's always room for beer," replied Kareem.

"Great, because just under three miles away is a great local brewery with a beer that's a Phoenix classic," replied Charlie.

"A Phoenix classic? We can't pass that up," said Carson.

After paying the bill, they made their way back to the parking lot, albeit slower than they had entered, thanks to full stomachs and sore legs.

Driving down McClintock Drive, turning right onto McDowell, and left onto Scottsdale Road, Carson turned into the Papago Plaza Shopping Center, a large shopping center with Adobe inspired shapes and color.

"Wow, this is cool," said Ty. "Where are we headed?"

"About halfway down on the left, you'll reach the spot," directed Charlie.

The large turquoise letters above the giant wooden doors showed they had reached their destination, *Papago Brewing.* Upon entering, they encountered an enormous statue of a portly, jolly monk, but continued toward the back of the building, past several round wooden tables.

"I love this large room and all the seating," said Ty.

"There's another room off to the side here," Charlie said, pointing to the left. "I love to sit at the bar. They have a great selection of beers on tap and an impressive inventory in those coolers."

Tegan walked up to the coolers, staring at the over five hundred different bottled beers from around the world.

"What a great beer selection!" Tegan said.

"They are available for on-site consumption or to take home. Plus, we have thirty taps to choose from," announced the server. "Do you want to sit at the bar or at a table?" she asked.

"Let's do a table. Easier to talk," suggested Kareem.

"Right this way," the server said as she sat them at a table near the bar.

"What's this Phoenix classic beer you mentioned, Charlie?" asked Carson.

"The Papago Orange Blossom. It's awesome on draft, and they have cans. One of two beers they produce, both well-regarded," said Charlie.

"Orange Blossom? A Mandarin Wheat beer?" read Ty.

"Yes, that one and the Coconut Joe. It's a coconut and coffee stout are what they are known for," replied Charlie.

"Then we need one of each," proposed Carson.

"I will bring you each an Orange Blossom to start, and then follow it with the Coconut Joe," suggested the server before returning to the bar to pour the drinks.

"So, what's the next step with this mysterious camel?" asked Charlie.

"It was quite the rude awakening at the river," replied Carson. "We are fairly certain that was the animal you saw. It was just so unusual to see a camel, but we couldn't get a good look at it because it was too far away when we made it out of the tents. We need to head back to the river and see if we can follow the tracks, or project where he might have gone and see if we can pick up evidence elsewhere."

As they were discussing the plan, the server returned with the Orange Blossoms.

"River? Are you guys going tubing? That's one of my favorite activities during the summer. Renting a tube and floating down the Salt River with a small raft of beer floating behind me," she said.

"No, not this time. These guys are investigating a mysterious animal I saw the other day out in Mesa," said Charlie.

"Mysterious animal? Sounds intriguing. Is it related to that one on the news this morning?"

"What news?" asked Carson.

"The story started the other day about a body of a guy they found in Goldfield," she answered.

"Yeah, we heard about that. Did they have more information?" asked Ty.

"Today they said the man died of a massive heart attack. Apparently, something ran up on him and scared him to death. The interesting thing was the animal might have trampled him. They found hair from an animal on his body," she added.

"When we arrived Charlie mentioned they found long strands of red hair on the body," responded Carson.

"Yes," she replied. "The results from the lab came back, and it was conclusive to camel hair."

The group at the table looked at each other hearing that.

"But the interesting thing about it was -" she added.

Carson interrupted, "More interesting than matching to a camel when there are no camels in Phoenix?"

"Yes. The interesting thing was the hair seemed to suggest the animal was between one hundred and one hundred fifty years old," she added.

"What? Camel life spans on average are about fifty years old," said Tegan. "That would be unlike anything ever seen."

"They said there were a few scattered reports of the animal this week. Those who saw it said it appeared to have a red glow about it. This hair was red, but wasn't glowing, so they were probably seeing things," she said.

"Any idea where it was last seen?" asked Kareem.

"I don't know. One guy interviewed was in Tempe," she said.

"Tempe isn't far from here. I say we check it out," suggested Charlie.

"Definitely, although I am dragging with all the action today. Maybe we hit it up tomorrow?" said Carson. "We got little sleep last night, and that hike did me in."

"I'm down for that. Right now, I want to relax and enjoy this beer," replied Ty.

"Me too, and this beer is great. I can see why it is a local classic. Tastes like a liquid old-fashioned creamsicle," reminisced Tegan.

"Definitely good orange and vanilla flavors. This would be quite enjoyable on a sultry afternoon," added Ty.

"Yep - not too heavy and with a nice, unique flavor. Makes me want to lie by the pool, or float down the river like the server suggested. Without thinking, I could make three disappear in ten minutes," said Carson.

After finishing the beer, the server returned to check in.

"Ready for the next round?" she asked.

"Ready when you are," added Kareem.

She returned to the bar and poured five pints of the Coconut Joe. Placing them on a round serving tray, she returned to the table.

"We used to make an Irish Milk Stout called Elsie's that was basically an Irish car bomb in a glass. It was a rich milk stout with one pound of Irish Cream flavored coffee beans added per barrel and a very popular drink. This is Elsie's cousin, Joe. He's a little more approachable for light beer drinkers. We match the bite of roasted coffee with a hint of coconut sweetness on the finish. It has easily become our most popular dark beer," she added.

Kareem reached for the pint in front of him. "I'm a big coffee fan," he said just before taking the first sip. As he started in, his face revealed he was fond of the beer. "Lovely coffee aroma followed by a clean coconut flavor and background cocoa malt."

"That first beer was a creamsicle. This one tastes like a Mounds bar," Tegan said.

"And that coconut tastes natural. Not the artificial taste you get in some beers. Solid coconut-laced brew that hits the entirety of right flavor notes," Ty.

"I love that the Phoenix market is growing in great craft beer, and some of the O.G.'s, like these two, are still prominent," said Kareem.

"The classics are timeless," added Ty.

After finishing the pints, Carson called for the check.

"It's been a long day. I am ready to go to the hotel and chillax," Carson suggested.

"Did you find a place?" asked Charlie.

"Yes, I booked a couple of rooms at the Best Western in Chandler on Ray Road and Arizona Avenue. And if we are going to hit up Tempe tomorrow, it isn't too far," Carson replied.

The group paid the bill and left the brewery, satisfied once again with the great selection of Arizona beer. They stopped by Charlie's apartment to drop him off.

"I will call you tomorrow to check in. Maybe we can do something in Tempe while we investigate the area," suggested Carson.

"Sounds like a plan. Have a good night. Get some rest. Maybe we can do another small hike tomorrow. There's a short, but decent spot in Tempe we can hit up," added Charlie.

"Will do. Catch ya later," responded Ty before they drove off to check into the hotel for the evening.

CHAPTER 7

HOUSE OF HEAT

Wednesday, March 16, 2016 (PM)

It was after noon when Carson and Ty woke up in the hotel room. Carson picked up the nearby cell phone and saw a message from Tegan thirty minutes earlier.

"Looks like they've been up for a while already."

"Are they still in the room?" Ty asked.

"Not sure, but I know I'm hungry," added Carson.

"Me too. That was quite the day yesterday. Camelback is no joke," Ty stated. "I slept like a baby last night."

"Charlie mentioned hiking somewhere today. I hope it is easier because I can't do Camelback again," Carson said, analyzing his level of discomfort with an awkward stretch.

Tegan returned the text stating she already ran three miles

on the hotel treadmill. Now she and Kareem were watching TV and waiting for the guys.

"We should join them and get the day started," Carson said as he pulled his head through the opening of a gray t-shirt with a cartoon chupacabra standing over a goat.

"I believe in chupacabras?"

"Seeing is believing," Carson said.

"I need one that said the chupacabra bit me," remarked Ty.

"That's likely a limited population. Probably have to design your own on Zazzle," replied Carson.

"Speaking of biting, I am in the mood for something different. Not the same pizza, burgers, and bar food that we frequently get. I love those things as much as the next guy, but it would be good to mix it up a bit," said Ty.

Tegan and Kareem knocked on the door of Ty and Carson's room.

"Mix what up?" asked Tegan.

"I'm already thinking about lunch. I guess we missed breakfast," said Ty.

"Yes, something different sounds good," said Kareem.

Carson searched for restaurants in the area on his cell phone and reported the results.

"Near to us we have Thai options, Mexican, ramen, Chinese, and Caribbean."

"Caribbean? That's my vote!" responded Ty.

"No objections here," said Tegan.

"It says they have authentic Jamaican cuisine prepared fresh daily from scratch using both local and imported spices," added Carson.

"How far?" asked Kareem.

"About one mile."

"Let's go. We can have lunch, and then check in with Charlie afterwards," suggested Kareem.

Carson drove up Arizona Avenue where, just past Warner Road, he found the shopping center housing Hot Pot Caribbean Cuisine.

Inside, the yellow and green wall was separated by a band of black and a band of red. Reggae music played over the speakers. Daily specials were displayed on a mounted menu behind the glass counter.

They walked to the counter to get a closer look at the options. A young woman came from the kitchen, ready to take their order.

"Do you know what you'd like? The specials today are curry chicken, curry goat, oxtail, and jerk chicken," she said with a Jamaican accent. "We also have mango wings or jerk wings."

"Mango wings sound fantastic," said Carson. "We can split it if you want?"

"I am going to order the oxtail, but I will share some wings with you," said Ty.

"I want the jerk chicken," said Carson. "That's one of my all-time favorite dishes."

"What do you guys want for sides? You get two," asked the server.

"Rice and peas and the plantains," ordered Ty.

"Same for me," added Carson.

Kareem stepped up and ordered the jerk chicken with the same sides. Tegan chose the curry chicken, also with the same sides.

"It will be just a few minutes," the young woman said. "Sit anywhere you'd like."

They took a table close to the counter and enjoyed the music.

"I dig a place like this. A real laid-back casual spot with a homey vibe," Ty replied, lost in the sounds of Buju Banton, Shabba Ranks, and Elephant Man.

"They have some super comfy-looking chairs over there for those waiting for takeout," observed Kareem.

"They have a fish fry the first Friday of each month and live music," Carson said, reading a poster hanging on the wall.

"The atmosphere is perfect. I love the small seating area. It's close and has a communal feel. The reggae music really completes it. I just need a cocktail and a beach," added Tegan.

Moments later, the young woman returned from the kitchen with the food. "There's also rum cake in the cooler if you're still hungry after this," she added.

She sat the plates in the middle of the guests as they took in the food's aroma.

"This looks and smells amazing!" responded Carson. "I can already smell the spice from the jerk chicken."

"Do you have any hot sauce?" asked Ty.

"Yes, I can bring some out for you," the server replied.

"Pro tip - brown rice and peas are good, but even better with hot sauce," Ty stated.

Carson cut a piece of the chicken and took a bite. Instantly, his eyes closed, and his face reflected a happy reaction.

"The spice is just right! I love jerk chicken, and this is to die for!"

"Why are you cutting? You're among friends. Pick it up and eat with your hands," scolded Ty.

"The flavor is amazing on this curry chicken," stated Tegan. "And the plantains are excellent."

"How's the oxtail treatin' you?" asked Carson.

"The meat is fall-off-the-bone perfect, and this sauce. So damn good, I would eat it on an old shoe! It's the best I have had in a while!" Ty added.

"Looks like Charlie's checking in," Kareem said, looking down at his vibrating phone.

"Is he ready to go? Tell him we will meet him in Tempe," Carson said, licking his fingers after finishing the wings.

"He suggested meeting up around 5 p.m. He has a few errands to run. That time of night will give us a good glimpse around sunset," replied Kareem.

Ty searched the Tempe area online while the others finished their lunch.

"That works for me. We know sunset also stirs up many animals. Maybe we'll get lucky and spot the creature. There is a parking lot on the map between Ash and University. We can park there and walk Mill Avenue," Ty suggested.

Kareem texted the suggestion to Charlie, who acknowledged with confirmation.

"We're all set," said Kareem.

Later that afternoon, the team arrived at the parking lot off of Ash. Ty walked to the parking meter and paid for three hours while the others stretched in preparation for another hike.

"This mid-eighties weather and low humidity is perfect," said Tegan.

"Hopefully we can find some leads or maybe the animal itself. We have been close behind it so far, and I don't want the trail to get cold," said Carson.

Charlie pulled into an empty spot and walked over to the group.

"How are you guys feeling today?"

"A little sore, but otherwise awesome. We slept in a comfortable bed, had Caribbean food for lunch, and now we are ready to see what we can find on this mysterious camel," replied Ty.

"Mill Avenue is a good place for people watching. It's the hot spot in the town. We might see a bit of everything, especially after nightfall," said Charlie.

"Austin is known for being a little weird too, so we'll fit right in," suggested Carson.

"This hike will be much easier than yesterday. It isn't long and not as strenuous as yesterday. It is a steep hike, but it's steady and a paved trail. We can get to the top in about twenty minutes with little difficulty," noted Charlie.

"As long as it isn't like Camelback, I'll be fine," said Tegan.

"We can head out of the parking lot and cross over Mill. The entrance is right there by the light rail tracks," said Charlie. "The official name is Hayden Butte Preserve Park, but most people call it 'A' Mountain," he said, pointing at the giant letter on the side of the mountain.

"Why the giant A?" asked Ty.

"There used to be a school here called The Tempe Normal School, and the class of 1918 installed giant letters on the mountain. The school changed its name to Tempe State Teachers College in 1925. The students changed the letters to be only a T. When the school changed names again in 1938 to Arizona State, students changed the letter to an A," reported Charlie. "Sometimes you see rivals from University of Arizona come up and paint or alter the letter."

They crossed Mill Avenue, stood at the base of the mountain, and looked up.

"It doesn't seem that bad," said Kareem.

"It's not. It is a popular Tempe. It's very easy, but gives a magnificent view of the surrounding areas. You can see Arizona State University just down the light rail tracks. The football stadium is near the tracks and the basketball stadium is just on the other side. Across the street from where we parked is Tempe Town Lake. That's very popular also," said Charlie.

The team walked through the semi-empty parking lot and came to the entrance of a dusty, rocky trail that wound its way up a heavily trafficked trail that was about a one-mile round trip.

"This is a fun little hike at night with really delightful views at the top," commented Charlie. "The lights in town and on the lake are spectacular. That's why I wanted to come out a little later so you can check out an Arizona sunset."

"I like this one already," said Carson as they started up the paved trail.

As they continued the steep climb up the mountain, the sun sat in the west. The sky over the lake turned yellow, orange, and red as the sun dipped below the peaks of Papago Park.

"They say Arizona has some of the best sunsets," said Ty. "I can see why," he said as he turned the last corner and reached the top of the trail. The summit was just beyond a small fence.

"I would do this every day," said Tegan. "Even though it's steep, I'm not even winded. It was a nice relaxing hike and yet close to all the commotion of Mill Avenue. No excuse not to enjoy nature when it's this easy," she said.

"Check out the view. I didn't know Phoenix was this green. From up here looking back toward Tempe, there are many more trees than I expected," admitted Carson. "And a lot of little bodies of water in parks, Papago, Tempe Town Lake, that looks like Kiwanis Park over there, and we passed some lakes in Chandler coming out here. Little oases scattered among the urban desert," he said.

They looked around from the top of the mountain and saw maybe a dozen other hikers sitting on the rocks watching the sunset on the lake.

"The good news is that once you get down the mountain, you are right on Mill Avenue, where there are dozens of restaurants and bars. It's the evening and weekend hangout spot," said Charlie.

"What's that building down there?" asked Tegan, pointing to a large white building at the foot of the mountain.

"That's the old Hayden flour mills plant. Charles Hayden founded it in 1868. Legend says he was trying to make his way up north, but the Salt River flooded, and he couldn't pass. While waiting for the waters to subside, he stood on top of Tempe Butte, which is where we are right now. He didn't see the trees and houses that we see today. What he saw was fertile land, and he realized it was the perfect spot to establish the flour mill," said Charlie. "The company is still in business today. That building is part of the original mill and is now a tourist site. It's the mill that gives Mill Avenue its name."

"Hard to imagine the river being that high back then. There isn't much to it now," said Ty.

"No, it's mainly dry in this part. Tempe Town Lake is a man-made lake, but there are spots of water in the river. You can see from here it running in front of Tempe Marketplace and behind the 202 near Sloan Park," said Charlie.

They sat on the rocks at the butte's summit for several more minutes, relaxing and taking in the views against the nightfall background.

"There is descent lighting up here, even at night, but we should begin the return and see what clues we can uncover around town," suggested Charlie.

"According to Joshua Gates, if you want to uncover the scoop on local legends and sightings of strange things, you check out the local taverns," reported Carson.

"My man," replied Ty.

"Mill Avenue has plenty of nightlife. Further up the street at South Mill Avenue at West 6th Street is a spot called World of Beer that I enjoy," replied Charlie.

"I've heard of that place. Not this one, but others around the country. Out of Florida, right?" asked Kareem.

"That's right. This one here opened in 2012 and it's nice. Friendly people and great beer selection. They rotate the handles frequently and keep a well-stocked cooler from around the world," replied Charlie.

"We have a couple in Texas also," replied Ty.

As they reached the base of the mountain and walked through the parking lot, they sensed Mill Avenue coming to life. The distant clangs of the light rail bell, the sights of streetlights illuminating, the smell of sugar cones from a nearby ice cream store, sounds of people laughing and having a good time in the open-air patios, and music from street performers combined to create an exciting atmosphere.

They crossed the street and walked south toward World of Beer. As they did, they passed an older Black man with a white beard and long dreadlocks. He wore a red knit Rasta hat and green t-shirt as he played an acoustic guitar and sang about surviving changes on Mill Avenue. The sign in front of his tip jar read *Walt Richardson.* They stopped and listened briefly to the soulful sounds of the street performing storyteller. Ty reached into his pocket and dropped twenty dollars in the jar as he bobbed his head to the song.

"That's awesome," Ty said. "I love hearing regular cats performing on the street and loving their craft. That's the soul of the city."

Walt nodded his head, acknowledging and thanking the group while he continued singing *Mill Avenue.* The group continued on as other walkers stopped to listen to music that complemented the night air and gentle breeze so well.

World of Beer was just another block away, past the ice cream shop, the Arizona State team shop, an old bookstore, and an ATM. The bar is in what used to be the old Tempe National Bank building. They remodeled the building to include patio dining, a small outside bar, and two levels of indoor seating. The bar boasted an extensive selection of craft beer with over five hundred and twenty bottle varieties and fifty rotating beers on tap. In the back of the building, the old bank vault remained and provided a secluded area for drinking or private parties.

As they walked through the door and into the large bar, the sight of the coolers and their contents amazed the travelers.

"I get it. I'm still impressed every time I come in," said Charlie. "Just the sight of the bottles causes me to gasp. It's hard to find that level of selection in town. They have a loyalty program that allows customers to earn prizes, at least in other states. Arizona laws do not permit rewarding people for drinking beer, so we kind of get hosed on the deal. However, I have a few points. Not like those guys on the loyalty board up there," Charlie said as he pointed to a tall chalkboard by the front door listing off the top ten loyalty members.

"Damn, that's a lot of beer," Carson said, looking at the bottom of the board. "Those guys have over two hundred and three hundred beers. How do you get a point?"

The bar's general manager approached them. He was bald headed and had a long gray beard. His North Carolinian accent was warm and friendly.

"You get a point for each unique beer you drink," the GM answered.

"Unique beer?" asked Kareem.

"Either a different beer, or it can be a different type of vessel. A can is a point, a draft is a point, and a bottle is a point. But if you have two cans of the same beer, that's just a point," the man from the Tar Heel state clarified.

"So these guys, they may have drank more beer than listed, but they have had three hundred *different* beers?" asked Kareem.

"That's correct," replied the general manager.

The team continued scanning the list.

"Jesus, look at the leaders. Two guys have about five hundred. Some person named *The WOB Father* has over six hundred, and… is that a typo? *Vanilla Heat* has over fifteen hundred different beers?" questioned Carson.

"Nope, that's correct. Vanilla Heat, he's the man. Absolute legend. He comes in regularly, and actually…" the man said scanning the bar, "that's him at the end of the bar," replied the general manager, pointing to a man a few seats away.

"The WOB Father has an impressive lead over the rest of the back, but Vanilla Heat has more than doubled him. Fucking legend is right! I've got to meet this guy," said Carson.

The group approached the man sitting at the end of the bar. He wore glasses, an orange Phoenix Mercury ball cap, jeans, and a navy-blue t-shirt with a Spider-man 2099 logo.

"Excuse me? Are you *The* Vanilla Heat?" Carson asked.

"Yes, that's me," said the dashingly handsome man as he turned to meet his unknown visitors. He may have been in his mid-forties, but could easily pass for early thirties. He was a mix between George Clooney and Brad Pitt.

"You've had all of those beers?" asked Tegan.

"Yes, I have. I come here every few days on my way home from work. They have a great selection, and the people are nice. Especially this guy," he said, pointing to the GM. "Everything I know about craft beer I learned from him, so I keep coming back," replied the pulchritudinous man.

"You must drink a lot of beer," said Kareem somewhat rhetorically.

The man pointed to a plaque on the wall that read *In Dog Beers I've Only Had One.* It included his name and loyalty award status printed below. It was one of the few loyalty awards he received before the city forced the bar to cease distribution of earned incentives.

"I drink a lot of beer, but not as much as most of the people that probably come in here. I just learned the system and work with it," Vanilla Heat replied humbly.

"How so?" inquired Carson.

"As my friend said, it's a point for every unique beer in a different delivery method. When most people go out for beer, and they go to different places around town. Mostly, I come here only. I like to try a variety of beer, but as much as I may like something, I only order it once. Instead of the menu, I order based on the World of Beer app, which I have set to filter out the beers I've already had. When I look at the app, it shows only the beers I haven't had, so I know I'll get a point for it when I order."

"We'd be honored if we could join you for a beer. Do you mind?" asked Carson.

"No, not at all," Vanilla Heat said. "Let's move over to a table so we can all talk," he said.

Tegan and Kareem snickered to each other while commenting on how charming the man was. Immediately after moving to the table just a couple feet from the bar, a customer walked in and took the vacated spot at the end of the bar.

Bobbye DePaul was about six foot two, with broad shoulders, and a slim figure. She had long black hair that cascaded to the mid-point of her back. Just passed her shoulders, the black gave way to a dyed blue, continuing to the ends. Her soft features, with high cheekbones complemented by soft pink lipstick. Wearing a black leather miniskirt, a loose black tank top, and black fishnet stockings, she gave the impression of hardcore punk rock. A tattoo on each leg peeked from the edges of the skirt. Another tattoo, a flock of flying birds, was on her outer forearm. She had a feather behind her left ear and a sun tattoo on her upper right shoulder. She signaled to the bartender with a raise of one of her larger than average fingers. In a soft, but deeper voice, she ordered a beer.

"Do you still have the Barrel Aged Piehole Porter?" she asked.

"Yes, we still have it," replied the bartender. "But probably not for much longer."

"One of those, please," Bobbye ordered.

"How did you get the name Vanilla Heat?" Charlie asked.

"That's an interesting story, ranging between PG and R depending on the audience. But that's one for another time. Let's just say I earned it on a vacation in Jamaica. Who knows? Maybe one day I will write a memoir and tell the full story."

"You've had a ton of beers. I'm sure you get this all the time… what are you drinking, and what's your favorite?" Ty asked.

"Right now I am drinking a Tahitian Honeymoon, which is a mead from Superstition Meadery up in Prescott. I don't drink mead very often because of the sweetness, but I enjoy it when I do. It makes me feel like Beowulf," Vanilla Heat said.

"Mostly I like IPAs and stouts. I don't have a well-developed sense of taste for the subtle flavors people write about in beer reviews. IPAs and stouts have a strong enough flavor that I can taste and enjoy them. One of my recent local favorites is Nativity in Black by North Mountain. That's top-notch if you can get it. They're on Dunlap Avenue in Phoenix. That's one of the rare times I went somewhere other than WOB. I don't get up there much, but I stumbled upon the release in one of the Facebook groups I follow. Immediately, I made the trip. Well worth the trip," said Vanilla Heat. "The White Russian from SunUp Brewing is phenomenal too, and they have it here."

"And what about IPAs?" asked Tegan.

"Right now I am really digging The Roosevelts from Arizona Wilderness. It's an Imperial IPA and is so good. Actually, they have many excellent beers there right now. The brewery is on the Gilbert-Chandler border. Have you been?"

"No, we are actually from Austin. We just are in town visiting this guy," Ty said, jerking a thumb toward Charlie. "We are also investigating a strange creature."

"Strange creature? Cool. I like paranormal stuff. Cryptids, aliens, and that sort of thing."

"You like strange, paranormal things *and* craft beer? You could be one of us," replied Kareem, enamored.

"Well, I like it on television. I have encountered a few unexplained things in real life, and I didn't really like it then," Vanilla Heat admitted.

"There's some strange stuff here in the building," the bartender said as she checked in on the table.

"Really? Like what?" Carson asked.

"Late at night after we've closed. I've been downstairs alone and heard footsteps. My dog was with me one night and he was terrified," she said.

"Animals always know," replied Tegan.

"You've come to the right place," Bobbye said, overhearing the conversation. "There's a lot of weird shit around here."

"What kind of weird shit?" Carson asked.

"You name it. The Phoenix Lights, the Turtle Man of Tempe Town Lake, Greys, centaurs, and that camel thing that was on the news yesterday," she said.

"Camel thing?" asked Vanilla Heat

"The reporter said it killed some guy in Goldfield. This camel scared him into a heart attack. Then they spotted it in Mesa, and yesterday here in Tempe somewhere," she said.

"That's actually why we're in town. We saw it first-hand," added Kareem.

"What? So it is real? Where?" asked Bobbye.

"We encountered it along the Salt River after visiting Goldfield. Early in the morning, it came running through camp and knocked down the tents," said Carson.

"But there are no camels around here," Bobbye said.

"Not anymore," said Vanilla Heat as the overhead music began playing a song by Ludacris.

"Anymore? What do you mean?" asked Carson.

"There used to be during the Civil War," Vanilla Heat added.

"Civil War? I never really thought about Arizona being in the Civil War. Wasn't it just a state in 1912? I thought it was part of Mexico during the Civil War," replied Kareem.

"It was the Territory of Arizona back then and claimed by the Confederate States of America from 1861 to 1865," Vanilla Heat reported. "Secretary of War General Jefferson Davis created the Camel Corps because he believed they would hold up better in the dry, scorching desert than a horse would. But the experiment didn't last long."

"That's a piece of interesting history. You know your shit. I would love to learn more about the use of camels in this area and what happened to them," said Carson.

"And smart to boot," Kareem swooned, leaning in and holding Tegan's upper arm and shoulder as Salt-N-Pepa's *Whatta A Man* played on the bar's radio. She shared the doting and dazzled expression regarding the charismatic, total package man.

"My advice would be to head out to West Phoenix. Check out Marble Hills University. There's a professor there named Dr. Sedona Williams. He's an expert on Arizona history and can probably give you more details," Vanilla Heat suggested.

"Ain't that some shit?" said Bobbye.

"What about this Turtle Man you mentioned?" Ty asked Bobbye.

"Some giant turtle that people say is under the bridges around Tempe Town Lake. I don't think it has hurt anyone and people say it's probably just shadows, but I've heard rumors. I love to take the paddle boats out on the lake, and I've never seen it, but you know, people talk," she said.

"You ready for another round?" the server asked as she returned to the table.

"Oh, damn. Sorry. We were so into our conversation we hadn't looked at the menu. How about you surprise us? Something local, something different for each of the four of us. I don't know if Charlie wants something different. It's all new for us, so anything is a treat," said Carson.

"I will have a Barrel-Aged Sirius Black, if you still have it," replied Charlie.

"Yes, that's still on, although we're almost out," said the bartender. "I will be back with that and four random locals," she said.

"That Turtle Man does sound interesting. And did you say centaurs?" asked Carson.

"I have heard reports out on the Salt River Reservation and even up into Navajo Nation around the four corners of people seeing centaurs. I don't know though. That seems sketchy," Bobbye added.

Carson paused briefly, recalling the strange statue he found last fall at Cody's Emporium in Burlington. It was a wooden carving from the Salt River Pima-Maricopa Indian Community in Arizona and depicted what Carson thought to be a centaur. He remembered thinking it was unusual because Native artwork usually depicted things in their surroundings that they experience themselves. It seemed out of place when he saw it last year, but now, he wondered if they really experienced these creatures. Maybe the carving was their rendition of what they saw. His thoughts were interrupted as the server returned with the drinks.

"I will just put them here in the middle and you can decide who gets what," she suggested. "I have a Camelback IPA from The Phoenix Ale Brewery, Magic in a Barrel Pale Ale from Huss, Fall Maple Strong Ale from Dubina, and Peanut Butter Husstler also Huss," she said.

Bobbye stood up and joined the table, enjoying the conversation about the strange happenings in the area.

"Oh, Vanilla, we have some of those cans of your beer if you want me to bring them. We tried the canning system on them and made about twenty," the server added.

"Really? That's great. Can we get them? Maybe these guys would be interested in taking some home. Bobbye, you want some too?"

"What is it?" Bobbye asked.

"About six months ago, I brewed a beer with my friend from here and some guys from Cartel Brewing. We made an Imperial Porter brewed with BLiS bourbon and vanilla maple syrup, aged on Copper City bourbon oak, vanilla beans, and scotch bonnet peppers on Nitro and named it the Real Vanilla Heat," Vanilla Heat stated.

"Jesus, that sounds like a mythical beast itself," replied Ty.

"Real Vanilla Heat? Named after you?" asked Tegan.

"Yes. It was only on draft for a limited time, but they wanted to test out their new Dixie crowler system, so we tried it out to see what would happen. Sounds like we could have a couple of cans each," Vanilla Heat offered.

Bobbye, Charlie, Carson, Kareem, Ty, and Tegan each took two cans, and Vanilla Heat had eight left to take home.

"I should probably check out and head home. See what the family is doing. We just had a quinceañera for my daughter the other day. I should get back and spend some time with them," replied Vanilla Heat.

"Quinceañera? When was that?" asked Charlie.

"It was Friday out in Mesa," he replied, as he handed his card to the bartender.

"Mesa? Was it at Pearl's?" asked Charlie.

"Yes. It was such a good night. She had a great time, and the band was spectacular," Vanilla Heat added.

"Hey, thanks. I am in the band that performed at the party," replied Charlie.

"The party you were playing at, when you took a break outside and saw the camel," Carson asked Charlie. "Was your daughter's party?" he asked Vanilla Heat.

"I didn't see a camel, but yeah, it sounds like it was the same party," added Vanilla Heat. "Small world."

"That's some crazy shit," said Ty.

"I told you shit's crazy out here," said Bobbye.

"Good luck finding this mystery camel. Like I said, check out Marble Hills and Dr. Williams," said Vanilla Heat as he gathered the remaining cans of the Real Vanilla Heat.

He stood and shook the hands of each of the investigators, Charlie, and Bobbye.

"Nice to meet you all."

"Keep up the good work on the beer. Looks like you have quite the lead on the WOB Father," added Ty.

"I haven't seen him in a long time. I think I am safely in control of the leaderboard."

The General Manager returned to behind the bar and waved at the loyalty leader as he left.

"See ya, next time, Heat," the GM said.

"What else do you guys plan on doing tonight?" asked Bobbye.

"I'm not sure," replied Carson. "We slept in this morning. I am still fresh. Maybe check out more of Mill Avenue?"

"I am going to a show tonight down the street at a place called Yucca Tap Room, if you want to join me," said Bobbye. "It's on Mill, but far enough that we'd have to drive. It's a pleasant combination of a dive bar and a modern craft beer bar. They have music acts there frequently. They have all genres of music. Just the other day they had Edith Crash, a French singer-songwriter who performs in French, Spanish, and English. That was chill. Tonight is Dreadnaught, a metal band from Melbourne, Australia. Should be wild," she said.

"The combo of a craft beer bar and a dive bar sounds interesting enough for me," suggested Tegan.

"Cool, I can get us in. I'm good friends with the head of security," Bobbye replied.

The bar was busy for a weekday. The group entered the craft bar side and slowly navigated their way between people and pool tables.

While the craft beer side had many people, the dive bar side was packed wall-to-wall.

"Guard your loins. Sometimes people get handsy," advised Bobbye.

The opening band was getting started, causing the lively crowd to bounce to the music, bounding and slamming off each other to start a mosh pit. Bobbye led the way as she knifed through the crowd and found a small opening at the side of the bar. She motioned for six beers, all of them Hamm's Premium. The bartender sat them on the bar top and opened each. Bobbye dropped twenty-five dollars on the bar to include the tip and began handing them to her new friends.

Each took a cold can and attempted to make their way through the crowd to a spot on the floor where they had a better view of the band and could enjoy the atmosphere. They raised their arms above their heads and pressed body to body through the gyrating people until they reached a small opening near the back of the crowd.

Dreadnaught took the stage, opening with *Scenester,* and the crowd returned a head-banging response. Bobbye began to dance within the crowd as the band moved into playing *Push*. She thought about the conversation earlier and the mysterious camel from the news, which she learned from her new friends, was real.

"If there is a wild camel in the desert, I hope you find it and capture it. We can't have strange creatures running up on people and scaring them to death," she said through loud music.

"What?" replied Carson loudly.

"She said we have to catch the camel," shouted Kareem

"We are going to head to that school tomorrow and see what we can learn. Figure out what we're up against," replied Carson.

They finished the beer and Charlie made his way to the bar to get a second round for everyone. The band played *The Game* as he returned with fresh cans for everyone. They drank and danced for the next hour while the band played, and the raucous crowd showed their approval. When it was over, the lights came up, but their ears continued to ring. They made their way outside and stood in the parking lot. The cool night air felt good after being in the tightly packed bar for a couple of hours.

"Woo, what a rush," Bobbye said. "So much fun. Thank you for coming out and hanging with me tonight."

"Even though it's late, I worked up an appetite in there. Where's a good place to eat this time of night?" Carson asked.

"Other places I've lived, you usually go to the Waffle House or maybe IHOP after going to the club all night. We have those places here, but in Phoenix, you go to a hot dog stand and get a Sonoran hot dog," replied Bobbye. "Now I kind of want one."

"What's a Sonoran hot dog?" asked Ty.

"Besides the best late night eats in the state and delicious?" asked Bobbye. "It's the most popular hot dog in Arizona, especially Phoenix and Tucson. The best ones come from dogueros operating small hot dog stands that pop up at night. Seems to be frequently in llanteras or next to an auto repair shop," she added.

"What's a llantera?" asked Carson.

"It means tire shop in Spanish," replied Charlie.

"I told you guys down in San Antonio my Spanish was rusty," Carson responded.

"In the evening, guys take over parking lots, erect tents, and set up grill carts. The bun is usually a top-split bolillo roll, which is sturdier than a regular hot dog bun. They wrap the hot dog in bacon, and then grill it. Next comes the toppings: usually pinto beans, onions, and tomatoes, but most places have a toppings bar where you can add cheese, spicy salsa, mushrooms, or pickles. Top it off with mayo and a large chili on the side. The flavors are delicious, and they put just enough of everything together to where it's not soggy," she explained.

"How much are they?" asked Ty.

"About five dollars," she replied.

"Damn. Sounds like it would hit the spot," Carson said.

"How lucky are we that we met someone who loves food and craft beer just as much as we do?" asked Carson.

"A girl's gotta eat," replied Bobbye.

"I live off Broadway if you guys want to follow me. There's a glorious stand close to my apartment. It's called Tacos & Dogos Don Nico, and it's the best," Bobbye said.

"Why not? It's been a fun evening, and if it's the best wiener in town, we gotta try it," replied Kareem.

"Well..." Bobbye hesitated, with a raised eyebrow and pursed lips. She shot a quick wink at Kareem. "And they have great tacos, too. You have to top it off with a Mexican coke," Bobbye added.

They followed Bobbye to the cash-only hot dog stand in the parking lot of the llantera. A large canopy tent covered several tables and chairs, providing ample seating for the business. The parking lot was full, despite the late hour on a weeknight. The food arrived at the table by the owner. They spent the rest of the night enjoying the food, the company, and weather.

Finishing the hot dog, Carson and Kareem went back for more, placing an order for two street tacos each; birria for Carson and cabeza for Kareem.

Afterward, they stacked the empty plastic trays in the table's corner and hugged Bobbye, thanking her for the fun evening. She wished them well on their search for the creature and for an enjoyable rest of their trip. Carson handed her a business card as they returned to their cars.

CHAPTER 8

RISE UP, MIGHTY OAK

Thursday, March 17, 2016

The Kia Soul driven by Carson pulled into the campus of Marble Hills University, home of the Mighty Oaks, at Thomas and 15th Avenue in West Phoenix. He stopped at the security gate to ask for directions to the Summerset Building, where they planned to meet Professor Sedona Williams prior to his 1 p.m. Arizona and Federal Government class. The guard pointed to a large parking garage to the left of the security checkpoint, then pointed to a building just down a sidewalk promenade. Carson thanked the man and pulled around the guard shack and into the garage, luckily finding a parking spot on the first level.

As they exited the vehicle, Carson filled the others in on the conversation he had with Dr. Williams earlier in the morning.

"I reached out to see if we could talk to him about the history of camels in Arizona. He teaches a government and Arizona history class that meets this afternoon. He said he would be in his office before lunch," said Carson.

The Summerset Building was a small, one-story building. The second one on the right from the driveway that looped the guard shack. Opening the door, students flooded the hallway, leaving from one class to the next and some heading to lunch. The investigators found room 103 and entered. Dr. Williams was inside speaking to a student after class. The team stood in the back, waiting for the conversation to conclude. When the student left, Carson approached, extending a hand to the professor.

"Dr. Williams? Carson Quinn. We spoke on the phone earlier this morning," Carson affirmed.

"Oh, yes. About the camels? Few people talk about that interesting topic around here. You don't think of camels being in Arizona, but they briefly used them in the nineteenth century," Professor Williams described. "I am headed back to my office between classes. We can talk there if you wish," he said.

They entered a large office within the Summerset Building. There was a round table and three chairs in the office for discussions with students, a large wooden desk, and a light oak peninsula desk, credenza, and hutch. He walked to the credenza and poured coffee from the pot into a mug that had been on his desk. Afterward, he reached into the top drawer of the desk, removed a plastic packet containing toothpicks, and dropped one into the coffee.

"A toothpick for your coffee?" asked Carson.

"It's a nicotine toothpick," replied Professor Williams.

"Oh, does it help in trying to quit smoking?" asked Ty.

"I don't know. I don't smoke. Nicotine, in small doses, calms the nerves while creating a rush of energy, and has a mind-clearing effect similar to caffeine. Drop one in a mug of black coffee and it's like being a reporter working in a 1940s newsroom without the clouds of smoke and sexual harassment," Professor Williams replied.

"I have never heard that before," said Ty.

"It's a nice little kick," the doctor replied. "Gets me going. What do you want to know about camels?" asked the professor.

"We are interested because there are recent stories about a camel in town. One scared a man last week, causing him to have a heart attack and die. There have been sightings around town the past few days, and we've even gone out to look for it ourselves," Carson stated.

"And we saw it. From a distance," added Ty.

"If you would have been around in the mid-1850's you would have seen several," replied Dr. Williams. "Major Henry Wayne proposed the first camels in the southwest in 1848. He thought camels could carry at least twice the amount of weight as horses or mules, and because they didn't need as much water or as frequent breaks, they could track Native Americans back during the wars. The military also planned to use them for postal service duties. In 1850, the US Secretary of War, Jefferson Davis, proposed the US Army purchase camels as a regiment," the professor stated.

"Where did Davis get camels and how many did he need?" asked Tegan.

"It was initially voted down, but eventually, in 1854, the government agreed to spend thirty thousand dollars to purchase seventy-two camels from the Middle East. They arrived in 1857 and worked carrying supplies in the southwest, but ultimately they deemed the experiment unsuccessful," the professor said.

"Why was it unsuccessful? It would seem they would actually work well in the region," asked Kareem.

"You're right. It well suited them to travel through the region. However, camels are a little stubborn and the soldiers didn't like them very much. Plus, they scared the horses and often ran off from camp during the night," Professor Williams added. "Reports also said that Henry Wayne and David Porter, who were in charge of the Camel Corps, made some poor hiring decisions. Since camels were plentiful in the Middle East, they assumed anyone from the area would be a good camel handler. They hired six men to be camel drivers and tutors to the Army's muleteers and a Turk named Elias to be the veterinarian; however, the men they hired lacked training in those areas. In fact, stories reported the veterinarian's treatment for a sick camel, whatever the ailment, consisted of tickling the animal's nose with the tail of a chameleon," the professor replied.

"That doesn't sound very trained," replied Tegan.

"No, but Wayne was convinced of the value of the camels and sent Porter back east to bring back more. In Camp Verde, he showed the angry troops what the camels could do by having it kneel on command. He loaded it with two large bales of hay that were larger than what a mule could carry, and when the troops scoffed that no animal could carry that load, Wayne added two more. The camels walked with the load effortlessly and the troops changed their mind," the professor said. "One of the camel handlers was an Arab named Hadji Ali, but the locals called him Hi Jolly. Because of his longevity with the Army, they knew of him for his work with the camels. So much so that when he died, they erected a commemorative monument over his grave and topped it with an effigy of a camel," replied the professor.

"Where is that located?" asked Carson.

"To the west of Phoenix, in a town called Quartzsite. Hi Jolly's grave is in a cemetery there, and I think that would be a good place to visit. Maybe you will find more historical clues there," Dr. Williams added.

"So what happened with these camels?" asked Ty.

"Good question. After the war, the government had no use for the camels. They auctioned many of them off, and they turned those that were not sold loose. Others ran off into the desert," Dr. Williams noted.

"Just turned loose in the desert?" repeated Carson.

"Yes, and stories of wild camels continued to be reported by people claiming they saw them roaming in the desert, especially in southern Arizona. Some of them were real sightings, but it also caused several legends and tall tales to begin," said the professor.

"What tales?" inquired Ty. "We love tales of mysterious creatures."

"The most popular is the tale of a camel known as the Red Ghost," Dr. Williams replied.

"Oh, that sounds creepy," said Kareem.

"That started in 1883 down on Eagle Creek, out near Clifton, Arizona. They found a trampled woman and, on her body and on a nearby bush, were clumps of reddish hair. They found large hoof prints around the area, but the locals didn't know what to make of it," continued the doctor.

"That sounds like the incident last Thursday in Goldfield. They found the body of a man trampled and they found red hair and large footprints around him," reported Carson.

"After that, they reported another sighting when a large animal ran into a tent also near Clifton, in which two miners lay sleeping. They could not identify the beast, but were awakened in the middle of the night when their tent came crashing down on their heads. They said they heard a loud scream and a sound of pounding hooves. When they emerged from the tent, they got a glimpse, but at a great distance. They described it as an impossibly tall horse crashing off into the brush. Again, upon investigation, they found large hoof prints and tufts of red hair left behind," the professor described. "It wasn't until a rancher named Cyrus Hamblin got a good look at the animal and could identify it as a camel. Hamblin was working on his ranch near the Salt River when he spotted the Red Ghost."

Carson and Ty shook their heads in disbelief.

"You might not believe this, Doc, but that same thing happened to us the first night we arrived. We camped along the Salt River to see if we could find this mysterious animal, and it ran through our tent as well," replied Carson.

"Interesting. Did you notice anything unusual about the creature?" asked Dr. Williams.

"More unusual than a wild camel in Phoenix?" asked Ty.

"After more incidents of the Red Ghost occurred, others besides Hamblin recognized the large animal as a camel. The weird thing was one rancher said the animal carried a rider, though the rider appeared to be dead. Naysayers were convinced it was merely the camel's hump," the professor stated.

"We didn't see a rider, but our friend Charlie spotted this creature last week and he claimed it had something on its back, but he couldn't make it out," said Tegan.

"It quieted the doubters of the Red Ghost when a party of five prospectors sighted the animal feeding on a mesa. They got within gunshot-range of the creature and fired," Professor Williams continued.

"Did they kill the Red Ghost?" asked Kareem.

"No, they didn't. However, what they did was scare it away. It took off and scuttled out of sight, but something fell from its back," the professor replied.

"What was it?" asked Kareem.

"A human skull with a few shreds of flesh and hair still clinging to it," answered Dr. Williams.

"Human skull? How creepy!" replied Tegan.

"Yes, and that discovery firmly established the Red Ghost as a living legend for nearly ten years to come," stated the professor. "Over those years, the sightings continued. Prior to losing its head, the thing on its back was a mounted rider. A rider that had died and was then just a skeleton strapped to the camel. Some theorized it was a captured soldier. Perhaps a Native tribe tied to the camel and released into the wild as a punishment. Others claim the corpse was that of a traveler who had tied himself to the camel as he grew weak from thirst, hoping that the camel would take him to water. Eventually, when the creature's reign ended and they could examine the body, they concluded the rider could not have tied the rawhide straps himself. So the mystery became whether the man was still alive when strapped to the animal's back," the professor concluded.

"So it was actually a real animal?" asked Ty.

"Yes, the Red Ghost was real. Whoever tied the rider made the camel suffer, and like most members of its species, the Red Ghost refused to suffer in silence. Although it killed only once, it attacked human beings nearly every time it encountered them during the first months of its agony. That aggression toward people fueled the fear of the Red Ghost and increased its frightful legend," the professor continued.

"Unreal. What happened to the camel? How did they finally stop the Red Ghost?" asked Tegan.

"The remaining accounts of the Red Ghost all told the same terrifying tale, that the camel still carried the strapped remains of a headless skeleton rider. It vanished into the night and disappeared for a few years. But then, in 1893, the Red Ghost made its last appearance," the professor said.

"1893? Didn't you say the first incident was in 1883? Ten years this camel roamed the desert as a wild animal?" clarifying Carson.

"That's correct," the professor assured.

"How do they know what they saw in 1893 was the Red Ghost?" asked Ty.

"On February 25, 1893, a rancher named Mizoo Hastings woke up and saw through the window of his cabin a big red camel grazing in his turnip patch. He used the windowsill to steady his shot and fired, killing the animal. When he went out to investigate the body, nothing remained of the corpse, though the animal bore the scars from the leather straps that once kept the rider in place. They had been on the animal so long that the straps had cut into the flesh," concluded the professor.

"What happened to the bodies? The Red Ghost and the skeleton rider?" asked Carson.

"That, no one knows. A mystery lost to time. The papers reported that after Hastings shot it, locals gathered from all around to view the dead beast. Although the rider was no longer attached, it was determined that the devilish skeleton riding the creature through the years was, in fact, a human skeleton that was tied to the animal with thick leather straps many years earlier. However, what became of the Red Ghost or the skeleton is unclear. The origin of the skeletal rider also remains a mystery," the professor stated.

"This is really wild," admitted Ty. "This story of the Red Ghost has many similarities to what has been happening around Phoenix over the past week. These stories seem like campfire tales, but they are from more than a hundred years ago. The camel they called the Red Ghost died, and this thing is alive now, so it can't be the same creature," said Ty.

"But it could be a descendant," theorized Carson. "The professor said there were dozens of camels, and they turned many loose. What if some of the other feral camels bred and over time, scattered herds of these mysterious camels formed?" he asked.

"If there were herds, I am fairly sure we would hear of more than one animal," Kareem responded.

"Remember the story on the news said they found hair on the body in Goldfield and when they tested it, they said the age was a hundred or more years old," added Tegan.

"Fascinating. The Red Ghost is a great tale of the Old West and of Arizona history, but not one with which many are familiar. I would be interested in learning more about what you find with this sighting. What if the Red Ghost is back?" asked the professor as he took a sip from his coffee.

"I don't know how a one hundred-twenty-year-old dead camel would be back, but… maybe?" Carson's voice rose in pitch, revealing the uncertainty in his response.

"Now we know that camels at least existed in Arizona. We don't know what happened to the Red Ghost's body, we don't know what happened to the skeleton of the rider, and earlier in the story, we also are missing the skull of the rider," replied Ty.

"The Red Ghost probably decayed over time, or it was the Old West and food may have been difficult to come by. Perhaps Old Man Hastings ate it?" replied Kareem.

"He could have. And the bones of the Red Ghost could have been discarded," added the professor.

"But what about the rider? Lost to the desert over time?" asked Tegan.

"There was a song in 1962 by The New Christy Minstrels called *Hi Jolly, the Camel Driver Song.* It says:

"Old timers down in Arizona tell you that it's true

That you can see Hi Jolly's ghost a-ridin' still

When the desert moon is bright, he comes ridin' into sight

Drivin' four and twenty camels over the hill," cited Professor Williams.

"One thing we know is that every legend has an origin, and those tales are based, even if loosely, in fact," responded Carson.

"What if that song has some truth to it? What if the Red Ghost truly is a ghost now and the skeletal rider is Hi Jolly?" Carson speculated.

"Charlie saw it at night. The camel ran over our tent at night, and the death in Goldfield was at night. Perhaps when the desert moon was bright?" added Ty.

"So if we, just for a theory, say it is Hi Jolly…" began Tegan

"then we should get out to Quartzsite," concluded Kareem.

"I can't promise meeting any ghosts, either of a rider or a phantom camel, but if you go to Quartzsite, you can meet Hi Jolly. His gravesite at least," said Dr. Williams. The professor looked down at his watch. "Hey, I've got to head to my next class, but it was great talking to you. I enjoy Arizona history and the similarity of the current events to the history is intriguing. Best of luck in your research," the professor said.

"Those who don't learn from history are doomed to repeat it," replied Carson.

"Maybe people today didn't learn from the past and are repeating it now," said Ty.

They left the building and returned to the sidewalk, cutting its way through campus.

"They have a coffee shop. Who's thirsty?" asked Carson.

Everyone agreed and headed toward the tall building labeled Student Union.

"It's in the back of this building according to their website," said Carson. "On the top floor."

The campus was beautiful, with many newly built or renovated buildings, a large grass field for lacrosse, and music playing from outside speakers. The sidewalks were teeming with students heading to class, most walking, but many skateboards, both regular and longboards. Carson remembered being younger and good on a skateboard, but speculated any attempt now would lead to injury.

They approached the back of the Student Union and walked to a wall with three elevators.

"Three elevators. They must get a lot of traffic here," speculated Ty.

Carson pushed the button, stepped back, and awaited an available elevator. They noticed a paper sign that hung on the metal frame of the final elevator. It read *Work order submitted for Elevator #3–Public Safety.* They looked at each other nervously and then moved in between the first and second elevator doors. Moments later, an elevator arrived. In the third bay. As the doors opened, they looked at one another, uncertain if they should get on.

The doors closed, and Kareem stuck a foot in to stop it from closing fully. They entered and pushed the button for the fourth floor. As the doors closed, Tegan broke the silence, saying aloud what everyone was thinking…

"I feel like we just took an enormous risk…"

The elevator creaked and moaned as it climbed. They listened to every sound, trying to analyze its source and severity. The elevator came to a stop, and the doors opened. Carson stuck his head out and looked around. A lobby sign identified it as the fourth floor.

"Looks like we made it," said Carson.

The doors opened into a large room with sofas, chairs, bookshelves, and large televisions, creating a comfortable area for students to relax. Closer to the coffee area, the line was long, showing it was a popular hangout spot for students.

"This coffee shop is really nice, especially for a college campus," said Kareem.

"Brewed Awakenings is a student-run and managed coffee shop not only giving students the ability to earn money while in college, but allowing them to gain work experience. Most of these students are working on business degrees. Therefore, they get to see some concepts they learn about in action. Plus that work experience is good after graduation when they are looking for jobs," said Carson.

"I want something cool. I am going to try that Monsoon. Maybe the Coco-Mocha with dark chocolate and coconut," said Tegan.

“Maybe a Blackberry Jasmine iced green tea for me,” said Kareem.

“An iced drink is definitely the way to go. That lineup of Monsoon’s looks good. I’m getting the Avalanche dirty chai with shots of espresso and a white chocolate twist,” said Ty.

They reached the counter by the time Carson determined his order.

“Bee Sting for me. The honey, cinnamon and a splash of coconut sounds pretty good,” he said.

“Hot or cold?” asked a young girl with freckles and full, natural hair.

“It is one of our popular choices,” the young barista behind the register said.

Minutes later, another young student walked to the counter with four drinks and called for Carson. They picked up the order and took the stairs instead of the uncertainty of the elevator.

“I checked out the map of this part of town. I thought we could stop by this bottle shop not too far from here, then maybe get some food?” said Ty.

Five minutes later, Ty pulled into a strip mall parking lot at Central and Thomas. The car’s passengers peered through the windows, checking out the neighborhood.

“Are you sure this is the place?” asked Carson.

“Yes, this is it. I’ve chatted with some people online and they say this is the place to go on this side of town,” Ty reported. “They have a killer to-go section and an excellent bar selection, but no food.”

"I really want tacos. Is there a good taco place around here?" asked Carson.

Kareem looked blankly surprised at Carson. "Are you kidding me?" he said. "They are literally everywhere. I would put the Mexican food in Phoenix near the top of the list in the country," he wagered.

"That might be the first time I am overlooking beer and focused on having lunch," said Tegan

"It's close, but no. I can't call it," pondered Ty.

"We can look at the cooler, have a drink at the bar, and grab lunch. Or if we have more beer, the food can be dinner," suggested Kareem.

They walked inside the bottle shop and began looking at the selection of bottles and cans. The retail area was spacious with bright lighting, while the bar area off to the rear of the store was darker and more relaxed. Business in the front. Party in the back.

They walked in and, as their eyes began adjusting the dimmer lighting, they found their way to the longer bar. It was mostly empty, as most people in town were still working. Another benefit of traveling and being in their line of work.

"Thanks for coming in. What can I get you today?" asked the young bartender.

"I think I will need a little more time," replied Carson.

"Yeah, that's quite the beer list you've got there," added Ty.

"We get some good stuff in. Some hard-to-get stuff we can do growlers or crowlers on most of them. We have a growler station back out in the back of the bottle shop area," said Franklin.

Looking up at the menu, Ty pulled up a chair. "Mother Bunch Cherry Popper Porter," he said.

"If we are going with interesting names, give me the Scotchy Scotch Scotch Ale from Grand Canyon," added Carson.

"The Heroes 19," ordered Tegan.

"That's a good one from Prescott Brewing," said Franklin. "It's a smooth brown ale that was a collaboration brewed in honor of the nineteen firefighters who died fighting the Yarnell Hill fire."

"That's a magnificent tribute. Is it popular?" she said.

"It is only available for a limited time and proceeds benefit the victims' families, so it has been moving quickly," replied Franklin.

"I didn't get the Sex Panther earlier in the trip, so let me get that one," concluded Kareem.

"That is an excellent local Porter. San Tan did a marvelous job with that one. It's seasonal and very popular," stated Franklin. "I will be right back with the drinks."

"So, what's the plan with this camel?" asked Ty. "We know what we are up against now. Do we go after it? And if so, where?"

"*Do* we know what we're up against?" inquired Kareem. "We know camels don't live for a hundred years, and we learned from Dr. Williams that they killed the Red Ghost in that turnip patch," he recalled.

"We saw it, and it matches the description. It follows the legend, but the timeline can't possibly work," added Tegan.

Carson took a sip of his beer and took a quick cough as the intensity surprised him slightly. "Bitterness with some roastiness," Carson reported. "We need more information. Remember, Dr. Williams told us about the history of Quartzsite? I think we need to get out there and have a look around," he said.

"How far is it out there?" inquired Tegan

"About two and a half," replied Carson.

"Five hours of driving seems like a long way for a hunch," stated Kareem.

"True, but I think we need to go to the beginning and look back. We can make a weekend of it. Drive out tomorrow, stay Saturday and back here on Sunday," Carson outlined.

"That sounds like a good plan. Might as well check out the town and that cemetery Dr. Williams told us about," Ty stated as he finished the beer. "Speaking of good. That's a nice smoked cherry porter. It's like a dark chocolate-covered cherry with some sweet cherry, bitter chocolate, and a nice mild smoky finish," he observed.

"A hundred years doesn't seem like that long ago when thinking about mysterious creatures. Remember, some of the first sightings and legends of Champ went back hundreds of years to the Native Americans of that region," said Tegan.

"The Native Americans were here too. Hard to imagine it was still the wild west then," said Carson. "They founded this area, and we can still see some petroglyphs and sites."

"I would like to get a look at some of those petroglyphs to see if they depicted The Red Ghost," Kareem added.

"Art was very important to them to express themselves and their world," said Carson. He again thought of the strange statue from Cody's Emporium. "Maybe it wasn't a centaur after all…," he said aloud.

"Centaur? What are you talking about?" asked Ty.

Carson looked up at his friend. "No, nothing. Just thinking of our trip to New England," he said. He returned to his thoughts on the oddly shaped statue. Not quite a centaur, and not quite a horse. Maybe it was the Red Ghost and its mysterious rider? What if the local tribes saw this back then? He completed the last sip of his beer, thinking of the possibility.

"So, we lost Carson in thought… What about this dinner? What are we having, and where is it?" asked Teagan.

"Just a couple miles from here, close to McDowell on 16th Street," replied Kareem. "And it's a great treat. A gourmet taco shop that has been on *Dinners, Drive-thru, and Dives.*"

"Well, then. That's just my game," replied Carson.

"But a little more upscale than a dinner or a dive," added Kareem.

Just over two miles away, they arrived at La Santisima, a gourmet taco shop known for its variety of regional Mexican specialties, with an emphasis on the cuisine of Mexico City and the Yucatan. They were fortunate to find a car leaving from one of the limited parking spaces in front of the restaurant. The avocado green building façade included the restaurant's name and a large bust of a woman in *el Día de los*

Muertos makeup and an oversized feathered hat, suitable for the Kentucky Derby.

Opening the giant wooden door, they found the seating inside to be as limited as the parking spaces outside. Luckily, they found a table large enough for the four of them. The large wooden furniture from the tables to the bar and cabinets, and the buffet containing an expansive fourteen-item salsa bar, coupled with the colorful seating and artwork by Mexican artists, created a comfortable and homey environment.

They were already reviewing the menu when the server arrived at the table with four cups of water.

"I am Yvette, and I will be your server today. Have you looked over the drinks?" the young woman asked.

"Jamaica for me," said Tegan.

"I want the horchata," ordered Kareem. "I've never seen it served with fruits and pecans before. Sounds interesting."

Carson and Ty also ordered the horchata.

"Coming right up," Yvette said with a smile.

"Everything on the menu looks good," Kareem said as he perused the menu. "An enormous selection of quesadillas, burritos, and, of course, tacos."

"What did they feature on the *Triple D* episode?" asked Carson.

"One thing he raved about was the Oaxaca Black molé sauce," replied Kareem.

Carson continued to review the menu. "Looks like you can get that on the tacos, quesas, or burros," Carson responded.

"I think I will go with the burrito."

Yvette returned to the table with a notepad.

"Did I hear you say you wanted the molé burrito?" she asked Carson.

"Yes, please," he said.

"How about you, sir?" she said, turning to Ty.

"Sign says gourmet taco shop, so I have to try the tacos," suggested Ty. "Mix and match three. Since he said the molé was good, let me get the Oaxaca black molé chicken shark taco, the Baja Sur dogfish shark, and the Sonoran carne asada," he concluded.

"Are rice and beans okay?" Yvette asked.

"Yes," replied Ty.

"I will go with the quesadilla," replied Tegan. "The La Condesa Mahi Mahi quesa," she said as she sat her menu on the pile with the others who already ordered.

"That's with our handmade corn quesadillas," replied Yvette.

"Saving the best for last," teased Kareem. "Guy said the molé was so good he would eat it right out of a jar with a spoon. I can't pass that up. Then the Aztec tinga taco, which is a specialty in Mexico City. That Mayan cochinita pibil taco comes from the Yucatan where they take the pork shoulder, and they slow cook it wrapped in banana leaves. Let me get that one also," he reviewed.

The food arrived and the hungry investigators took a bite of the food. Carson's face immediately following the first bite reflected his now shared opinion with Guy Ferrari on the mole sauce.

"Damn. Welcome to Flavor Town," he reviewed. "I have had some decent molé sauce before, but this is maybe the best. The depth of rich flavors. So complex," he said.

"This horchata is probably the best I have ever had. The only thing that might make this better is a solid beer," Ty added. "We already hit up Kings. I'm not sure what else is around here that we should try."

A man from the next table looked over and listened in on the conversation for a bit. Soon, he joined in.

"Excuse me. I heard you say you were looking for some good local beer around here?" the man said.

"Yes, we are in town for several days and always enjoy trying the local beers," added Carson.

"There are some good places in Phoenix. In this part of town, I usually go to Kings. I'm actually looking forward to this summer because there is a new place opening in July on 40th Street and Thomas called Helio Basin Brewing. I hear they have some excellent beer planned, but I am also excited because they have a chef in the kitchen," Geraldo said.

"A chef? In a brewery?" asked Ty.

"Yes, she is an up-and-coming chef in town who offers some creative forged and Native American-inspired dishes," reported Geraldo. "I like beer, but as you can see from my waistline, I like food, too."

"Don't we all," said Carson, patting his own stomach.

"Helton Brewing Company is just five minutes from here between Arcadia and uptown Phoenix. They opened a few months ago. I think they typically have a Scottish ale, an IPA, a milk stout, and a lager of their own and a couple of guest taps. They have between twelve and eighteen beers on tap," said Geraldo. "They have a giant building and space for an outdoor beer garden," he said.

"Sounds like a nice way to end the evening," said Tegan.

They finished the meal and called for the check. Yvette came over with the bill.

"Anything else I can get you before you go?" she asked.

"No, we're all good here. Thank you for everything. This was wonderful," replied Kareem.

They pulled into the driveway of Helton Brewing and parked next to a giant building that looked like a tire warehouse from the outside. Walking inside, the size of the facility impressed them. It included an indoor bar with additional table seating, a grain room, tank room, a tasting room, as well as a spacious outdoor beer garden. It boasted an enclosed beer garden with multiple opened garage doors allowing enjoyment of the beautiful spring evening. Pool tables provided a pleasant opportunity to pass the time with friends while enjoying the beer.

They walked to the patio and found some empty yellow metal chairs next to a wooden bar across from an unused pool table.

"Hey, Carson. Whatcha say we rack 'em up?" inquired Ty.

"I'm down. Let's put our order in first," Carson replied. He turned to Kareem and Tegan, who were reviewing a menu left on the bar top. "Do you know what you want?"

The brewery named the beer by style rather than a crazy name.

"I want the Northeast IPA," replied Kareem.

"A plum saison, please," added Tegan.

Ty and Carson walked inside to the main bar to place the order. They looked around the large interior space in the main room as they approached the bar.

"Evening, gentleman. What'll it be?" asked a young, bearded man.

"Can we get a Helton nitro milk stout, a Northeast IPA, a plum saison...," said Carson.

"... and the single hopped pale ale," added Ty.

"You got it," said the bartender.

The bartender returned with the beer and Carson handed him the cash. Each man grabbed two drinks and headed back to the pool table where Kareem and Tegan were awaiting.

Ty walked over to the table and began racking the balls. He placed one ball on top of the others and drifted the rack back and forth before giving it a sudden jar, causing the ball to fall into the open hole. With his fingers inside the rim, he moved it back and forth until it stopped in a tight formation on the foot spot.

"Have you thought about our trip tomorrow?" asked Ty as Carson placed the cue ball and lined up his shot.

Carson slid the stick across his circled fingers repeatedly. After a third pass, he connected with the ball and sent the balls flying with a loud *Crack!* The number seven ball found the corner pocket.

"I say we drive to Quartzsite, tour the cemetery, and speak to some locals in the area who may know something," replied Carson calmly. "Five ball in the corner pocket," he said, lining up the next shot. He took the shot, and it went in.

"From Dr. Williams we learned about Hi Jolly, and it sounds like he was well-respected there. I think there may be some connection between Hi Jolly and the Red Ghost. Two ball, corner pocket."

He shot, and the ball hit the lip of the pocket, rebounding a few inches away.

Ty stepped up and looked at his options on the table.

"Ten ball, side pocket."

After a few passes across his fingers, he let go of the shot and it found its home.

"The cemetery can provide some clues into the past, but what about today? Fifteen ball, side pocket."

"Quartzsite is famous for its swap meet. It boasts the largest open-air flea market in not only the country but also the world. It has over two thousand vendors of rocks, gems, minerals, fossils and everything else imaginable, drawing more than a million visitors each year with a wave of RVs. This is one of the last weeks of the season. With all of those shoppers and vendors, maybe someone knows something," Carson said.

"Let's hope we can turn up something. Eleven ball, corner pocket," Ty said. He sank the shot and the game, and drinks, continued into the night.

CHAPTER 9

IRON WHALES & RUSTY NAILS

Friday, March 18, 2016

Leaving Chandler around 8 a.m., the group encountered early morning congestion, typical of all Phoenix highways. It took more than an hour to make the drive from the east valley to Goodyear, where, after passing Highway 85, it finally dissipated. Just over ninety minutes later, they were coming up on the small town of Quartzsite, known to some as the *Desert Phenomenon*.

With Ty driving, Carson searched his phone for the location of the Quartzsite Historical Society as they approached the city limits. By the time Carson found it on the phone and called out to Ty, they already passed the Central Boulevard exit.

"There's another exit just up ahead we can take. US-95 to the right," said Carson. "Then turn on the first street to the right."

Ty turned right onto the exit ramp and followed US-95 as it passed gas stations, a Carl's Jr., and became an industrial park area of town. Ty drove twenty-five mph down the small two-lane road and slowed down further as they approached a building with beige aluminum siding.

"What's that thing in front of the building?" asked Ty as he pointed toward a red sculpture standing in front of the Gem World building.

"I can't see it from here. Turn in there," suggested Carson.

The white metal gate was open, but only one car sat in the parking lot. Ty pulled in and drove to the front entrance of the building. To the left of the door stood a statue of a creature. Ty parked the car, and everyone exited to get a better look.

"It's a camel," said Kareem.

"A red camel," added Tegan.

The sculpture was tall, made of metal scraps and what appeared to be tire rims. The owners painted it red with white legs.

"What do you make of that?" asked Carson.

The door opened as of the store's employees exited carrying empty cardboard boxes for the trash.

"Howdy," said the tall, middle-aged man with a scraggy salt and pepper beard. Wearing boots, jeans, and suspenders, he gave the appearance of a man who may have had a hand in mining some gems located inside the building.

"What is this sculpture?" asked Tegan.

"Oh that? That's Georgette. She's kind of the store's mascot, I guess," said Virgil.

"I need to get a selfie with that pretty girl," replied Kareem.

"It's interesting that it's a camel out here in Arizona," said Carson, attempting to feel out Virgil for more information.

"Camels are pretty big out here. Camels influence this community's history. There's even one on our city emblem, police department patches, and our local flag. During the Civil War, the military brought camels to Arizona. They made Georgette out of car tire rims. Her head was once a motorcycle gas tank, and her legs are automobile tie rods. The city originally commissioned a local businessperson to construct the creature. Plans called for it to stand in front of his flea market, and then they it they left it to rust when he went out of business. When the owner of this store bought the flea market, he inherited ol' Georgette. However, she wasn't as good looking as she is now. One of our employees, Lily, helped clean her up and gave her a fresh coat of red paint and some jewelry. Kind of returned from the dead, I guess you'd say," Virgil said with a grin.

"That's a very interesting story," said Carson, looking closely at Georgette. "We just came from Phoenix, and they are having a problem there with a camel," he added.

"A camel? Today? The camels round here disappeared around 1900," said Virgil.

"It is an interesting connection," said Ty. "They have spotted this camel around town, and they say it's responsible for one man's death. That camel is also red, almost a glowing red. We stopped by Marble Hills University and learned the history of camels and Hi Jolly, which is why we wanted to come here. The professor talked about a creature called the Red Ghost, which was a camel from around the time you mentioned, but like Georgette here, it seems to have returned from the dead," he concluded.

"The tales of the Red Ghost are well known out here, but mostly campfire stories and urban legends I figured," said Virgil. "If you want to see some of the local stories, the historical society is just down the road, and they have some good artifacts from the history of the town. Hi Jolly's tomb is also down the street. Turn left after the Yacht Club and it's right there," continued Virgil.

"Yacht Club? There are a lot of strange things in this town," replied Carson.

"If you enjoy looking for creatures and strange things, you might stop down to Hassler's RV Park just before the historical society," said Gavin.

"Thanks, we'll check that out too," said Kareem.

"Now, if you'll excuse me, I'm going to dump these boxes and then go to the little boys' room to see a man about a horse," said Virgil.

The group headed toward the car, thanking Virgil for the information on Georgette.

"That was certainly interesting," said Tegan. "Seeing a large red camel out here in the desert brought back memories of the creature we saw by the river. And the comment about Georgette coming back from the dead?"

"Right? Another synchronicity that connects to the reports we are following," said Kareem.

"Let's hit up the historical society next," said Carson. "Then we'll check out that RV Park afterwards. I think local museums are a great way to get a feel for the area when investigating these creatures," he said.

"Many things that are forgotten by the modern world are clues that are sitting in those old, local museums," said Ty.

The Quartzsite Historical Society was just about a mile down US-95. Also known as Tyson's Well Stage Station Museum, the museum sat where the original adobe stage station, built in 1866. They restored the building in 1980, with walls that were still structurally sound being kept and others rebuilt. A shell of stabilized adobe brick protected the original walls.

As they approached, they saw the original assay shack from the Mariquitta Mine, which provided a look into the everyday life of the miners from that time. The yard also contained a little village of cement and stone houses, and just to the west, the ruins of the old Oasis Hotel.

Walking inside the station house, they glanced around, seeing the ceiling of the main room comprising saguaro ribs and one room retained a dirt floor for authenticity. The original fireplace was not only still in place, but still operational during the winter months.

"Good morning. Welcome to the Tyson's Well Stage Station Museum," said Cooper, serving as the museum's guide. "Let me know if I can show you around," he added.

"Thanks. We wanted to stop by and see a little local history," responded Carson.

"The museum is small, but we have a lot to see. We have artifacts gathered from interested local citizens, as well as photographs, books, newspapers, and out in the yard, you probably saw some of our old mining equipment," replied Cooper.

"Newspapers, photos, and books sound interesting. Anything about the Camel Corps that used to be out here? Or Hi Jolly?" inquired Ty.

"Or the Red Ghost?" asked Carson.

"We have some items. Right this way," Cooper said as he led the group into a small room.

Tegan sat down in a chair in front of an old wooden desk as Cooper removed a book of newspapers from the shelf and sat it in front of her. He wiped dust from the front cover and opened the book, carefully turning pages until he stopped at a particular paper.

"This is from 1883. It's the Mohave County Miner, a weekly newspaper from Kingman. This paper contains an article about the death of a woman in Eagle Creek. Early one morning, two men rode out to check on the livestock, leaving their wives at the ranch with the children. About midmorning, one woman went down to the spring to fetch a bucket of water while the other remained in the house with the children."

"We heard about that story. This newspaper reported on it?" asked Carson.

"This article reports on the verdict of the jury in the hearing regarding her death," replied Cooper.

"Jury? Wasn't it reported a camel trampled the woman?" asked Ty.

"Yes, but the coroner from Solomonville held an inquest and was highly suspicious of the story. Except for the horribly battered state of the body and the remarkable hoof prints, other members of the family attempted to convince him that the woman was murdered," replied Cooper.

"Why would the family kill the woman?" asked Tegan.

"We don't know. When questioned by the coroner, the surviving woman from inside the cabin spoke of a beast *red, very tall, and ridden by a devil.* The coroner didn't believe her and felt it was about to cover up what really happened. But in the end, the jury returned a verdict of *death in some manner unknown*," responded Cooper.

"But they did not specify it was the Red Ghost?" asked Kareem.

"No, just that it was unknown how she died. Back then, there were many tall tales in the West. Here's another newspaper article about a sighting of the Red Ghost," Cooper said as he ran his fingers across the spine of the albums and pulled out another binder.

"I can see where there are a lot of tales from the West that are suspect," said Ty.

"The West was wild. There weren't a lot of people, but there was a good supply of whiskey. Some people were known to spin a good yarn, as they say. Those that had a reputation of such were dismissed by the paper," Cooper responded.

He sat the album on the table and turned the pages until he stopped at another issue.

"This one talks about a man who reported seeing the Red Ghost along the Black River in eastern Arizona. However, the paper attempted to dispel that by pointing out that the same man had once seen a flying bear and a mountain of gold. Word of the Red Ghost spread unstoppable throughout the territory," Cooper stated.

"Like Kobe in the fourth quarter," replied Ty.

"Um… yeah," said Carson.

"Of course, the papers ran the story of the creature's death at the hands of a farmer when it was finally stopped," said Cooper.

"That's what we are interested in learning more about," said Carson. "There are some who think the Red Ghost is back and currently running amok in Phoenix," he continued.

"I don't see how that could be possible," replied Cooper. "That was a long time ago and we haven't seen reports of any descendants over the years. If there were stories about feral camels, we would have heard them. I don't believe it would just start now out of nowhere," said Cooper doubtfully.

"We think it's unlikely too, but we wanted to come out and explore where the legend may have started," said Kareem.

"Then you will want to visit the cemetery where Hi Jolly's grave lies. That cemetery is just half a mile from here," Cooper said.

"Sounds like we should head there next," replied Ty.

They thanked Cooper for the information and while heading out of the museum, Kareem put twenty dollars in the donation jar.

As they drove US-95 toward the cemetery, Tegan noticed several RV parks. One across the street from the Historical Society, and others on each side of US-95.

"What was the name of that RV park the guy at Gem World said we should stop at?" Tegan asked

"Was it Hassler's?" asked Kareem.

"Yeah. I think that's it up on the right. Should we stop?" she asked.

"He said there were some strange creatures there," replied Carson. "Why not? We have time."

Ty turned right into Hassler's RV Park and found a spot up front. Getting out of the car, they walked the streets within the community.

"Wow, check out these sculptures," said Tegan.

A large metal scrap giant cactus stood to the side of the office, labeled with the words *Hassler's* across the front. Small metal birds guarded the office just underneath the ramp to the office and a series of what appeared to be grist mill wheels on the opposite side.

As they walked through the parking lot looking at sculptures around the office, the property manager joined them. He was tall and slender, about 6'2 and 165 pounds, with gray hair and an enormous nose. He was wearing jeans, a tucked in red shirt, and drinking a cup of coffee in a large mug.

"Can I help ya?" asked Nile Finley.

"Hello, sir," replied Tegan.

"Name's Nile. Nile Finley. Ya looking for a place?" he asked.

"No, we are just visiting town, and someone suggested we stop here and check out the sculptures," said Carson.

"Well, in that case, I'll show ya around," he said jovially.

They walked down one street and Nile pointed out palm trees, velocipedes, and cowboys with six-shooters, large elephant feet, and a huge hand made of bolts that reached out of the ground to grab a vine crafted from reinforcing rods.

"These are really cool sculptures," said Tegan.

"Thank ya', Missy. I hate lettin' things go ta waste, especially if they're things I can use to create something else. 'Round the corner is what I consider my masterpiece," Nile said proudly.

As they turned the corner and came into a central location within the park, they saw an enormous creature, a whale that measured about twenty feet long and six feet tall. Nile made the animal of horseshoes and iron rings, and it sat next to a water fountain.

"Wow! That is a truly magnificent creature," said Kareem.

"I never thought I would see an iron whale," said Carson.

"How many sculptures do you have here?" asked Tegan.

"Over fifty," replied Nile.

"We enjoy finding hidden and unexpected animals," said Ty. "Actually, we're researching one now and came out to Quartzsite to see if we could find some clues," he added.

"You don't say? What animal is that?" asked Nile.

"It's one that seems to have a connection to the early days of this town. The Red Ghost," replied Carson.

"Yep, I know about that one. He's got ties out here from the turn of the century," Nile stated. "The prior century," he added.

"What we are trying to figure out is how an animal that was said to exist around 1900 could be spotted today in Phoenix," added Carson.

"Much longer than the lifespan of a regular camel," added Ty.

"First thing you gotta know is The Red Ghost. He ain't no ordinary camel," stated Nile.

"We've heard a lot of stories about it getting shot multiple times until they finally killed it," said Tegan.

"Some say it glows, kind of like a red aura around it," added Kareem.

"That's because he's back from the dead," Nile said calmly.

The group looked at each other with shocked expressions.

"Back from the dead?" asked Carson.

"He's become supernatural," Nile added.

"H-How can that be?" asked Ty. "That stuff's not real. I mean, I'm down to investigate cryptids and I think there are many things out there we haven't seen yet. But supernatural?" he said dismissively.

"Thing is, they shot before the Red Ghost and it continued running. He didn't lose his rider, but the rider commanding him lost his head. Kept running," said Nile.

"We heard that story at Marble Hills," said Carson. "The professor said the animal was shot and the rider's head fell off. But he didn't say if it was ever found or what became of it," he added.

"Oh, they found it," said Nile. "A local miner found the head and kept it at his home. Thing is, after some years, the head disappeared and no one had seen it since," he replied. "Until recently, that is," he concluded.

"Until recently?" asked Tegan.

"Rumor is someone bought it at the swap meet," Nile responded.

"The flea market just down the road?" asked Kareem.

"Yep. Typically runs from January 1 through the end of February. 'Cept this year, it's run a little longer. Last weekend starts tomorrow," he added.

"Tomorrow? Looks like we're spending the night in Quartzsite," said Carson.

"Yep. There are many local vendors at the swap meet. One of the largest rock and mineral shows not only in Arizona, but in the country," said Nile. "But they have a lot of other vendors too. Sculptures, jewelry, and other trinkets and odds and ends," replied Nile. "Stuff from all over Arizona. I heard a guy was wandering around looking at the tables and picked up an artifact. The vendor selling it thought it was some replica skull, but turns out it was the head of the rider of the Red Ghost. This guy bought it for a few dollars and afterward was all excited and left," reported Nile.

"Sounds like he must have been looking for it for a while," said Carson.

"That's what they say. Said he had been searching for it for years and finally tracked it down to this vendor at the swap meet," said Niles.

"Do you know who this guy is?" asked Ty. "Or what he would want with an old skull?"

"Some say the skull belongs to an ancestor of the man who bought it. Some say the rider controlled the Red Ghost for years and whoever possesses the head of the rider can control the Red Ghost. Others say the rider was the devil himself, and having the skull of the devil brings untold power to the holder," Nile said. He took a sip of coffee. "Or it could all be bullshit. I don't know."

"That a twist I wasn't expecting," added Carson.

"That's some *Sleepy Hollow* shit," said Ty.

"But what I don't get is if the rider was the one who lost his head, how does that make the Red Ghost supernatural?" asked Kareem.

"One mystery that hasn't been able to be answered over the years is the identity of the rider. If it was a man who was killed or eventually died, he still rode that camel for several years. The leather straps kept him bonded to the camel and eventually cut into his flesh. Some say when the man died, his spirit bonded with the camel. That's how he still commanded him to ride throughout the years. When the rider lost his head, the spirit was part of the Red Ghost. I don't know why they are running around terrorizing the city now, but it seems both are back," revealed Nile.

"We know the Red Ghost is real. He ran through our campsite, and we got a brief glimpse of him, but this supernatural rider I am still having trouble with," replied Carson.

"If it were me and I was doin' the lookin', I would check out the cemetery tonight and see who knows what at the swap meet tomorrow before they leave town for the season," suggested Nile.

"Sounds like a good plan," said Tegan as she reached out to shake his hand. "Thanks for the information. This one gets weirder and weirder, but at least we have some direction to go on," she said.

They parted ways, and the group headed back to the car with Carson taking driving duties. He sat in the car and fiddled with the radio until he stopped on a song with a cumbia and Afro-Latin beat. He paused, thinking about the next stop in pursuit of the Red Ghost's origins for a moment, and bobbed his head to the baritone sax, bongos, and a heavy cumbia beat.

"What is that? I really dig it," replied Carson, entranced by the song.

Ty held up his cell phone and hit an app on the home screen. "App says it's *Me Voy Pa' Porce* by La Misa Negra," Ty responded.

Carson turned up the radio a bit, still focused on the song. A few minutes later, he snapped back to the present.

"Okay, so the cemetery is back west, and that's also the direction of our hotel. The cemetery isn't going anywhere. I'm thinking we stop for a drink first," suggested Carson.

"I won't say no to that," replied Ty.

Carson looked at his cell phone and attempted to locate a place nearby. "Here's one that is just down Central," read Carson.

He put the phone down and the car into drive. Just over a mile later, he stopped in front of the parking lot of Tyson Wells RV Park & Market Center. "Looks like it is in here," Carson said as he leaned forward and glanced upward at the sign.

"Is this the swap meet we were going to visit tomorrow?" asked Kareem.

"This is the place, but they aren't open long enough to have a look around. We can grab a drink and a quick bite to eat, then tomorrow do a full sweep.

Looking at the gravel lot in front of him, he continued. He pulled into a deeply graveled parking lot and felt the tires sink into the rock. It was slow going, and he wondered if only a vehicle with 4-wheel-drive could navigate the lake of gravel. He risked it and continued, eventually parking next to a large truck camper in an area of the lot that seemed to have a reduced amount of gravel.

"You take us to only the best places," Ty said sarcastically.

"Expand your horizons," replied Carson.

Walking past booths selling crystals, antiques, and camper accessories, Carson led the way while looking down at the walking directions on his phone's GPS. Finally, they found Beer Belly's Adult Day Care, a seasonal open-air bar littered with monkey decorations and funny bumper stickers. They walked through the two posts holding up the *Welcome to Beer Belly's Adult Day Care* banner

Ty looked over at a clipboard hanging with a few sheets of paper and an attached pencil. The board read, *Day Care Sign In*. He got up and walked over to it.

"Well, might as well do it up right," he said as he signed the group in on the sheet and returned to his seat.

Kareem reviewed the menu and assessed the situation. "Live country music, some chicken sandwiches or hamburgers, and a few non-microbrews," he said.

"What more do you need?" quipped Tegan.

A woman in her late sixties, sitting at the bar next to Tegan, turned toward the group while holding her Bud Light.

"That is all you need," said Margaret Chalmers, a lifelong resident of Quartzsite. "You just pull up a seat here at the bar and watch the ebb and flow of the seasonal inhabitants. They don't got the *gourmet* food or beer. That's not the point of this bar. The point is just to soak up the Quartzsite vibe!" she revealed.

"So far, I am digging the vibe," replied Ty.

"Just you wait until the music starts up again right over there on that stage," Margaret said as she pointed to a wooden platform near the back of the roped off boundaries of Beer Belly's.

"Sounds like a good time," added Ty.

"It is. Tonight we got one of the bests, Agnes Hartman. They call her *The Singin' Snowbird.* And tonight they got the food wagon if you are hungry," Margaret said.

Moments later, an elderly woman took the stage holding a microphone. She had long gray hair flowing from under her black cowboy hat, a red short-sleeved t-shirt over a black long-sleeved shirt, and a black bandana tied around her neck. Her husband, Freddy, accompanied her on the guitar.

Margaret leaned over toward Tegan. "She's superb. They come every year and usually close it out the last weekend," she said.

"I can't wait to hear her," Tegan said with a warm smile.

Freddy began strumming the guitar and Agnes began with *Daddy and Home*, a song occasionally interjecting some verses of yodeling, originally performed by Jimmie Rodgers in 1928. The crowd cheered for her singing and mastery of the yodel.

"Now I will do a song from 1902 that you may have heard from Patsy Cline around 1963, *Bill Bailey Won't You Please Come Home*," announced Agnes.

Again, following the rendition, the crowd applauded approval. Agnes smiled and bowed to the fans.

"Thank you. You're all too kind," she said with the crowd again showing their approval.

"Now Freddy's going to switch over to the banjo and sing a song for you all tonight," said Agnes to the crowd.

Freddy propped the guitar up against a bench sitting at the back of the stage. A man to the side handed him a well-worn banjo and Freddy walked to the mic.

"This one goes back to 1843… but I don't go back quite that far," Freddy said as the crowd chuckled in response. "Dan Emmett wrote this one, but I remember it from Grandpa Jones on the *Grand Ole Opry*," he added.

He began picking the banjo while Agnes played an old acoustic guitar as they performed *Old Dan Tucker* to the crowd's enjoyment.

The group hadn't noticed Carson went to the bar and placed an order and was now returning with four Budweisers.

"Here ya go. I also checked out the food options and the hamburgers look pretty good," said Carson.

"I think I will go with the chicken sandwich," replied Kareem.

Ty stood up and announced he would get the food.

"Three burgers and one chicken?" confirmed Ty.

Everyone agreed and turned their attention from the music back to the investigation at hand. Margaret was completely immersed in the singing and no longer paid attention to the group's conversation.

"So we have to focus our attention now on the rider and not the camel," said Carson.

"The rider that no one in one hundred years has identified?" asked Kareem.

"Yes. But we know someone recently purchased the head," replied Carson.

"Allegedly," said Kareem. "Nile said he *thought* the guy bought the head, but we don't know for sure. He might be just going from hearsay," downplayed Kareem.

"Maybe, but the transaction in question went down here at the swap meet, and that's where we will work on tracking down this seller," said Carson. "We're already here so if it's nothing, that's what it is, but I think we have to investigate the possibility."

Ty returned with the sandwiches and passed them out among everyone.

"We should head out to the cemetery soon. They are going to close here at six, and sunset is 6:38 p.m. That should be enough time to check out the tomb before it gets dark," said Carson.

"Where are we staying at tonight?" asked Kareem?

"The Super 8 just down the road from the cemetery. There's a store called Roadrunner Markets. We can pick up some beer for the evening," added Carson.

Tegan crumbled up the wrapper from around her burger and tossed it on the plastic tray. "Sounds like a plan. I'm ready to learn more about this Red Ghost," she said.

The others finished up and readied the table. As they walked out, the music was still going. Agnes concluded with *I Want to Be a Cowboy's Sweetheart*, made famous by Patsy Montana in 1935. They looked back and Margaret was still enjoying the show.

"Looks like their last weekend is off to a good start," said Ty.

"And ours isn't so bad either. Hopefully, we will get some more clues at the tomb and tomorrow at the swap meet," replied Carson.

Carson drove two miles from Beer Belly's, just behind Gem World, down a narrow blacktop road leading into the cemetery. Several cutouts of camels lined the roadway leading into the graveled parking lot. Getting out of the car, they stopped at a small informational kiosk that contained a map of the cemetery and biographical information of many of the people buried in the cemetery.

There was no grass in the cemetery. The ground was hardened dirt, and the gravesites bordered by rocks or petrified wood and covered with gravel. According to the map, Hi Jolly's tomb was in the pioneer section.

"Check that out," Ty said, pointing to a large marker that appeared to be made of wood and marble. It read *Quartzsite* and featured a pyramid and three camels. Spotlights placed in front of each camel illuminated the sign at night.

"This town certainly believes in the connection to its past and the camels that were here," replied Carson.

Tegan walked over to a large brown sign, the typical design of a national monument or historic place, and read biographical information about Hadji Ali, the man who the locals knew as Hi Jolly.

As they began walking into the cemetery, they stopped at another sign. This one framed by a wooden border and posts. It detailed information and contact details for the cemetery management.

"Will you look at that?" asked Kareem. "Check out the bottom of the panel."

Detailing the name of the cemetery as Hi Jolly Cemetery and providing more information contacts as the local library and the Tyson Wells Stage Station Museum, the sign contained a large image of a camel and the inscription:

Legend

The camel atop the Pyramid symbolizes the legend of

The Red Ghost that roamed the desert, terrorizing

man and beast with what amounted to a corpse

tied to its back.

It continued to say rumor has it the ashes of Hi Jolly's favorite camel were included in the bronze time capsule on the tomb.

"So they are tying the Red Ghost to the tomb of Hi Jolly. That's a little odd, isn't it?" asked Tegan.

"Now I am more excited than ever to check out that tomb," said Carson as he removed a pamphlet from the sign's brochure holder.

They continued through the barren cemetery and headed to the tomb, a large pyramid monument with a standing camel on top of it made it impossible to miss, even without the benefit of a map. They reached the grave and stood in front, staring in awe at the site. A small, round, black plaque set into the ground revealed the National Register of Historic Places added the tomb to their list in 1949.

"Wow, that's something else. More than I was expecting," said Ty.

The pyramid stood approximately ten feet tall and was made of multicolored petrified wood and quartz with the copper camel at the top. The brochure revealed the locals loved Hi Jolly so much that when he died, they built the special tomb for him.

"The brochure and these monuments all say they don't really know the origins of the man. They are uncertain if he was from Greece or from Syria. They know when he arrived, and they loved him, but they didn't care where he came from. Sounds like the people in this town back then accepted immigrants for who they were and what they did more than many experience today," said Kareem.

"The tomb was dedicated on January 4, 1903, and they placed plaque from the government in 1936," read Tegan.

Carson pulled out his phone and searched for more information on the man in the tomb.

"So that explains that mystery. It says his mother was Greek and his father was Syrian. Of the original camel drivers the US hired, all were of Greek origin. It says people viewed him as a living legend until his death in Arizona. That's cool," Carson said. "Oh, get this - once, insulted because they had not invited him to a German picnic in Los Angeles, he broke up the gathering by driving into it on a yellow cart pulled by two of his camels," read Carson. "It says he was born Philip Tedro, but after going to Mecca on a pilgrimage, he called himself Hadji Ali. He reverted to Philip Tedro later in life and he had two children," concluded Carson.

Ty scrutinized the pyramid and its assembly. "This is really cool. For regular citizens to just come together and build this. The artisanship is rugged, but good. Black malapai rock, petrified wood, gold-bearing quartz, and natural red, white, and blue rocks are very artistic and symbolic of the area. The government added a cemented plaque to the front, but the rest is nice. This round black piece below the sign appears to be the time capsule mentioned on the sign. There is a lock on it. Someone at the museum probably has the key. I wonder when they plan on opening it?" investigated Ty.

"It sounds like he had an interesting life," said Tegan. "How did he die?"

Carson continued to scroll through the information retrieved from the internet search.

"Interesting. It says Philip Tedro died walking along the old desert road from the Colorado River to Wickenburg on December 16, 1902, at the age seventy-three. The legends have it that Hi Jolly was searching for one of his camels when he died. It says he found the camel during a sandstorm, but the next day people discovered him dead with his arm across the camel's neck. That became one of the man's most enduring legends. Newspaper accounts report that to his dying day, Hi Jolly believed that a few of the camels still roamed the desert," Carson read.

"Sounds like he was right. Didn't they say they found a wild camel in 1946?" asked Ty.

"Yes, and one even later than that in California," replied Carson.

"He certainly loved the camels. It connected everything about him and this town to those camels," said Kareem.

"I wonder what happened to the children?" asked Tegan.

"This other source says he married Gertrudis Serna from Hermosillo, Mexico, in November 1859. Her parents were Catholic, so he gave his nationality as Greek because the church would not approve of her marriage to a Muslim," stated Carson. "The previous article stated they had two kids, but this one says they had three children together: Amelia, Minnie, and Fernando Serna Tedro."

"I wonder if any of their descendants are still in the area?" Tegan asked.

"Looks like Amelia Tedro married George Ernest Smalley, but she died January 17, 1943 in Los Angeles County, where Amelia worked as a dressmaker. They had no children. George had two children from a previous marriage. Minnie Tedro married Charles William Hansford. He died of smallpox and she died December 3, 1958 in Rialto, California where she was working as a tailor and lived with her mother and nephew Arthur Smalley. Fernando Serna Tedro was born in Tucson September 1891, but other than working as a carpenter in a railroad shop, there wasn't much information on him. It shows in the 1920 census he was in Los Angeles County living with George and Amelia," revealed Carson.

Ty was still admiring the pyramid and ran his hands across the surface of the stones when he felt indentations causing him to move in for a closer look. He stared at the rocks for a moment, then pulled out his phone and used its flashlight to get a better look since the sky was losing light.

"Amazing. Some of these stones also feature ancient still visible petroglyphs. It's faint, but now that I feel it and get a good look. I can see some of the artwork," Ty said.

As he continued to feel the stone's surface, he felt another marking that caused him to stop. He pointed the flashlight at the rock near the bottom center of the pyramid structure.

"That's odd. It's like an engraved circle, but it's not a clean circle," said Ty. "It also feels sharper, which makes me think it is newer than the rest of the monument."

The others walked around to the side and looked at what Ty was seeing. The indentation was circular, but some lines ran inside the circle.

Carson bent down and grabbing some dirt from the ground, rubbed it on the engraving.

"That's not a circle. That's a serpent," he said.

"A serpent?" asked Tegan.

"Yes, or sometimes it is depicted as a dragon. Those lines inside are legs. It's called the Ouroboros, first used prominently in Ancient Egypt. The serpent is consuming its own tail and serves as a sign of being in a cycle. Some say the cyclical nature of the year, some say infinity, and others say it represents the beginning and the end of time or the cycle of death and rebirth," explained Ty.

"They use it in Egypt?" asked Kareem.

"First in Egypt around the 14th century BC. However, it also appeared in the text of early alchemy and Gnosticism around 400 AD. Since then they have used it in Greece,

Persia, and even with modern theorists such as psychologist Carl Jung," said Carson.

"So pulling from what you said, it is a symbol that represents death and rebirth that was used in Persia?" asked Ty.

"Like Hi Jolly and the Red Ghost!" added Tegan.

"That's what I am getting at. Someone added this symbol to the tomb. Hi Jolly was the famed camel driver in this area. We saw the symbolism of camels all around this town. The story about him dying in the sandstorm seeking the lost camel, only to find it, and both of them die. That sign over there mentions the Red Ghost. That song the professor at Marble Hills mentioned about Hi Jolly still seen and heard riding through the night leading twenty-four camels. We know he left his family in 1886. The first Red Ghost story we heard was from 1883. The last was in 1893. This tomb says Hi Jolly died in 1902, but cowboys found him. We don't know when he actually died. The timeline is very similar," said Ty.

"Similar, but can't be the same. When Mizoo Hastings killed the Red Ghost, they saw its body. The rider was missing, and we didn't find out what happened to the Red Ghost's body, but I think there are too many years between that incident and 1902 when Hi Jolly is buried," added Carson.

"The first reports of the Red Ghost hit the papers and local gossip, then three years later Hi Jolly leaves his family. Maybe he went searching for the Red Ghost?" suggested Kareem.

"I agree with Carson," said Tegan. "But we know Hi Jolly was the best camel driver around and we know there are ashes of a camel buried in this tomb with him. What if the symbol that means death and rebirth brought him and the camel back, but it's not the original Red Ghost or its rider? What if it is Hi Jolly and his favorite camel, Topsy?" asked Tegan.

"I like where it's headed, but I don't think that's quite it," said Carson. "We know Hi Jolly died in 1902. Who are the other riders? We heard Yiorgos Caralambo, or Greek George, lived to about 1913. Therefore, he's out. Let me check this article again," said Carson.

"I don't think they fit the timetable. When the Red Ghost first appeared, it was 1883, and the rider was not only dead but also a skeleton. The Camel Corps started in 1857, so our rider had to have died somewhere between 1857 and 1883. These people dying in 1902 and 1913 don't fit the bill. What about other riders?" asked Kareem.

"The rumors about Hadjiatis Yannaco, or Long Tom as they called him, are that he took some camels and joined the Ringling Brothers circus. The other five guys, I see little information," said Carson as he reviewed his phone.

"We may want to hit the Quartzsite Public Library and see if we can find any information on the other five riders. Maybe they have some death records or information about what happened to them after the war," suggested Kareem.

"That's a good idea, but looks like they closed at 5 p.m. today and don't open again until Monday," said Carson, looking at the phone. "I can put a call in to the librarian Monday and maybe they can send us information when we are back in Phoenix," he suggested.

"Sounds like we put that on hold," said Ty. "But I think the symbol on Hi Jolly's tomb is unusual and possibly a clue."

"I don't think there's much else we can do here tonight," replied Carson. "Let's hit up the market, grab some cans to go, and get a good night's sleep. Tomorrow we check out the swap meet and see what we might find there. After that, head back to Phoenix and figure out what this Red Ghost is up to," outlined Carson.

"Sounds like a plan. Not to be disrespectful to the dead, but this pyramid is impressive, and I think it is a good clue. I'm going to take a selfie before we are in total darkness out here," said Kareem as the others headed toward the car.

A few miles later, they parked in front of another beige building, this one with beige aluminum siding at the top. With two large road runner cutouts on each side and white signs each reading *Beer, Wine, Deli, Ice, Snacks, ATM, Lottery,* and *Liquor*, Roadrunner Market was a general store that was listed as one of the top locations in town for craft beer.

"Tegan and I will run in and get some beer. You guys keep it running," suggested Carson.

"Sounds good to me. I am tired from thinking about that cemetery and the Red Ghost," said Kareem.

Tegan and Carson went inside and began wandering down the aisles of refrigerated cases holding meat, eggs, milk, and vegetables, eventually finding their way to the beer section. Once there, they found an enormous selection of beer, including a metal shelf display containing specifically craft beer.

"Let's grab a couple of six packs and head over to the hotel," suggested Ty.

"This one looks good," said Carson, picking up a six-pack of black cans of Uncle Bear's Peanut Butter Cup Porter. "Pick another one," he suggested to Tegan.

"They have an excellent selection of local beers. How about something from Mudshark? I don't think we've had them yet," Tegan said.

"I think you're right," said Carson.

She grabbed a six-pack of Desert Magic from the shelf. "An IPA always does the trick. Right?" she said.

A man stepped beside her and grabbed a six-pack of Four Peaks Peach Ale. He looked at Tegan's selection and spoke.

"Ever had their Lunacy?" he asked.

"No, I haven't," she replied.

"It's a witbier. They make a peach version too. Only on draft, but man, it's worth finding. Twelve percent, but so smooth," he replied. "I like the regular, but that peach gives it some added sweetness and a ton of peach. One of the best around."

"Thanks for the tip. I will keep an eye out for both," replied Tegan with a smile as she grabbed the six-pack and headed to the register with Carson.

Later, sitting on the floor of their room at the Super 8, they drank the Uncle Bear and Mudshark cans while plotting their next moves.

"Hopefully we can get to the end of the connections in Quartzsite tomorrow and find out information on that missing skull," said Carson.

"I can't wait to check out that flea market and see what we can find," said Ty.

CHAPTER 10

SWAP MEET

Saturday, March 19, 2016

The group arrived back at Tyson Wells Market Center Swap Meet just after 9 a.m. and prepared to search the entire location for clues. Yesterday didn't afford time to search the flea market, but it was the principal item on today's itinerary.

"Let's talk to some vendors," said Ty.

"We learned from Nile that there's a rumor someone purchased the skull at this swap meet. We don't know that actually happened, and we don't know what vendor," said Ty.

"He said it may be mystical," said Kareem.

"Watch ya self," interrupted Carson.

"Not that Mystikal," said Kareem.

"We could look at vendors selling rocks, vendors selling skulls, mystical crystals, or God only knows what else," sighed Tegan.

"That's why I wanted to come back early today. There are tents and vendors all over the place, selling everything imaginable. General swap meet stuff to tons of rocks, fossils, and crystals," said Carson.

"We heard this is one of the largest rock and mineral shows, perhaps in the world. It will be challenging to cover everything," added Kareem.

"I read during the RV swap meet that the town's population increases from just over thirty-six-hundred people to over a million," said Carson.

"That's a lot of people!" replied Tegan.

They stood in the middle of the dusty path between the tents, just gazing in awe at the number of options. Over three thousand vendors attend the annual swap meet.

"There are tables full of one-dollar crystals all the way to high-end vendors selling individual pieces for thousands of dollars," said Ty, looking around.

"I say we just pick a row and start walking," suggested Carson. "It will not get any easier just standing here gawking at it."

They walked down the outside row of tents, looking at the items on the tables, and greeting vendors and fellow shoppers. Vendors and visitors from all over the world come to Quartzsite to attend this swap meet and gem show. They met vendors from Morocco, India, Mexico, Mali, Afghanistan, and a dozen other countries represented.

The entire site was several acres in size and included not only rocks, minerals, and gems but also other swap meet items, such as comic books, jewelry, and guns. Carson stumbled upon a vendor selling Old West relics, bolero ties, old books, petrified wood, and Native American art. Kareem found a table with a large arrowhead collection, including a cheap bin of common, well-worn arrowheads for just a couple of dollars each.

Ty found a vendor selling handmade cedar tables and chairs with large, rustic legs that looked like driftwood. Tegan walked around the corner of the row and ran into a vendor with dozens of cattle skulls laid out on the dry, dusty ground.

"Hey, Carson! I found some skulls over here," she said, calling to Carson and the others.

The guys joined up with her and scanned the rows of skulls.

"Pretty impressive, but only cattle. I don't think we will find a human skull here," Carson said.

They continued down another aisle and saw an assortment of turquoise rings, necklaces, and toe rings. Another vendor had Native American pottery and modern novelty items, such as cookie jars in the shape of animals and a few resembling politicians and celebrities. Another vendor also sold cookie jars, but more vintage. All items at his tent were perhaps not antique, but old: Old bottles. Old roller skates. Old plates. Old tools. Old books. Old photos. Old lunchboxes, you name it.

On the opposite side of the row, Carson examined a table of wooden sculptures. The artist was a middle-aged man named Douglas from the Salt River-Pima Indian Community. The intricately designed carvings reflected the artisanship that likely took years to master. The carvings depicted eagles, horses, coyotes, ducks, and other animals native to the area. Carson's eyes darted to another carving, a red cedar carving of a man riding a horse. He picked it up and examined it closer. The details revealed it wasn't a man, but a skeleton, and the horse was a camel.

"Excuse me?" asked Carson

"Yes, sir. How are you?" responded Douglas.

"I'm good, thanks. Can you tell me about this piece?" replied Carson.

"That's the Red Ghost of Arizona," said Douglas.

"Really? I've heard some of those tales," Carson continued.

"They're not tales. The Red Ghost was real and rode the desert in the late 1800s. Some of my ancestors saw it on the reservation around where Scottsdale is today," Douglas replied.

Carson looked at some other editions of the Red Ghost that were close to being finished, but still rough around the edges. He leaned over and picked one of them up.

"Now these remind me of a sculpture I saw up in Maine," remembered Carson. He stared at the statues and chuckled as he sat it back on the table.

"When I saw it, it was rough like this. The man and the animal were indistinguishable, and I thought… I thought it was a centaur. But I couldn't understand how Native American art would have a fantasy creature like a centaur," said Carson.

"Where was this statue from?" asked Douglas.

"It was from here in Arizona. The section in the store labeled it as Salt-River Pima," Carson replied. "It thought it was unusual to see a piece from here all the way in Maine," he added.

"It is possible it was an early design. One of my nephews got a scholarship to Maine College of Art and moved to Portland two years ago. He went to learn to paint, but made some money selling wooden carvings. I taught him everything he knows about woodworking," Douglas gloated.

"I wasn't familiar with the Red Ghost then, so a centaur was the only thing that came to mind," said Carson.

"When you said the art depicts what we see, the Red Ghost is something we saw. Around the Salt River and down into Apache Territory, where settlers were fighting Geronimo, the Red Ghost was there," said Douglas.

Carson looked at him for a moment, taking in his tale. "Some say he's back," replied Carson.

Douglas looked on silently.

"Some say a man brought the Red Ghost back from the dead by finding the skull of the rider. A head that someone may have purchased at this swap meet recently," said Carson steadily.

"I know nothing about that. The Red Ghost is more than a hundred years old," said Douglas.

"Yes...," replied Carson.

"But there are... ways, I suppose. Old ways," replied Douglas.

"What ways?" asked Carson.

"The Navajo and Apache were known in the region for what the settlers thought was witchcraft. In the Navajo culture, a Skinwalker is a type of harmful witch who can turn into, possess, or disguise themselves as an animal," replied Douglas.

"I have heard of Skinwalkers, but I don't think we are dealing with that," said Carson.

"The Diné believe there are natural places where powers for both good and evil are concentrated, and we can harness those sacred powers for healing or harm. Medicine men use these powers to heal and aid members of their communities, while those who practice Navajo witchcraft seek to direct the spiritual forces to cause harm or misfortune to others. We know this type of Navajo witchcraft as the *Witchery Way*, which can use human corpses in various ways such as tools from the bones, and concoctions that are used to place a curse, harm, or kill intended victims," added Douglas.

"I don't know about human corpses, but we saw a symbol on a gravesite yesterday. A symbol that is tied to death and rebirth," said Carson.

"Rebirth of the Red Ghost to harm or cursing others, perhaps…" implied Douglas.

"I wasn't sure what we would find on this journey, but I didn't think it would be witchcraft," replied Carson.

"Witchcraft doesn't accurately apply because this form of Navajo spirituality has little to do with the practices and beliefs of European witchcraft. It is simply another aspect or set of ways within the existing Navajo spiritual culture. There are four basic ways of Navajo witchcraft: witchery, sorcery, wizardry, and frenzy," stated Douglas.

"That's interesting," said Carson.

"Navajo witches believe objects such as hair or personal items can be used for good or evil. Within Navajo spirituality, the supernatural and the physical worlds tightly intertwine. Pieces of physical objects like bone, hair, or other items hold strong supernatural properties that can be manipulated. Mostly, only a thin line separates the living from the dead, the good from the evil, and the medicine man from the witch," continued Douglas.

"Which of these four ways would involve bringing back the Red Ghost?" asked Carson.

"The Witchery Way focuses on corpses in their rituals and ceremonies," said Douglas. "You mentioned a skull. That could be part of the ceremony. The symbol on the grave may be connected, but the witch would need more. If this were the Red Ghost, he would need the bones of the Red Ghost," said Douglas.

"If the rumor is true, this guy has the skull. We've seen the symbol, but the bones of the Red Ghost… we don't even know where those bones ended up. I can't find information on what became of those," replied Carson.

"Most regard sorcery as a branch of the witchery way," said Douglas. "Sorcery is essentially an enchantment by a spell. The witch doesn't need to encounter the target personally at all. He must merely get something personal from the target and bury with flesh or other material in a grave under a lightning struck tree. He would then recite a spell in a chant or as a song. Then the spell is cast," revealed Douglas.

"Wow. That's some shit. However, we don't know who or what the intended target is in this case. I don't know if I buy it, but let's just suspend disbelief for a moment and assume that's all true. If it is, and someone found the skull here, and maybe found the bones of the Red Ghost, it could explain why these sightings started in March," said Carson.

Ty arrived drinking from an orange, yellow, and green can. "Find anything?" asked Ty.

"Yes, Douglas here has filled me in on a lot of background information on how the Red Ghost may have returned," said Carson. "What are you drinking?"

"Cactus Cooler. I got it over there from a vendor," Ty revealed.

"What is a Cactus Cooler?" inquired Carson.

"It is a Southwest, or at least Arizona favorite. An orange-pineapple soft drink. It's quite good," reported Ty.

"Orange-Pineapple? Why cactus? Shouldn't it be called prickly pear soda or something?" asked Carson.

"There's a cactus on the can?" replied Ty.

"Doesn't seem like a good reason," replied Carson.

"It can quench the thirst of a cactus frying under the scorching desert sun?" added Ty.

"I'm not buying that either," stated Carson.

"Fred Flintstone's favorite drink was called cactus cooler on *The Flintstones*?" continued Ty.

"Nope," said Carson.

"I don't know… but it's good. And if we had some tequila, maybe some peach schnapps, a little orange juice, and drop a Red Bull in there?"

He paused, setting the can down on the table and flexed while releasing a "Woooo!" imitating Ric Flair.

Tegan and Kareem joined up with the others at the booth.

"So what's the plan?" asked Tegan.

"We're on the right track. We need to keep looking for the vendor who may have made the sale," replied Carson.

The next booth had a collection of old comic books acquired from a recent estate sale. Kareem stopped and flipped through the long boxes of bagged comics.

"Man, I used to love comics growing up," Kareem said.

As he flipped through, he stopped on the fourth issue of *Ghost Rider* and pulled it out.

"Ah, this was one of my favorites. I used to have this one," Kareem said.

"That doesn't look like Ghost Rider," replied Carson.

"That's the original Ghost Rider, from 1950. Before he was Johnny Blaze and the demon on the motorcycle, he was the Phantom Rider and Carter Slade," replied Kareem.

"That's cool. He looks like an actual ghost on that cover. He and the ghost horse jumping from the grave and the tombstones in the back are like Boot Hill. How did he get his power?" asked Ty.

"He's not really a ghost. He's dressed in a phosphorescent white costume, with a full-face mask, cape, and the white hat.

He received his outfit and his white horse from Flaming Star, a Native American medicine man," revealed Kareem.

"Interesting. Many parallels to our mystery. A ghost camel instead of a ghost horse, and a rider who is a skeleton instead of a phantom. Both may have received their powers from a Native American medicine man," replied Carson.

"If the trees on the cover were cacti instead...," added Tegan.

Kareem slid it back into the box dejectedly.

"I can't believe this is $250. I paid about $3 for it as a kid. I wish I didn't sell my collection," Kareem muddled.

"How did Flaming Star transfer the power to the Ghost Rider?" asked Tegan.

"Flaming Star prayed to his god, Manitou, for power. When Manitou appeared to Flaming Star, he instructed him to find the glowing dust from the heavens and enchant the costume with it. He who wore it would become the *He Who Rides the Night Winds*, or the Ghost Rider. One night he saw a meteorite fall to earth and the glowing tail flowing behind it. He located the crash site and collected the dust for storing until he found a would-be champion. He also found a skull shaped item he called the spirit stone. He gave the dust to Carter Slade and told him to capture the ghost horse called Banshee," said Kareem.

"So dust from a meteor, a hero, a dead horse, and a mysterious skull?" asked Carson.

"Yeah, that's how it happened in the comic," replied Kareem.

"The symbol on the grave might have returned the hero, the bones of the Red Ghost relate to the ghost horse, the skull of the original rider creating a source of power to be transmitted to the rider relates to the skull that was possibly found here," replied Carson.

"What about the meteorite? There have been no meteor strikes in Phoenix recently that I have read about," replied Tegan.

Carson began pacing and scratching his head, then ran his hand along his beard, which he did occasionally when he was in deep thought.

"Recently…," he replied. "Yes, not recently. But there's that meteor crater about thirty-seven miles east of Flagstaff," Carson replied.

"Yes, we talked about that on the flight up here," added Ty. "It's the world's best-preserved meteorite impact site on Earth."

"But how would you get there?" asked Tegan. "Yes, you can visit the site, but isn't it a national monument or something now?"

"Yes, there is a visitor's center, it's closed off, and the website says there is no hiking," said Kareem, looking at his phone. "That's how they preserve the site so well."

"So it's unlikely this mystery man could have hiked there to get meteor dust," replied Carson.

"Hey guys, how about this?" replied Tegan, reviewing internet search results. "It's not a meteor, but it was something from the sky and something unknown," she added.

"Unknown? Sounds like that's up our alley," replied Ty. "What are we talking?"

"The UFO crash site at Dreamy Draw Recreation Area," Tegan replied. "It's at the base of Piestewa Peak, on the north side of the city, the second largest peak in the Phoenix Mountain Park, formerly known as Squaw Peak. And we already climbed the largest one. Camelback," she said.

"It's in town? That seems more convenient to the case," replied Carson. "Maybe we should check it out," he said.

"UFO's and ghost camels? Why not?" replied Kareem.

"Let's focus on aliens in Phoenix later. Right now, we still need to find what's here in Quartzsite," suggested Ty.

"And we still have a lot of ground to cover," Carson said, looking around the swap meet.

Walking past a vendor selling hundreds of different license plates and another selling metal sunflowers, the group continued and came to a vendor selling driftwood and walking sticks carved from wood. Continuing on, they found an outdoor table covered with various rocks. Not gems as they saw yesterday at Gem World, but colorful rocks, arrowheads, and a few crystals. What caught Carson's eye was a white pyramid in the center of the table.

"Hey guys, that pyramid strikes me as symbolic of the pyramid atop Hi Jolly's grave. Nice collection of crystals and other rocks," replied Carson.

Ty looked over at another table from the same vendor.

"This table has some larger rocks and crystals," Ty replied.

"Some of these are very raw. The rock hasn't been carved out or polished," stated Carson.

As they were looking at the table, an older man walked over. "See anything ya like, just let me know," stated Arrow Burgess, a vendor with long gray hair working on his eighteenth season at the swap meet.

"You've got a lot of nice stuff," said Kareem.

"Thanks. Been collecting it for a while. I pick it up in the off season, then bring it out here every winter," Arrow said.

"How do you keep up with all of it?" asked Tegan.

"I don't. Not like I used to. I get stuff in, pick stuff up at estate sales, and sometimes just have people drop stuff off if they are cleaning house. As I get older, I find it harder to stay on top of it. Sometimes stuff sneaks in. I didn't know I had," replied Arrow.

"Oh?" inquired Carson. "This stuff is unique. I bet there's a lot of demand for it."

"Sometimes there is. Sometimes people just like to buy it and call it a souvenir from the Old West vacation they took. Sometimes there's folks looking for specific items," Arrow added.

"You get a lot of people asking for specific things?" asked Carson.

"A time or two. Mostly, the older groups know what they are looking for. Then you've got the New Age people looking for specific crystals. Sometimes people looking to buy and resell because we sell cheap here. Other times, I don't know. Some people looking for things and I don't really know what for," Arrow reflected.

"Like what? What people?" asked Ty.

"Seems of late, miscreants, ne'er-do-wells, and hooligans," said Arrow.

"Sounds like trouble," replied Tegan.

"It can be. This guy came around recently and fit the description of all three, I'm afraid," reported Arrow.

"Really? What happened?" inquired Kareem.

"This guy from back 'round Phoenix way came up and was looking at my table. He was rough with some items. He rubbed them and scratchin' at the rocks. I told him not to do that. Those rocks are raw and if he was interested, he could buy it, cut it down, and polish them to his liking. I figured he had a shop or something," remembered Arrow.

"Did he?" asked Carson.

"No, I reckon not. He was disrespectful. Called me a dumb old man. Said I didn't even know what I had," stated Arrow.

"That's not cool," said Ty.

"No, no, it's not. But he was right. I just got some stuff in over the prior couple of weeks and hadn't really had the time to go through it. He picked up something large that I thought was a crystal still in the raw rock. He said it was something else. What I thought was rock was thick-hardened mud. He said it was a skull of some sort. I couldn't see it, but that's what he claimed anyway," said Arrow.

"A skull? Did you sell it to him?" asked Carson.

"Yeah, he took a liking to it and I just got it in. After he said it was a skull, I didn't want it. Not really what I sell here. He asked what I wanted for it and I didn't know. I just said *how's twenty bucks sound?*"

"What did he say?" inquired Tegan.

"He jumped right on it. Handed me the twenty. It was so quick I knew I probably messed up," stated Arrow.

"Did you get his name?" asked Ty.

"Actually, I did. By accident," said Arrow.

"How'd you do that?" asked Carson.

"He bought something from another vendor and left the paper bag as trash on my table. It had the credit card receipt with his name on it. Before that, when he first came up and was makin' small talk, he said he lived out in Guadalupe out in Phoenix," stated Arrow.

"Guadalupe? That's that small village just outside of Tempe and Phoenix," said Kareem.

"Yeah, that's the place," said Arrow.

"Who was he?" asked Ty. "What did he look like?"

"Just some punk kid. Well, not a kid, probably late twenties or early thirties. A kid to me. I think he's mestizo, with a kind of punk rock look. Long hair on the sides but spiked up on top. Sleeveless black rock band shirt, black jeans, boots. You know the type. Angry at the world," described Arrow.

"Had you seen him around here before?" asked Carson.

"Nope, and I hope he doesn't come back. Johnny," the man recalled. "That's his name. Johnny Stamps. I remembered it because it was kinda different," stated Arrow.

"You seem like a nice guy with a lot of interesting things. It's not cool he treated you like that," said Tegan.

"He was angry, but when he left, he was excited about his purchase. Sounded like he had been looking for it, or something like it for a while," said Arrow.

"Any idea why he wanted it?" asked Ty.

"Not a clue. I was just glad to get rid of him and make twenty bucks," replied Arrow.

"We appreciate your time. Hopefully, the rest of your weekend will be peaceful," said Kareem.

"Yep, tomorrow I pack up and head back home. Until next season," stated Arrow.

Walking away from the table, the group knew Arrow was the unsuspecting man who sold the skull. Now they had a name and a location to check out: Johnny Stamps of Guadalupe.

"So maybe Johnny Stamps came out here to visit the grave of Hi Jolly and carve the symbol. If that thing Arrow sold him was the skull of the original rider…" Carson said.

"Which would make sense because it was encrusted with mud and we learned the skeleton rider's head was shot off, but not found," added Ty.

"Right. Probably fell to the ground somewhere and over time became covered in mud. The summer sun out here can dry the mud and bake it into brick or a hard ass rock," continued Carson.

"He would still need to find the camel's bones, which we don't know what happened to them either, and he would need something to enchant it with," added Kareem.

"Which we think, at least based on your Ghost Rider story, we might connect it with Dreamy Draw," stated Tegan.

"I think we are good here," said Carson. "We've hit this small town pretty hard and found what we were looking for regarding the skull. I don't know there are any clues left. Let's grab some lunch, check out of the hotel, and head back to Phoenix. I'm interested in returning and paying Johnny Stamps a visit. See what he knows," proposed Carson.

"Good plan," reviewed Ty.

"Let's hit up Quartzsite Yacht Club. See what it's all about," suggested Carson.

The large gray and white bar and motel, the Quartzsite Yacht Club, reminded the group of some of the dive bars back in Austin. A large, open space with plenty of seating, pool tables, and a stage in the corner for local performers and karaoke singers took Carson back to his days as a regular at Giddy Ups. The bar was busy with college basketball on the television and locals enjoying a few beers before heading out of town for the season. The blue walls displayed several maritime artifacts and read *Quartzsite Yacht Club* above a captain's wheel.

The stage was empty, as was a table directly in front of it. Kareem walked over and secured the seats as Ty raised a hand, responding to the server acknowledging their entry and directing them to sit anywhere.

"This is a cool place," said Kareem, looking around at the furnishings.

"Right? I would expect this along a lake or the ocean. But in a desert? There isn't any water close to here," replied Carson.

"What's with it being called a yacht club?" Tegan asked as the server arrived at the table.

"Hello. I take it ya'll are visiting?" asked Pepita Ayers, a longtime employee at the Yacht Club.

"Yes, we are from Texas, on our way back to Phoenix," replied Carson.

"This bar used to be The Jigsaw back in the 1970s. When it went up for sale, Al Madden purchased it and thought it would be funny to name it The Yacht Club. He decided he would sell memberships to anyone who qualified, which back then was ten bucks. It caught on and people started joining. With improvements to the bar, the membership continued to grow with members from all around the country. Now we have over ten thousand members and can boast of having the largest membership in the world," replied Pepita.

"That's some story!" responded Ty.

"We've got some good food, good music, dancing, and cold beer," stated Pepita.

"What beers do you have?" asked Carson.

"Miller, Michelob, some craft beers like Shock Top. Mudshark, Goose Island," said Pepita. "We have a couple of Arizona beers on tap too," she said.

"What's on tap?" asked Tegan.

"We have a few from Sleepy Dog Brewing, our brewery of the month. We have The Belly Rub, which is a Belgian Tripel. Wolfpack is a double IPA, Coco's Imperial Chocolate Stout, and Feisty Chihuahua Pilsner," she replied.

"How about one of each?" asked Ty.

"Coming right up. Any food catch yer eye?" Pepita inquired.

"I think we're good. Just the beer, then we gotta head back to Phoenix," said Carson.

"Sounds good. Do you want me to close out when I bring the beers?" Pepita asked.

"That'll be great," replied Carson.

A few minutes later, Pepita returned with the beers and the check.

"I'm surprised to find these beers here," said Kareem.

"Most of our customers prefer the big beers, but we try to have something for everyone, and the craft beer market is growing. Keeps people coming in when we can carry a wide variety, and we like to support the Arizona beers as much as we can," Pepita stated.

Tegan took the Belgian, Ty the Pilsner, Kareem the IPA, and Carson the Stout.

"This might be one of the best double IPAs I've had," Kareem stated. "Try this," he said, offering it up to the others.

"This stout has a nice cocoa and malt taste," Carson said, reaching for Kareem's beer to sample it as well. "That is nice!" he said after taking a sip of the double IPA.

"One thing we still have to figure out is where the bones of the Red Ghost ended up," spoke Ty. "I think we have found a lot of clues on the other things, but if this guy brought the Red Ghost back, that's the missing piece," he said.

"We know Mizoo Hastings shot the Red Ghost, and that was the end of him, but those stories mentioned nothing about its bones," said Carson. "We have to find out where Mizoo Hasting's farm was," he added.

Tegan picked up her phone and began searching online for clues. A couple of attempts produced no results. When she typed the keywords Mizoo Hasting Farm Arizona, multiple results showed for a subdivision. She clicked the first link and saw photos of houses available for sale.

"Hey guys, there's a subdivision called Hastings Farms, and it's in Queen Creek, Arizona," Tegan said.

"Queen Creek?" asked Carson.

Tegan opened the map application on her phone.

"It's a fairly large parcel of land in Queen Creek, which is southeast of Mesa. Less than twenty miles from where we're staying," she said.

"One thing I've noticed since being here in Arizona is there is a lot of housing construction," said Carson.

"Yeah, many times those companies buy land from farmers or from the family who inherited land from their ancestors. With Phoenix being one of the fastest growing cities in the country, that land is valuable, so it's tempting to sell and make a good profit," replied Ty.

"And they often name the subdivision in honor of the prior owner, so Hastings Farms… it wouldn't be unlikely that it was originally Mizoo Hasting's farm," replied Carson.

"If that subdivision used to be Old Man Hasting's farm, then maybe the bones of the Red Ghost were found there," said Kareem.

"Maybe Johnny Stamps found out about it? Queen Creek isn't too far from Mesa, and if the builder found something, they might want to keep it quiet. If reports hit the paper, it might force them to stop construction and turn it over to archeologists," suggested Tegan.

"Good point. And that would delay getting a return on their investment," added Carson. "But how would Johnny find out?"

"Maybe he has a buddy that works for the builder? Or maybe he works for them?" theorized Ty.

"I like it. Maybe he had a general idea of where the farm was, and if this is newer build, maybe he got a job working construction? That gives him an opportunity to search the land without drawing suspicion, and if he found it, he could hide the evidence and take what he wanted," said Carson.

"Looks like we've got Guadalupe, Dreamy Draw, and now Queen Creek to explore," updated Kareem.

"And they are still constructing houses in the subdivision?" Carson asked Tegan.

"It looks like construction started around 2014 and they are still building. Plus, multiple sections set aside for future construction a few years out," replied Tegan.

"Sounds like we have some work to do," Carson said, before he took a long drink from the glass.

"We better get back to town and get this show on the road," suggested Ty.

"It will be late when we get back to the hotel. We should rest up then visit Guadalupe tomorrow. Maybe we can run into Mr. Stamps," suggested Carson.

They stood up, dropped cash on the table to cover the tab, and headed to the parking lot to begin the long drive back to Phoenix.

CHAPTER 11

STAMP COLLECTOR

Sunday, March 20, 2016

Carson drove as they entered the tiny town of Guadalupe. From Tempe, Priest Drive transformed into Avenida del Yaqui, and the surrounding area gave the appearance of stepping into another country. While metropolitan Phoenix continually expands, the small one-square mile town of Guadalupe will remain its small size. With its surrounding man-made boundaries of Interstate 10 and the city of Phoenix on the west, Baseline Road and the city of Tempe on the North, the city of Tempe on the South, and the Salt River Project's Highline Canal on the East.

It is a town with a cultural richness untouched, despite the high-tech changes taking place around it. It is a mixed Yaqui Native American and Mexican community of about fifty-five hundred residents with a very strong cultural and ethnic identity, maintaining Hispanic street names and storefronts with Mexican artifacts hanging, giving them a look different from traditional storefronts visitors are used to seeing.

El Tienges Mercado de Guadalupe, on the southeast corner of Guadalupe Road and Avenida del Yaqui, serves as the town center. The Mercado is a commercial shopping center designed in the fashion of a Mercado, with inward facing shops surrounding a central plaza. Carson pulled into the parking lot on the side of the Mercado.

"Seems like a good place to park and explore on foot since it's right in the center of town," Carson said as he exited the car and looked around.

As he turned his head, he caught an obstructed view of one of the town's central landmarks. Standing well off from the road, across a gravel driveway, sat a white-colored Spanish colonial church, Our Lady of Guadalupe Catholic Church. Besides the church, the rectory and Santa Lucia Pascua Yaqui Temple formed a complex that called out to Carson, even though he hadn't set foot in a church in several years. Kareem spoke, interrupting his gaze.

"I need to get a selfie with that church in the background, and then we should head over to the Mercado. Some stores may have information on Johnny Stamps. It's a small town, so chances are if he lives here, someone knows him. That farmer's market across the street might be a good place to start," Kareem suggested. "I can also smell the carne asada cooking from somewhere nearby. It's Sunday. I wonder if they have menudo?"

"Are you hungry already?" asked Ty.

"I'm usually hungry," replied Kareem. "You know that."

The Guadalupe Farmer's Market was a small beige-colored building with a painted mural of a cornucopia and a garden on the side facing a terracotta-colored strip mall containing a tattoo shop, a barbershop, and Loreto's Mexican Food. To the left of the Farmer's Market was a small parking lot. Although the mural on the side said Guadalupe Farmer's Market, the front read, *Mis Amigos Food Mart.*

Ty held the door open, and Tegan walked in first. She stopped and looked around at the business.

"Looks like the farmer's market sign is old. It's a general store now," she said.

As they entered, a man behind the cash register greeted them. "Hello. Name's Enyeto," said the young man with long black hair. "Anything you're looking for?"

"We are," said Tegan.

The man smiled as she walked closer. "What are you looking for? I will see if I can help you," said Enyeto.

"We're looking for a guy," replied Tegan.

"Oh, maybe I can help you," Enyeto said, removing his cowboy hat.

"We're looking for a specific guy. We don't know a lot about him, but we think he lives around here. Late twenties, long black hair. Kinda of spiky on top. He's a little edgy and usually angry," she said.

"His name's Johnny Stamps," replied Carson. "Do you know him or have seen him around?"

"Don't recognize the name, but the description sounds like a guy who was around here a few weeks ago, causing trouble," replied Enyeto.

"What kind of trouble?" asked Kareem.

"Just the normal stuff. Too much to drink, disturbing the peace. Although someone tagged the wall down by the barbershop next door. Don't know if that was him or not," said Enyeto.

"Thanks," replied Carson. "We'll check it out. Thanks for the tip. At least we know he lives around this area."

"This graffiti that you mentioned. Did you get a look at it? Do you know what the person painted?" asked Ty.

"It was just a circle with some lines, but I don't know what it was supposed to be," replied Enyeto.

"You have seen nothing else strange around here, have you? Like a large camel?" asked Kareem.

"Camel? No, certainly nothing like that here. Although, now that you mention it, I heard something like that on the news," Enyeto added.

"The animal is definitely here in Phoenix, and that symbol sounds like a similar symbol we saw out in Quartzsite on a grave," said Carson.

"If you want to get a better look at it, I think it's still on the wall next door," said Enyeto.

"We appreciate the help," replied Tegan as she reached into her purse and removed a business card. "Here's my card. If you see Johnny Stamps or a camel, call me," she said.

Leaving the mini mart, the group headed next door to the strip mall to look at the graffiti. They found the small symbol on the wall underneath the windowsill of Loreto's. Ty knelt down to get a closer look at it.

"This is the Ouroboros, the same symbol we saw on Hi Jolly's grave," Ty revealed.

"That means we are definitely close," said Carson. "It had to be Johnny Stamps. Let's go inside and see if anyone saw who did it."

The inside of the restaurant was colorful: white tile floors, orange walls, with yellow booth seating. The counter was also yellow with a large menu with color photos of all the items that spanned the full length of the counter. A woman stood behind the counter waiting to take the order of the group as they entered.

Kareem noticed a white board daily special menu mounted on a black stanchion to the side of the counter.

"Nice, they have menudo," read Kareem.

"You know what you want?" asked the young woman behind the counter.

"Hola, Señorita," said Kareem, still looking at the daily specials.

"¡Hola! Mi llamo Lark," replied the cashier with an accent.

"Hello, Lark. Unfortunately, we can't stay to eat," replied Carson, giving a glance toward Kareem. "We noticed the graffiti outside your window and wondered if you may know who did it."

"Some young punk," replied Lark. "He comes around here and hangs out in the parking lot, sometimes harassing the customers," she said.

"That doesn't sound good for business," responded Ty.

"No, it isn't. People mostly ignore him, but sometimes we have had to call the police and run him out of here," said Lark.

"Do you know his name?" asked Tegan.

"I think it's John, or Johnny. Something like that," Lark responded.

"That's the same guy we are trying to find," added Carson. "Do you know where he lives? Is he around here?"

"I know he lives around the area, 'cause he comes around here a lot. But I don't know exactly where. We filed a police report on the graffiti, so they might have more information," stated Lark.

"Thanks for your help. We'll keep looking around the area. Hopefully, he turns up," added Carson.

"Good luck. I hope you find what you're looking for," said Lark.

As they exited the restaurant, Kareem was a little disappointed.

"I really thought that carne asada was coming from there, but that's a no. Looks like they cook orders up as we place them. That smell wafting through the air has me hungry. There's nothing like the smell of carne asada on the grill. Maybe there's a carnicería on one of these side streets," he said.

"Calm down, Toucan Sam. We're here to find Johnny Stamps, not lunch," replied Carson.

Kareem stopped and looked around, smelling the air. "They say to go with your gut, and right now my gut says it's time to eat," replied Kareem. He scanned the area and pointed further up Avenida del Yaqui. "That way," he said.

They began walking and less than half a mile later turned down East Calle Encinas.

"Smells like it's coming from this direction," reported Kareem.

They passed a small house with yellow siding and black numbers reading 5537. A small white wooden porch projected from the front of the house and a middle-aged woman was sitting on an old wooden chair, smoking a cigarette. She watched the group of strangers walk down the street. They stopped to allow Kareem a moment to detect the scent of the carne asada.

"We're very close," Kareem replied.

Carson turned and noticed the woman on the porch. "Good afternoon!" he said with a cheerful wave.

She said nothing, but raised her hand to respond to the gesture.

"Say, we're looking for a guy that lives around here. I wonder if you could help us out?" asked Carson.

The woman stood up and walked out into the grassless front yard where the only thing other than dirt was a bed of rocks circling a small tree in the front yard. As she walked closer to the group, she took a long drag on her cigarette and blew a puff of smoke into the air.

"Hello. I am Carson, and these are my friends Tegan, Ty, and Kareem. We are searching for information about a man from town. We're hoping you might know him?"

She took another deep hit from the cigarette before she spoke in a gravelly voice.

"I'm Cheyenne. Cheyenne Armijo. What can I do ya for?"

"We are trying to find Johnny Stamps," replied Ty.

She took another puff on the cigarette and gave a smirk and slight chuckle as she inhaled.

"Yeah, I know Johnny. Haven't seen him for a few days though, but he stays up the road a piece," she replied.

"Do you know where?" asked Tegan.

"What kind of trouble has he got into this time?" Cheyenne asked.

"Right now, we just want to talk to him and ask some questions," replied Carson.

"Questions? Sounds like the law," said Cheyenne.

"No, we're just some people looking for answers," said Carson. "You haven't seen any camels, have you?"

"Only camels around here I've seen are the ones I'm smokin'," added Cheyenne. "Come to think of it, Johnny was talking about a camel recently. Said he was working on something. Something big," she said.

"Big? Like what?" asked Tegan.

"Don't know exactly. But he mentioned something about ghosts. I told him I don't believe in that ghost shit. That's when he said it wasn't actually a ghost, but a camel. Something from the past he was researching and said it was going to change things," she continued.

"Change things?" asked Kareem.

"Something to focus all his pent up anger on, I reckon. He always gets worked up when talking about family and ancestors," she said.

"And this anger management project has to do with a camel?" sought Carson.

"I don't know about anger management. Sounded like revenge," she said.

"And that didn't startle you?" asked Ty.

"Naw. He talks a lot but doesn't do too much harm. A few minor run-ins with the cops, but just stupid shit. He still thinks he's a kid and gets into mischief," Cheyenne said.

"So he's been missing a few days?" asked Ty.

"Guess so. About a couple weeks since I saw him last. But he lives over near the church with the Whitaker twins. Maybe he came back. Could be just lying low," said Cheyenne.

"Where can we find the Whitaker twins?" asked Tegan.

"They're over on the next street, Calle Iglesia. It's a little gray house with a wooden porch. A couple cars in the front yard. They usually are grillin' out front," Cheyenne replied.

"Grilling?" repeated Kareem.

"Yeah, they have a big grill and usually do up some carne asada and sell it to the neighborhood or just whoever happens by," she said.

"That's what I smelled!" added Kareem. "I knew someone was grilling asada around here somewhere."

"Can't miss the smoke and delightful smell," replied Cheyenne.

"Thank you for your time," replied Carson. "We will see if we can find the Whitakers, and hopefully Johnny Stamps," he said.

The others started to turn and walk away. Carson stayed and commented on Cheyenne's lawn ornaments.

"That's kind of unusual. You don't have grass in your yard, but you have lawn ornaments?"

"Those? Those are my frogs," Cheyenne responded.

"They're a little bizarre, if you don't mind me saying so," replied Carson.

"They are definitely unique," answered Cheyenne.

"I've never seen frogs standing up, bipedal," continued Carson.

"My sister up in Ohio sent these to me. I like frogs, and even though I don't have grass, it's something to put in my yard and look at," she stated.

"Frogs kind of freak me out," admitted Tegan after stopping and waiting on Carson. "Especially big ones, and if I ever saw a weird bipedal one, I don't think I would ever go back to… Ohio, did you say?"

"Yes, that's right," said Cheyenne. "I like things from local shops and artists. My sister came to visit last fall and brought these with her. They are weird, but kinda cool," Cheyenne replied.

"You can definitely keep them. They give me the willies," Tegan concluded.

"Hey, thanks again for your help. Enjoy the rest of your day," replied Carson as he and Tegan started walking to catch up with the others headed toward the church and the smoky smell of the grilled asada.

It was only a few minutes later that the group reached Calle Iglesia and looked for the Whitaker's home. As they walked closer, the smell of grilled carne asada intensified.

"Look, just up ahead. Smoke," Kareem pointed out.

They arrived in front of a small house with a picket fence. Most of the posts were white, but several were unpainted, showing signs of recent repair. Two tall palm trees stood on each side of the dirt entrance that served as a driveway. The house looked like unpainted cement, with three wooden posts holding up the roof. An older model Toyota Celica sat in the driveway and two men were outside operating the grill near a window-mounted air conditioner unit covered with a large garbage bag.

"Looks like this is the place," replied Ty.

Carson called out to the men. "Hello!"

The men turned around and one walked out to greet the visitors. The other man continued to operate the grill, turning the meat with metal tongs.

"Hello," the man said to Carson. "We're selling plates: carne asada, beans, and macaroni salad for ten dollars. Comes with a Coke. How many would you like?"

"Sure smells good," said Kareem. "I noticed it half a mile away down by the Mercado!"

"The smoke is our free advertising," said the man, laughing.

"It's very effective," replied Tegan.

"Name's DeQuan, and that's my brother Dychon over on the grill," replied the man.

"I wasn't expecting to see a couple of Brothers grilling traditional Mexican food and serving it up in the community," replied Ty.

"Yeah, we're one of a kind around here. We grew up in this neighborhood and were influenced by the Latino and Native culture we saw everywhere. We put a little of our own spin on the final product, but people around here embrace it and now we're out here every weekend until we sell out of food," replied DeQuan.

"We came for the food… or at least I did," said Kareem. "But we're also looking for a guy that lives around here. Someone down the street said he might stay with you. Johnny Stamps?"

"Man, punk ass dude. He was staying here for about six months, but a couple of weeks ago, I guess he moved out. Took most of his stuff and left without saying nothing. Still owes a couple months' rent," said Dychon.

"About two weeks ago? Someone else said she hadn't seen him around since then as well. Any idea where he went?" asked Carson.

"Naw, last time we talked, he said he was working on something and was going out of town for a couple of days. I was happy because when he said he was working, I thought that meant he was going to pay the rent. Instead, he just disappeared," stated DeQuan.

"He left some shit in his room. We boxed it up and were going to throw it in the trash if he didn't come back this week," replied Dychon. "You can have it if you want since we're just going to toss it."

"Sure, maybe there are some clues in there that may help us find him," replied Tegan.

"If you find him, tell him he owes us five hundred bucks," added DeQuan.

DeQuan turned and walked into the house. He returned a few minutes later with a small banker's box and handed it to Carson.

"That's the last of his shit," replied DeQuan.

Carson opened the lid and peeked inside. Seeing several miscellaneous objects, he closed the lid and decided to look at it back in the hotel room.

"Good luck finding him," replied Dychon. "He plays in a metal band called Shamanic Wind. They play at some small clubs around town. Maybe you can find him there?"

"Any idea where his most recent shows were?" asked Carson.

"I know he played at Yucca Tap Room recently and Chopper John's up on Indian School Road, but those were a couple of months ago. He plays wherever he can get a spot. The Nile in Mesa is another spot he plays," DeQuan replied.

"Thanks. We'll check it out," responded Carson.

"Before we head out," said Kareem, "let me get a plate to go," he replied, holding ten dollars in his hand.

After leaving Guadalupe, the team drove into Phoenix for a beer and dinner. Exiting the 202 Highway onto 24th Street, they traveled toward the Green Gables neighborhood of Phoenix at the intersection of 24th and Oak, where small businesses and neighborhood houses made up the community. There they found Wren House Brewing Company, a brewery in an old house. When searching for a location, the brewers fell in love with the home's character. The main 1920s bungalow house transformed into the taproom and the remodeled garage used for brewing. After opening in June 2015, Wren House moved toward the top of the Phoenix craft beer scene.

"I have heard great things about this place and wanted to check it out while we are in town," said Carson.

Walking into the brewery, the group paused and looked around. Immediately it felt homey - and it was a home. The main room of the building was the taproom, with bright white tile behind the bar and on the counter. Metal black seating for ten patrons spanned the front and one side of the counter, while a large blackboard behind the bar showed the beer menu. There were a couple of smaller tables in the room with seating and a large wooden table nearly as long as the bar counter against the inside wall. White exposed beams on the ceiling showed wooden flooring above. There were smaller rooms that used to be bedrooms now used for additional seating. The brewery had a feeling of comfort that often is missing, even in small craft breweries. The group sat at the large table and soaked in the atmosphere and character of the old house.

"We have some space at this table. You guys look over the menu and I will run to the car and get that box we got from the Whitakers," said Carson.

When he returned, the group reached decisions on what beers to get. Ty ordered the Black Caddis, a dark porter brewed with chocolate rye that gave the beer a rich chocolate-coffee taste. Tegan followed with Lady Banks, a gose made with Celtic sea salt, rose petals, chamomile, and hibiscus flowers. Kareem selected the Olmec, an imperial stout with cacao nibs, dried chiles, and vanilla beans. Carson looked over the menu and immediately made his selection.

"Is that a sign or what?" asked Carson. "I have to go with the Hi Jolly," he said, looking at the American wheat ale brewed with local wheat, desert wildflower honey, chamomile, and elderflower.

He sat the box on the table and walked to the bar to place the order. He made two trips carrying a beer in each hand and sat at the large table, immediately taking a sip from the beer.

"That's fantastic. Clean tasting, slightly sweet, little floral notes. I really love when breweries take local ingredients and use them in the beer. This local wheat and wildflower honey not only make an excellent beer, it gives it a local flavor," said Carson.

Ty took a drink of the Black Caddis, one of the first beers Wren House brewed.

"I see what you did there," replied Ty.

"As Brad Pitt said in *Seven*, '*What's in the Box*'", asked Tegan.

Kareem took a sip of the 12.5% stout. "I was thinking Justin Timberlake," replied Kareem.

"They both work," said Carson. "Let's have a look, shall we?" Carson removed the lid of the banker's box and reached inside, pulling items out one at a time. First, a notebook. "This looks like a sketch pad," he said, looking at the cover. He opened it up and flipped through the pages.

"Partially used. It looks like Johnny is an artist. There are some drawings of skulls, what appears to be the name of his band. Like a logo or something."

"Maybe a design for a t-shirt?" suggested Ty.

"Good call. Maybe that," added Carson.

He passed the sketchpad to Tegan and reached back inside the box. Tegan began flipping through the pages of the book.

"He's talented. There's a couple sketches of camels in here," she said.

"We have some music to listen to on the trip," said Carson, pulling out four CDs. He glanced at the cover and turned each over to look at the back.

"Hmm. I am not familiar with these groups. We have *One Nation Under*, a 2001 CD from the group Blackfire. They appear to be a punk rock band from Arizona. The second album is *Sagebrush Rejects* by the group I Don't Konform, another Native punk band from Arizona. Next, ... oh, these guys have scary make up. Another metal band from Arizona called Mutilated Tyrant with the CD... something I can't pronounce. I don't recognize the language," read Carson.

Ty looked over the I Don't Konform CD.

"It appears the genre is called Rez Metal or Diné metal, per the back of the CD," read Ty.

"One more," said Carson as he removed the final CD. "*Welcome to Reality* by Resistant Culture, another Rez-Metal band, but from Seattle," said Carson.

"The guys we spoke to this afternoon said Johnny was in a metal band, so it would make sense he would listen to similar music," said Kareem.

"What else is in the box?" asked Tegan.

"Looks like the Ace of Spades playing card, a couple hair ties, a key to who knows what, a day pass to Tonto National Forest dated Saturday March 5, a printout of a map of the Piestewa Peak Dreamy Draw Trails, a menu from the Queen Creek Olive Mill, a rusty nail, and a USB drive," revealed Carson.

"That's an interesting combination of items," said Kareem. "What can we make of it?"

"We thought to explore Dreamy Draw, and there is a map in this box of the trails, which means he likely did or intended to explore the area," said Tegan.

"And the Queen Creek Olive Mill. We said Mizoo Hastings' Farm where the Red Ghost was killed is now a subdivision in Queen Creek," added Ty.

"Maybe the nail was used to etch the symbol on the monument out in Quartzsite?" suggested Kareem.

"And God only knows what's on this USB. We'll have to save that for the laptop back in the hotel," replied Carson.

Carson sipped his beer and reflected on the case. He thought about their conversation and wondered how many other conversations had taken place around this large table. Not just here at the brewery, but its previous life. It looked old, and no doubt was in someone's house previously. Many important conversations take place around the kitchen table, and this conversation was no different. This table. The house. *How many people have enjoyed them over the years and what important conversations were had?* he pondered.

Ty interrupted his thoughts.

"Hey, buddy. I know you probably missed it because, well, you always miss it. Notice anything above the shelves behind the bar?" teased Ty.

Carson turned his attention toward the woman working behind the bar and then noticed the shelf behind her. Above the shelves was a mounted trophy head of a jackalope with two medals hanging around its neck.

"That's a nice touch. I definitely dig this place now. The jackalope - the animal that has eluded me the longest," Carson said jokingly.

"I'll drink to that!" said Ty.

"Speaking of that, let's get another round," suggested Kareem. "I feel right at home in this brewery and at this table. It's very comforting, like actually being home."

"That's a good call. That barrel-aged imperial porter, Who Hit John, was calling my name," replied Ty.

"Since they have another Berliner Weiss on the menu, I need to order that Globe Miami Weiss," stated Tegan.

"Can you get me a Jomax? A coffee oatmeal stout sounds pretty good," replied Carson.

"And a Señor Gallo lager for me," added Kareem.

"Those jackalopes always had a way of escaping, but hopefully this Red Ghost won't escape us much longer," replied Carson.

"I feel we are getting closer to understanding the origin of the beast anyway," said Kareem.

"Yes, understanding is one thing. However, can we stop him? Can we end the torment the people in town have felt as it seems to be randomly wreaking havoc," answered Carson.

Deciding it was time to go, the group checked out and drove to a nearby spot Tegan wanted to try. Just three miles away, Barrio Urbano and award-winning chef Silvana Salcido Esparza, known for redefining Mexican food in Phoenix since 2002. One of the principal attractions of the restaurant was Chef Silvia's vision of guacamole. It was prepared table-side with a generous amount of avocados and pomegranate.

They drove through a side alley where an expansive mural covered the back wall leading to the Barrio Urbano parking lot. Walking through the back door of the restaurant, they found an empty table.

"We have to try the guacamole here. I've heard it is unlike any I've probably ever had before, and people just rave about how good it is," said Tegan.

The server approached with four menus and took their drink order. Ty and Tegan ordered the Limon Mexicano, a mixture of fresh lime juice, agave nectar, and sparkling water. Carson ordered a similar drink, a Naranjada, but made with orange juice instead of lime. Kareem ordered a freshly prepared kiwi agua fresca.

"Great. I will give you a moment to look over the menu and return with the drinks," said the young server.

It didn't take long until everyone narrowed down the menu and made their selection. Tegan ordered the classic chile relleno, a roasted poblano pepper filled with a blend of Monterey, Oaxaca and Chevre cheese, topped with grilled skirt steak, puff dough, and a crushed blend of tomato salsa and bleu cheese garnish. Ty chose the puerco con nopal, a seared pork loin topped with a tomatillo and nopal verde salsa. For Carson, it was the enchiladas suizas con longaniza. They were homemade corn tortillas filled with Oaxaca cheese and chicken breast, then finished in a tomatillo jojoque crema, Schreiner's longaniza sausage, and green squash. Kareem concluded the order with a selection of three tacos. He selected tacos azul: grilled skirt steak topped with chorizo, onion, cilantro, avocado slice, and bleu cheese; a taco de pescado borracho, which was fresh fish cooked in a Modelo especial beer batter, topped with cabbage, spiced rosarito aioli, avocado slice, pico de gallo. His last choice, a taco de arrachera: a grilled skirt steak topped with onion, cilantro, and an avocado slice. All the tacos came with a side of salsa tatemada.

"Based on what we saw in that box, especially the Dreamy Draw Trails map, we need to investigate it tomorrow," suggested Carson.

"That map and the menu to the Queen Creek Olive Mill mean we are on the right track to the probable location of the Red Ghost's skeleton," replied Ty.

"This case is distinct from anything we have investigated so far. Not only is it a cryptid, but it is a supernatural cryptid now, thanks to Johnny Stamps," said Tegan.

"We have to not only find the animal, but figure out how to stop it," said Kareem. "Maybe that means locating the animal, but it might also mean we have to find Johnny Stamps if he somehow is controlling it."

"I hope the USB can help us with those questions," answered Carson.

CHAPTER 12

LIVIN' THE DREAM

Monday, March 21, 2016

As Ty woke up, he yawned quietly and realized that Carson was already in full-research mode, sitting in his bed and working on his laptop.

"You're up early. What's good with it?" asked Ty.

"Just checking out this USB from Johnny Stamp's house," replied Carson. "There's some crazy shit on here."

"What kind of crazy shit? We specialize in crazy shit," Ty responded groggily.

"That we do, my friend. That we do," responded Carson. "There are some saved documents on here that show Johnny has been researching the Red Ghost and conjuration."

"Conjuration?"

"Yes, specifically reanimation and animal control spells," replied Carson. "There are pasted screenshots of conversations he was having on Reddit asking about the legend of the Red Ghost, and some emails from someone that appears, by their email address, to be connected with the Salt River Pima-Maricopa Indian Community."

"Any insight into why he was doing it? Why the Red Ghost?" asked Ty.

"Some of these documents appear to be poems he's written, Word documents that look like journaling of dreams, and some scanned images of what look like old letters. I am still reading them. The poems are very dark and mad at the world," Carson added.

"He is in a black metal band. There's some anger that comes with that," replied Ty.

"Yes, but it goes deeper than just playing in a band. These poems and journal entries show resentment and hate that didn't just come out of nowhere. It runs deep. Perhaps generations deep," replied Carson.

"I can see it," answered Ty. "I feel that myself sometimes too, but there's a right way and a wrong way to handle those feelings," he said.

"Looking at some of these spells, they have written notes related to the Red Ghost. It's his outline of what's needed to make the spell work," read Carson.

"What's it say?" asked Ty.

"It shows he needed to find the skull and carve the symbol into both the skull and the grave," said Carson.

"We know he completed those two steps," replied Ty.

"Yes. Next, find the camel skeleton and bring the reanimation sprinkle with interstellar cosmic dust," concluded Carson.

"Based on the reappearance of the Red Ghost, we can conclude he finished those steps. That meteor crater in eastern Arizona sounds like a logical place to find cosmic dust, but the map of Dreamy Draw means he likely went there. He must have found the location of the Red Ghost's skeleton out in Queen Creek. But why the Red Ghost and why use the grave of Hi Jolly? He wasn't the original rider, so what's the connection?" asked Ty.

"Maybe the connection is in these old letters?" replied Carson.

Carson opened the folder labeled *letters.* It contained scanned images of old letters, dozens of them. Carson clicked on one and opened it, skimming the contents.

"This is a letter to a woman. It talks about the camp of the Camel Corps and what they are doing," read Carson.

He reached the end of the letter. It was signed *Philip.*

"Philip? What Philip do we know related to the Camel Corps?" asked Carson.

"Philip Tedro!" replied Ty.

"Yes! Philip Tedro, also known as Hi Jolly," answered Carson.

He opened another and read it. Then another, and another.

"These letters are from Hi Jolly," said Carson.

“Why would he have letters from Hi Jolly? And where would he get them?” asked Ty.

“Good question. They talk about frustration with the direction of the Corps, mention of Greek George - remember he was another one of the camel drivers. These letters say they forced Greek George to turn the camels into the wild. He lists the original camel drivers: Greek George, Mimico Teodora (Mico), Hadjiatis Yannaco (Long Tom), Anastasio Coralli (Short Tom), Michelo Georgios, Yanni Illato, Giorgios Costi, and we know Hi Jolly was the other one,” said Carson.

“We knew Greek George moved to West Hollywood, Hi Jolly moved to Quartzsite, and Long Tom worked with the circus. We also know those guys died prior to the final sighting of the Red Camel, and we know Hi Jolly’s favorite camel, Topsy, was cremated with him and is buried in the time capsule on the monument we visited,” deducted Ty.

“Right. These letters talk a lot about Mico, and how he worked with one soldier to get him used to a new, aggressive camel. Mico was trying to break the wild beast. He said the soldier was afraid of riding him, but Edward Fitzgerald Beale, who was a friend of Kit Carson and Buffalo Bill Cody, and the guy who convinced Jefferson Davis to start the Camel Corps told him the way to break the camel was to get him used to the rider. They were pleased with the camel and figured once they controlled him, he could be the lead camel in the Corps. The journal talks about their attempts to work with the camel and rider,” read Carson.

“Who was the rider?” asked Ty.

“A soldier, William Avant. The camel was a Mt. Sinai dromedary named Spitfire. Avant was afraid of the camel and had difficulty learning how to ride Spitfire. So in order to teach him how, his fellow soldiers tied him to the top of the beast, thinking that would help him get over his fear," said Carson.

"Do the letters say what happened to Avant and Spitfire?" asked Ty.

"This letter says that after tying him to the camel, something spooked Spitfire and he ran off. Some troops attempted to follow on horseback, but could not keep up with the camel," replied Carson.

He continued opening letters and scanning the contents.

"This letter is dated six days after Spitfire and William disappeared. Hi Jolly says they continued to search, but were unsuccessful," Carson said.

"Are these letters to the same person?" asked Ty.

"Yes, they are all addressed to his wife Gertrudis in early 1862. We know they married in 1859 and had three children together," said Carson. "The Camel Corp sold off or turned loose the remaining camels in 1864. The disappearance of what they hoped would be the lead camel probably didn't help the future of the program."

"We know the Red Ghost's first sighting was 1883, and it died in 1893. If he escaped in 1859, that's twenty-four years from its disappearance to its first sighting. Hi Jolly died in 1902 so he would have heard the stories about the Red Ghost," added Ty. "I wonder if he tried to find the body? We heard stories in Quartzsite about him wandering the area looking for camels after the Army discharged him. Maybe he was searching for the Red Ghost?"

Carson opened another file in the folder.

"Hmm. This looks to be a PDF of Johnny Stamps family history on Ancestry.com," said Carson. "Looks like he took the free trial."

"Any information we can use from that?" asked Ty.

"Johnny Stamps was born August 13, 1989, which makes him twenty-six. The listed birthplace is the Phoenix Children's Center in Phoenix. Apparently, he was born premature. He has a younger sister, Dakota. His mother's name is Maria, and his father is Jesse. His father is deceased, but his mom is still alive. She was born in 1970 and his dad in 1967," read Carson.

"Not much there to go on related to this Red Ghost," answered Ty.

"Let's keep digging. The next generation, his grandmother, goes back to her birth in 1919. Grandma Guadalupe died at age sixty-seven in 1989. She was married, but her husband, Jasper, appears to have died in or at least around the time of World War II," said Carson.

He continued to look at the family chart and look back at the prior generation.

"Oh, now we're on to something!" revealed Carson.

"What is it?" inquired Ty.

"Grandma Guadalupe's father was Fernando Serna Tedro. He was born in Tucson September 1891, and earlier we learned he was included in the 1920 Census in California. He was about twenty-eight when Guadalupe was born. He died in 1963 in Tucson, Arizona. We know Fernando was the third child of Philip and Gertrudis, which means…" said Carson.

"It means Johnny Stamps is a direct descendant of Hi

Jolly," said Ty.

"Correct! And Hi Jolly was the best camel driver around. From the journal, we know William Avant couldn't handle Spitfire. Maybe Johnny sought the expertise of his great-great-grandfather possessed so that he could carry out his plan!" theorized Carson.

"Yes, there's the connection. Johnny is driven by anger and resentment at the world. He planned to take revenge by reanimating and controlling the Red Ghost. When he was alive, the Red Ghost caused torment in the area and took its anger toward humans out on anyone it encountered. Now it is a supernatural creature controlled by Johnny to do his bidding," said Ty.

Tegan and Kareem knocked on the door, dressed, ready to explore the trails of Dreamy Draw.

"Morning, guys. You look like you are deep into something. What's up?" asked Tegan.

"Just going through the files on the USB drive," replied Carson.

"Did you find anything?" asked Kareem.

"Did we? We found conversations and plans Johnny Stamps had regarding the Red Ghost, spells he used to bring him back to life and control him, and we found he is a direct descendant of Hi Jolly," responded Ty. "There is also a file that looks like a land deed, but I'm not sure of its connection."

"Wow! You've been busy," said Tegan.

"We know he definitely completed the first few items on the checklist, and based on the appearance of the Red Ghost, we can assume he successfully completed the spell," said Carson. "But I think we should still investigate Dreamy Draw and Queen Creek to see what clues we might find. Then we need to find Johnny Stamps and the Red Ghost to put an end to it and prevent any other deaths or injuries."

"As news continues to get out about the Red Ghost and people see it around town, they will be afraid to come out of their homes," suggested Ty.

As Carson drove up Highway 51, the group formed a plan for their investigation.

"So what do we know about Dreamy Draw?" asked Carson.

"We know there was a supposed UFO crash site at Dreamy Draw back in October 1947," replied Tegan.

"That's right. You mentioned that before," responded Carson. "What happened to that investigation?"

"Frank Scully wrote a book in 1950 where he claimed two men named Silas Newton and Dr. Gee told him they pulled two alien bodies from the wreckage in September 1947, and the remains were stored in a freezer until the Army picked them up," Tegan responded.

"1947? The Roswell crash happened in June or July 1947, so this was just months after that. Any chance it was just speculation based on the hype surrounding Roswell?" asked Kareem.

"Perhaps, but there's another story. Timothy Good wrote a book in 1987 that included a chapter called *Paradise Valley, 1947*. He claimed the UFO first hit at Dreamy Draw, then bounced or hopped to Cave Creek," said Tegan.

"Cave Creek? How far is that?" asked Ty.

"That's about twenty-three miles from Dreamy Draw to Cave Creek," answered Tegan.

"That's quite a bounce," replied Carson. "Like skipping rocks on a pond. The UFO would have to be going fast to bounce over twenty miles, and if it were, how would it just stop immediately upon the second hit?"

"And they have found no crash debris at either site, but conspiracy theorists say that's because the government cleaned it up. The focus of their claims center on the Dreamy Draw dam, which they say is useless and built simply to cover up the spaceship crash," responded Tegan.

"What about these two men, Newton and Gee?" asked Ty.

"People discredited them as con men and they were later arrested by the FBI for conning people into investing in fake deposits. They also say the dam theory doesn't hold up because the crash occurred in 1947 and the town constructed the dam in 1973. It is true there is no river or lake there where one would normally build a dam, but according to the civil engineers, the real purpose of the dam is to prevent flooding to the surrounding neighborhoods during monsoon season," added Tegan.

Carson continued driving up the 51 and the mile-long section of road near Northern Avenue before turning next to the sign, directing them to the park. The street meandered its way through the park entrance and passed a large wooden sign proclaiming Dreamy Draw Dam, and just behind the sign was the dam.

"There it is! Based on not seeing it on the maps and the

talk about aliens and conspiracy theories, I thought it would be some secluded area we would be lucky to find, but here it is, right in the open. No parking here, but there is a road that goes off to the side and is marked with a *Gate Ahead* sign," said Carson. "Let's keep driving and find a parking spot."

Even though it was still early in the year, noon-time temperatures in Phoenix were forecast to reach ninety-one degrees, and there hadn't been precipitation for weeks, making the hike warm and dry, a description that covers Phoenix much of the year.

"I brought the map from Johnny Stamps' box along so we could find what we are looking for, but looks like we won't need it to find the dam," replied Ty.

"Beside UFOs, I found a few other facts about this area, which increases the weirdness factor," replied Tegan.

"By all means, please share," said Carson.

"I have read some paranormal reports about a green lady specter seen on the dam at night. In addition, there used to be a cinnabar mine here where hundreds of miners died in the dangerous conditions. Cinnabar is a mercury sulfide discovered in the area in 1916. This area was the largest deposit and called the Rico Mine. Miners who worked there were in constant and direct contact with the mercury during the mining and the refining process of the cinnabar. This mineral had a significant effect on them because the townspeople who lived in downtown Phoenix and saw the miners came into town said they looked to be dreamy. Memory loss, mental confusion, and fatigue are just a few of the symptoms of mercury poisoning. Because of their dream-like state, the area became known as Dreamy Draw," said Tegan.

They parked in the main parking lot and started walking the paved bike path back toward the park entrance.

"The dam shouldn't be too far down this bike path. We might have to cut over back onto the road. I hope we can get a closer look because from what I saw driving in, it looked just like a gigantic pile of earth," said Kareem.

Unlike a poured dam in other sites around the southwest, this four-hundred-fifty-five-foot earthen dam seemed out of place in the surroundings. Looking closer at the dam, it was a well fenced off area with several *No Trespassing* signs covering the area.

"Seems like pretty top security for an earthen dam with no water behind it!" said Ty.

"I wonder if we could get a little closer?" wondered Carson.

Carson looked around and saw there wasn't much distance between the road entering the park and the dam. However, it was fenced off. While there was a road to the side leading up toward the dam, a gate blocked access. There was a lot of incoming and exiting traffic on the park entrance road, making it difficult for Carson to sneak around in areas he was not supposed to be.

Carson looked around and waited for a break in traffic to walk up the side service road while the others served as lookouts. Finally, he thought he had a chance and made a slow-jog break for it, reaching the gate in just a few hundred feet. He looked down and caught a signal from Ty waving him through. The gate was just a swinging bar and, although locked, it was easy to cross over. It looked like the gate was there to prevent cars and not people from entering. However, the trespassing signs were for people. Their presence caused Carson to pause and wonder what lurked just up the hill and the road turned out of sight.

Part way up the hill, beyond the crossing bar, Carson continued to walk up the street while attempting to stay out of sight from oncoming cars. He turned back to check the group and his progress when he saw the terrain just below where the group was standing. It was a big drop to the floor of the hill's base, which appeared to be a dry wash. While the group couldn't see it, from Carson's view, he noticed a large concrete box with a fence on three sides. He also heard a steady, low-pitched humming noise emanating from the ground. He couldn't identify a source, but it appeared to be coming from beneath the dam. He stopped and looked around, trying to find additional clues before finally continuing his climb further up the hill, hopefully to its summit.

The road came to a dead end at the top of the dam. He could see a road along the peak of the dam and the barren earth on each side. His nervousness increased when he saw a couple City of Phoenix trucks parked in a lot below. Having walked down the road from the parking lot to the dam sign, he had seen the gravel covered dirt road leading to that lot, but he noticed it was locked when they passed. Because of the bushes and trees, they did not see cars in the lot from the road. Fearing running into an employee in an area so heavily marked, he returned and rejoined the group.

"It is weird. Just the number of these no trespassing signs. I mean literally like every fifty feet and threatening thousand-dollar fines and six months in jail, among other Federal action if one so much as placed a boot on this thing. And for what? Like you said, Ty, there's no water anywhere around it, so they don't seem to protect people from falling in," said Carson.

They stood on the road looking up at the dam as Kareem turned and took a selfie with the sign in the background. Soon a middle-aged man walked by, headed back to the parking lot.

"Excuse me, sir," said Ty. "Are you from around here?"

"Yep, lived right around here my whole life," said the man.

"We're visiting from Texas and love the hiking here. Phoenix has some awesome trails," said Kareem.

"Yes, it does. The weather is boiling in the summer, but a lot of the year it is perfect for hiking," the man replied.

"Can you tell us about this dam? It seems kind of out of place," said Ty.

"Yes. Yes, it does. It's an unnecessary structure, if you ask me," he said. "If you could stand atop that knoll over there and overlook the project site, it would become immediately obvious. Even with our monsoons generating a flash runoff from the mountains to the south, there is natural drainage, which moves this runoff safely to the canals below. The mountains don't generate enough water to warrant it. Even when I was a kid, we used to bike and climb these trails and go up the mountain. Though the washes would run sometimes, the terrain has never generated enough water to flood the neighborhoods below," he said.

"It seems well maintained and the signs show it has Federal protection," said Carson.

"It's always been suspicious, if you ask me. Look around the site. If they built the dam to hold back water during times of seasonal monsoon flooding, who the heck built a road, a parking facility, a trailhead, a plumbed restroom and water facilities, and ranger station directly on the uphill side of it? If these mountains were ever to generate enough water to create flood conditions, which they never have yet, the facilities and structures would be under thirty feet of water if the dam were to do its job and hold back the runoff. How does that make any sense? How did that get approved by the city engineering department?" the man asked.

"Good questions. I know in Texas if I were to build a house in a potential flood plain, they would never approve it," said Ty.

"Another thing to think about - if this is a site of such sensitive civil infrastructure, one which requires signs threatening fines and jail time posted every forty feet, why is the western gate left open for trash removal vehicle access and the entire area used as a trash transfer station? Why is there a concrete guard shack on top of the dam complete with razor wire and what looks like communication aerials protruding from the roof if they stationed no one in it?" the man continued. "And look at that shack. Looks more like a hardened bunker for repelling an attack than a guard shack, as described in the Army Corp of Engineers report, if you ask me," he concluded.

"So if this dam is to block floodwater coming off the mountain, are there other mountains in town with dams like this?" asked Tegan.

"No, not a one," said the man. "The only dams I'm aware of are the ones used in the management of our rivers and canal systems. Are these mountains unique in their ability to accumulate mass volumes of monsoon runoff? Is it to protect the developments around these mountains? Because most mountains in the Phoenix area have high-end housing surrounding them," the man said.

"Sounds like a mystery," replied Kareem.

"You want to know a mystery? That sign down there that says Dreamy Draw Dam is two-sided. The back side of the sign would be unreadable unless exiting the fenced site," the man stated.

"That is unusual," said Ty.

"There are a lot of questions about this place. Do you think the stories about a UFO here are true?" asked Kareem.

"UFO? No, I don't think so. A lot of things here make little sense, but I don't believe in little green men," the man said.

"It would be great to get a closer look at that dam," said Carson.

"I mean, you could do it. See if the place really has guards on the other side of that crest. Maybe someone shows up and takes you away. Then you'd know, right?" the man replied.

"I don't think I want to know that way," Carson stated.

"Or maybe get back to the parking lot and see if you can get to it from the other side?" said the man. "It's rockier coming that way."

"Yeah, but we're so close right here. Just a little more up this road and it appears there is another road that runs the length of the dam," said Carson.

"Unless this is the one time there is someone in that block building," stated the man.

"True. I saw some cars in the parking lot when I started up the last time. It made me nervous enough to turn around then. I think it still feels that way," said Carson.

"We are more obvious as a group of five people standing on the side of the road. Drivers notice groups of people. They might not see, or at least draw their attention to, a single person," the stranger said.

"I just need to muster up the courage to get up there and risk getting caught," replied Carson.

"Find your balls!" said Ty.

"Hey, I'm the one risking getting caught by authorities," replied Carson.

"If only I had my running shorts," said Kareem.

The others looked at him.

"What? I could jog up this road and onto the crest of the dam. If they caught me, I'd just be honest and say I am from out of town and jogging in the park. I didn't know I wasn't supposed to be up here. It looks like the road went up here," said Kareem.

"And you missed all the trespassing signs?" asked Ty.

"And the *Gate Ahead* sign and the giant yellow metal gate that was locked?" asked Carson.

"… Yeah," said Kareem.

"You don't have to be a jogger," said Tegan. "You could be a hiker who is distracted by looking at her phone…. outta my way!" Tegan said as she slapped a straight-arm across Kareem's stomach and began walking up the hill.

The others walked back to the base of the hill, but turned their back and pulled out their phones so as not to be obvious and draw attention to Tegan. The thick bushes and trees helped provide some cover for her from cars traveling along the entrance road. Soon she made it to the top of the service road at the top of the dam.

The road ran the full length of the dam and led to the white building that served as a guard shack. She turned and looked down both sides of the dam. The side facing the park entrance was earthier and covered in trees, bush, and grass. They covered the opposite side with rock.

Tegan walked closer to the edge of the rock-covered side and looked down into the valley below. Pulling out her phone to get a better look, she pulled up the camera app and zoomed in.

In the valley below, approximately in the middle of the dam, she saw a white cement block building that appeared to be a water intake structure. She could make out a small pile of debris on the uphill side of the dam surrounding the structure, showing past water accumulation. Checking toward the guard station to make sure no one was watching, she climbed down the opposite side of the dam. The rocks slid a little as she descended, but overall, the footing was good. She continued further until she could reach the edge of the dam where the ground was more dirt than rock. She followed a subtle path that led to the valley below and into the dusty base of the wash. She minimized the camera and used the phone to call Ty.

"Hey, you guys should head back to the parking lot. I want to get a closer look at this structure. I can see the parking lot from here and I can use the wash to get back to the road and meet you there," Tegan whispered.

The guys thanked the man for his time and information, then began walking up the road to return to the main parking area while Tegan walked the wash floor toward the water intake unit.

Looking up at the top of the dam to verify no one was watching, she moved closer to the structure. On the front, she noted stark white paint serving as a high water debris mark. The structure itself was not tall, and the mark was only a couple of feet high. From living in Texas and having a heavy rain season, she knew washes run during monsoon season, and logs and debris get carried downwash. Were this dam not constructed, the existing natural wash in which the dam is located would have carried this material downwash. Still, looking around, she could not detect any sign there had ever been levels of precipitation sufficient to cause this dam to hold back any significant amount of water.

She looked through the metal grating on the top of the structure to the shaft below. It was dark and she couldn't make out any details to the ground below. Grabbing the grate, she discovered it was loose, as if someone removed and just sat back on top instead of locked down. She gave it a tug and could lift it up.

"That's odd," she said as she lifted the lid full off and propped it up against the side of the structure.

She gave the top of the dam another glance, and then turned her flashlight on, shining it down into the dark hole below. It appeared to drop at least six feet below. She theorized if water was high, it would enter this structure, so then it must go somewhere. If only she could get down inside it to explore. Looking around, she noticed something under the Blue Palo Verde trees behind her.

"I hope that's not a rattlesnake," she said as she walked over toward the trees.

It was not a snake, but a lengthy natural fiber manila rope, possibly abandoned by a prior visitor.

Maybe Johnny Stamps was here? she thought.

She grabbed the rope and walked back to the cement structure, tying one end securely to the metal grate. It wasn't too heavy for her to move, but had enough weight that it would stay propped against the structure. Even if it moved, it wasn't in danger of falling through the opening and stranding her in the hole. Before placing her phone into her jeans pocket, she texted Ty.

Change of plans. I found a rope. Going to rappel into this structure.

Too dangerous. You don't have a harness texted, Ty.

I'll be fine, she texted back.

You don't know what's down there. What if you get stuck? replied Ty.

I won't, Tegan answered.

She realized if this is an intake, there must be an outlet. Being an earthen barrage dam, the rocks and stones on this side identify it as the wet side. There should be a feeder canal, but she didn't see one. Another sign they didn't design the dam to hold or divert water.

Gotta run. Wait at the parking lot for me, she continued.

She inspected the area around the structure and again gave another tug on the rope to ensure it was sturdy. Satisfied, she doubled up the rope and sat on the edge of the structure. Thinking about the approach, she felt the safest technique would be the South African abseil.

She took the rope and wrapped it around both sides of her body, cradling the rib cage, then sliding around her back and through the legs, practically giving her a seat to descend. Since she didn't have gloves, she wrapped the rope around her wrist once to give as much control over the descent as possible. She dropped the other end of the rope into the hole and prepared to enter.

Good thing I didn't have a big breakfast. I might be the only one of us who could squeeze into this opening, she thought.

She twirled her foot around the rope, giving a single wrap around one of her legs and across the top of her shoe. She dropped one leg into the hole and gripped the rope with both hands before lowering the second leg and scooting off the edge of the structure. She descended the rope, going down hand under hand until she reached the bottom, approximately ten feet below. Once on the ground, she removed her cell phone and shone the flashlight, illuminating an underground tunnel system with concrete walls and ceiling extending north and south from the opening of the water intake structure. The southern passage appeared to go underneath the dam itself.

The underground tunnel was dark and quiet, except for a constant low hum Tegan felt was emanating from further down the southern passage. The air in the passage was stuffy, but cool. The walls felt smooth and cold to the touch as she slid her palm along the wall, entering further. Approximately one hundred feet from her entry point, she saw what appeared to be two doors, one on each side of the cement wall.

She walked toward the eastern wall and found a large steel door plastered with warning signs blocking the entryway. There was a small window in the door, but something clouded it over with dust and dirt from the inside, suggesting it had not been in operation for some time. A number pad device locked the door. She pulled on the handle to verify, but the door, as suspected, was locked. Her flashlight illuminated a *Danger: Do Not Enter* sign affixed to the front of the door and yellow text with additional warnings, but dirt covered some of the lettering, making it difficult to read. It was obvious that the door was designed to keep people from coming in, and maybe whatever was on the other side of it from coming out.

Turning her attention to the western side of the corridor, she found a similar door, but it was broken, and the heavy door was ajar. A crowbar laying on the ground was likely the tool used to gain entrance into the area beyond. She pulled on the door handle and it opened a little more, allowing enough room to glimpse inside. She jerked hard on the handle and the door moved another eight inches, allowing just enough space for her to squeeze past the door and into a large, open room.

She felt along the walls and searched with her flashlight in each direction, finally locating a switch. She flipped it on. There was another, different low hum, and then the old overhead lights turned on. They flickered and were dim, but provided enough light for her to see she was in some type of lab. She texted an update to Ty.

Found a tunnel under the dam and a lab, she texted.

WTF A lab? Under the dam? replied Ty.

Appears to be abandoned. Deep Underground Military Base? Tegan typed.

Thought those were urban legends, Ty replied.

Guess not, she answered.

Be safe, suggested Ty.

She put her phone back in her pocket and looked around the room. There were worktables, a small office, and in one corner what appeared to be a prison cell. She saw another door in the back of the room, but upon further investigation, it was locked. It would limit her search to this room. Knowing the other doors were all still locked, she theorized that whatever the prior visitor was looking for must have been in this room.

After walking through a room still in good condition with several shelves of books and materials, she found another room. This room, cluttered with overturned seats, a filing cabinet with a partially opened drawer and folders sticking up, and bottles knocked over on the tables, appeared to be a main working area of the past. The air was heavy and smelled of mildew and dust. She wasn't sure what exactly this facility was or even what she was looking for, but she was curious.

She found some opened notebooks on a nearby table containing scribbled writing on some pages. She flipped the pages and found notes and sketches of what appeared to be small, grey alien beings. She knew greys to be commonly reported extraterrestrial beings, similar to the alleged beings from Roswell. The notebook identified these beings as Zeta Reticulans and they were highly advanced members of a dying race on a mission to save their race from definite extinction. The notes stated aliens crashed at Dreamy Draw and the beings held in this location for nearly one month before the US Air Force transferred to them Wright Patterson Air Force Base in Ohio.

"Shit, they're real!" she said aloud in a hushed but startled tone.

She closed the notebook and took it with her, turning her attention to the filing cabinet. The drawer was jammed, but she got it back on track and operational. Inside there were dozens of manila tabbed folders, each with documents, other papers, and sometimes photos or sketches inside. She pulled out the cell phone and shone the flashlight on the folders as she thumbed through the contents. Some folders had names of creatures on the tab. Some were green hanging folders with thin manila folders inside. One such folder had a tab labeled *Bigfoot.* Other individual folders displayed handwritten identifiers reading *Ohio Grassman*, *Owlman*, *Yahoo*, and *The Cherokee Devil.* Other folders displayed names of locations such as *Loveland, Lee County, Plum Island*, and *Canter's Cave.*

She realized there were too many folders for her to take them all, but she could grab a few and bring them back to the guys as evidence. She grabbed about a dozen folders and sat them on top of the notebook on the table behind her. As she turned, her phone dropped to the ground. Luckily, it was unbroken, but as she bent down to retrieve it, she noticed the flashlight hit something shiny underneath a table behind her. She crawled over to the table and held the light under to get a better look. It was an old skeleton key on a string.

She stretched her arm as far as she could underneath the table and could barely reach enough of the string to pull it closer. She stood up and looked at the key, then turned her attention to the locked door in the back of the room. The lock responded with a Click! as she inserted the key into the lock and turned it.

Taking a deep breath, she turned the knob, and the door swung open. She gasped as she saw what appeared to be a damaged saucer-shaped craft. The hum she heard earlier was coming from the ship as it continued its constant song.

Still in shock, she raised her phone and snapped several photos of the craft. She texted one to Ty and closed the door as she cautiously backed out into the main room. Seconds later, her phone vibrated with a wide-eyed face emoji response from Ty.

She continued searching the lab room for clues, remembering their theory that Johnny Stamps needed some type of cosmic dust to make the reincarnation spell work. The spaceship in the other room proved something interstellar was here. She realized Johnny must not have seen the ship because that door remained locked. The prison cell at the other end of the room must be where they held the aliens until the Air Force arrived. If so, they transported the bodies from one room to the other, and this room connected them. She picked up a corked beaker from another table to use it to collect any dust material specimens she may find.

Against the back wall, a dirty, white cupboard stood with shards of glass on the floor before it. She realized this might be Johnny's doing. The doors remained closed on the cabinet, but the cupboard's weakness was the glass in the door. Inside, the cabinet contained multiple bottles of unknown liquid or solid substances.

The cabinet was mostly full, but an empty space in the front of one row showed something was missing. She shone her flashlight inside the cabinet and noticed the small bottles stacked four rows deep. The three remaining bottles in the row appeared to be the same small bottles of a blue powdery substance that had a faint glowing characteristic. The three bottles were the same as each other, but different from the bottles in the other row. Tegan speculated Johnny Stamps took the missing bottle.

She carefully reached through the broken glass and took the next bottle in the incomplete row. The glass from the door scratched the top of her hand, causing a slight redness as she attempted to extract the object. She felt a sharp, instant sting from the scratch but could complete the task.

Eager to show off her discovery and return to the others, she grabbed the bottle, the stack of papers and folders, and exited the room. Returning to the corridor, she continued heading south and looked for the floodwater outlet. It wasn't long until she reached a boarded-up section of the corridor.

There were gaps between the planks that would allow water to flow if it did flood, but it prevented large objects, including petite humans, from passing. Studying the boards,

Tegan put her Muay Thai skills to use and delivered a powerful side kick that knocked a board loose. A second side kick loosened another, creating enough of a gap to exit the tunnel.

On the other side of the barrier, she was in a corridor similar to her initial point of entry, but she could see light ahead. Emerging from the tunnel, she had a few scrapes and scratches and a layer of dust, but came away with what she hoped to find. She found artifacts about apparent cryptozoological studies and evidence the government had collected. Thick brush obscured the tunnel entrance, but beyond that, the path emerged into a deep creek bed in a valley below a steep hill. The creek bed was dry, but the brush in the valley and along the hillside was green. She saw a couple side-blotched lizards scamper away as she climbed. Something slightly startled her. A small canyon tree frog sat along the small boulders and rocks where the streams would run during wetter months.

"Yuck!" she exclaimed. "I hate frogs!"

The frog croaked as he passed. Unhappy about the frog, at least she was outside again, and the warm, fresh air was a pleasant change from the air in the abandoned lab. She climbed up the hill, bent over and attempted to balance herself with one hand while holding the evidence in the other hand. It was a steep climb, but she found herself beside the bicycle path on the opposite side of the road, just southwest of the dam. She could see Arizona State Route 51 just ahead and knew she was near the park entrance. Removing the phone from her pocket, she called Ty and asked them to pick her up.

"What was that photo you sent?" asked Ty when they pulled up to get her.

"I'll fill you guys in later. I need some time to process everything I saw down there," admitted Tegan. "But, I got this," she said, handing Kareem the bottle of blue dust.

"Are you sure this is the stuff?" asked Kareem.

"Fairly certain. There were four in a row, but one was missing. The door to that room was broken and the cabinet's glass door smashed by a prior visitor. It was someone looking for something, and since one was missing, I think it's safe to say this is what they took," she replied.

"Are you okay?" asked Carson, noticing the cut on her hand.

"The hand is fine. It will heal in a few days. The rest of the stuff, it's safe to say I'll need a drink. Or a couple to recover from," replied Tegan.

"I think we can arrange that," said Carson. "It's been a full day at the park, and you earned your beer."

Carson drove back to Tempe and pulled into a parking lot on the corner of University and South Ash Avenue between a long L-shaped brown building and a white brick building. Most of the parking spaces were full, but they were fortunate to find a car backing out as they entered. The others looked around at the buildings and area as Carson parked.

"This is an odd building. Looks like an old two-story motel," replied Ty.

"Nah, this place is great. Look around, it's a hotbed of activity," Carson responded. "A tattoo shop over there, a vintage clothing exchange on the corner, a vape shop in that white building, as well as a skateboard shop and a comic store. What more could you want? And this is Cartel Coffee Lab," he said.

"I was thinking something a little stiffer than coffee," said Tegan.

Ignoring the comments, Carson led the way to the door and held it open as the others entered.

"This place has some great coffee from the reviews I've read, but they also have beer. They brew their own and serve it right in the store," replied Carson.

"Now we're talking," said Kareem.

The interior was a colorful, hip mixture of tables, chairs, and decorations that created an inviting atmosphere. It was busy inside, mostly a younger college-age crowd sitting at long tables working on laptops, collaborating with friends, and enjoying the coffee.

"It smells wonderful," said Tegan.

"This space is much larger than it looks from the outside," acknowledged Ty. "Looks like a large bar back there, another room off to the side, and look, a table for us."

A young woman in a black long-sleeve t-shirt with long dirty blond hair and deep plum lipstick approached, pushing her large clear frame glasses further back on her nose.

"Hey, I'm Adler. Know what you want?" she asked.

"What's that IPA up there? I can't make it out," asked Kareem.

"F.Y.I.T.M. We call it, uh. Fight 'em," replied Adler.

"Fight 'em?" asked Ty. "Like fight them? I guess I can see it… FYIT–Fight…. M?" he said whimsically.

"Well…," she said, looking around the counter area. "Sometimes we call it…" she paused and looked around again. "Fuck You In the Mouth… because it is so hoppy, and… it hits you hard. Right in the mouth," she started.

"It's an acronym?" asked Ty.

"Yeah. Because it's an acronym… But we do vary the response based on the audience. You know, not everyone is into that type of response, so for others we can say it means Five Years in the Making."

"Well, both sound great to me," replied Kareem. "I will have one of those," he said with a smile.

"I will have the pale ale," said Ty.

"Desert Pale Ale for you," replied Adler.

"I had a drink the other day, in a crowler," said Carson. "It was called Real Vanilla Heat? An imperial porter. Any chance…?" he paused.

"No, I didn't even get a taste of that. We brewed it in collaboration with World of Beer down the road, and it didn't last long. Heard it was phenomenal though," she said.

"I looked at reviews online. We met the guy behind the name, and he gave us some cans, but I haven't tried them yet. Everything on Untappd and Beer Advocate mentions how good it is," replied Carson.

"I bet," she said. "And from what I hear, he's also phenomenal."

"No complaints from me," said Tegan, the recent memory of meeting Vanilla Heat causing her to smile uncontrollably.

"So… Plan B?" asked Adler.

"Bingo Bango Bongo," Carson said.

"Good choice. Probably my favorite beer right now," Adler stated. "And for you, Miss?"

"I want the Berliner Weisse," Tegan said.

"We serve the Great Save with a flavored syrup, like Woodruff or raspberry," Adler said.

"Raspberry," followed Tegan.

"Back in a minute," Adler replied before leaving to fill the drink order.

"After today, we've confirmed our theory about Johnny Stamps reanimating the Red Ghost," stated Carson. "I think we still need to head to Queen Creek tomorrow just to have a look at the farm, but then we need to put together the plan on finding either Johnny or the Red Ghost," he said.

"Hastings Farms is one of those master plan communities and the builder is Maracay Homes. Maybe they have some employment records on Johnny or maybe know where he is," suggested Kareem.

"Let me know if there's anything else I can bring you guys," Adler said, returning with the drinks.

The group took the drinks and sat at a nearby table.

"Speaking of records, what about those folders you brought back, Tegan?" asked Ty.

Tegan dropped her head and stared into her beer for a moment, collecting her thoughts before speaking about her findings earlier in the day. "I couldn't believe what I saw under that dam," Tegan responded. "I grabbed as much as I could, but it's just the tip of the iceberg. I don't know how many things were in that filing cabinet. I wish I could have grabbed more because I think there is a lot about cryptids that the government knows, and those files may contain the evidence. We need to have Jourdyn scan and digitally archive them in our system when we get back to Austin," she said.

"I can tell whatever you saw down there is weighing heavy on your mind," replied Carson.

"More like on my soul," answered Tegan.

"Let's focus on The Red Ghost and stopping it from terrorizing Phoenix, but maybe we can pay that dam a second visit before we leave town and bring back more of those files. Now that you've been there and know what to expect, it shouldn't take long to get in and out," he said.

"That might be an enormous asset to the T.I.M.E. Agency and our future investigations," said Ty.

"This beer helps. Very easy drinking. A little salt and a little sour, but not overwhelming in either direction. Delicious," Tegan said, taking a sip from The Great Save.

"A few of these F.Y.I.T.M.s and I might explore that lab with you," said Kareem.

"The good news is since I found the exit, we don't have to drop through that hole next time," Tegan said.

"When we finish up here, we should walk over to Taste of Tops and pick up some bottles to take home. Their website says they have over six hundred bottles and cans and it's just on the corner," Ty said.

"Good way to end the evening," said Carson.

"If you like the beer, check us out later this year. In a few months, the beer production is moving to a new location in Tempe and they are calling it The Shop Beer Company. It will have a larger brewing facility and a wonderful patio to enjoy some cold beers and this nice Phoenix weather on," said Adler as she dropped off the check.

"We may have to come back and check it out if they continue making great drinks like these," replied Carson.

CHAPTER 13

THE QC

Tuesday, March 22, 2016

The crowded streets of greater Phoenix faded into the background as Ty drove the group into the rural community of Queen Creek. A town that grew up from a 1919 railroad stop frequented by the Arizona Stage Company that still prided itself on its farming heritage. Schnepf Farms was part of that heritage, operating a large pick-your-own garden and orchards. It also provided a large farm-to-table style restaurant.

The town also featured newer ventures, such as the Queen Creek Olive Mill, a family-owned-and-operated one-hundred-acre farm with over seven thousand olive trees, noted as the only olive mill in the state. The town also housed one of the state's largest equestrian centers, featuring both English and Western equestrian styles.

"This is nice out here," Carson said as Ty drove down Rittenhouse Road, nearing Queen Creek. "Not as developed as the other parts of Phoenix, but still close enough to hit up town if you wanted."

"Probably won't be that way much longer. Looks like a lot of construction is happening," replied Ty.

"And construction is what we are looking for. You can stay on this road and turn on Cloud," suggested Kareem.

"That looks like the turnoff up ahead," Tegan said as she pointed toward a small gravel road with a construction trailer beside it.

As they pulled into the dusty driveway, several men passed in front of the car. A man in a different colored hardhat was standing on the opposite side of the road looking at oversized drawings, pointing, and yelling in every direction. Exiting the vehicle, Carson approached.

"What? Can I help you?" asked the site supervisor abruptly.

"Yeah, I wonder if you could help us find out where one of your former employees might be?" asked Carson.

"Former? I don't give a shit. I'm having a hard enough time with the current ones!" shouted the man.

"Look, you'd really be helping us and save time on our case if you could spare a few minutes," Ty said.

"Case? Are you guys cops?" asked the man.

"We're… investigators. So, can you help us?" asked Ty.

"Sure. Anything to help you… *investigators*. Say, what are you investigating?" asked the man.

"Something connected to Johnny Stamps. Know him?" responded Ty.

"Stamps… Stamps… Yeah. Come to think of it, a young man worked here for only like three or four weeks. That's his name," said the man.

"Really? Do you know where he is now?" asked Ty.

"What do I care? That bum did nothing while he was here. Always asking what everyone else was doing, but he did nothing. And he was shit on the bulldozer. Plowed up an area that was supposed to be left untouched until the next phase. Fired him less than two weeks ago after he stopped showing up. Good riddance!" responded the man.

"Do you know if he found anything… odd… while he was working for you?" asked Ty.

"Odd like how? He didn't get along with most of the guys, so everything he did was a little odd," he said.

"We think he found something on the site. Something, like a skeleton," said Ty.

"Skeleton? A person?" asked the supervisor.

"No, an animal," answered Ty.

"That's a relief! What kind of animal?" he asked.

"Camel."

"Camel? That's odd," the man responded. "That would be something that we'd have to report. Probably have to stop work for several weeks for an investigation and covering our own asses in case there's a lawsuit, ya know," he said.

"Maybe he found it and didn't mention it," addressed Ty.

"Who can say? I just know he stopped showing up, and I let him go," answered the man.

"Any particular things happen the last day you saw him?" asked Ty.

"I don't know," he said as he turned and grabbed a book from the desk shelf before flipping through the pages. "That last day he left early. Something about an emergency," said the supervisor.

"What type of emergency?" asked Ty.

"Didn't ask. Don't care to know details I don't need to know," said the supervisor.

"Isn't there some type of… process when employees leave?" asked Ty.

The supervisor gave Ty a long harsh look, as the conversation was not ending as quickly as he assumed.

"We should have a personnel file with H.R. in the trailer," he said with a tone reflecting his frustration.

In the trailer, the supervisor pulled on the handle of the filing cabinet containing the records of his employees, including Johnny Stamps.

"Looks like there is an address on file," said the supervisor. "An address in Gilbert off of North Greenfield Road. I shouldn't give you the information, but screw it. He was a pain in the ass."

"Any idea what he was doing before he left? asked Tegan.

"Nope. You could ask his partner, Jaxson. He's back there on the bulldozer," pointed the supervisor toward a man in a Phoenix Rising FC jersey and jeans.

The group approached the bulldozer as Jaxson finished dropping a load of dirt into the bed of a dump truck. He saw them approach and stopped. As he got off the dozer, he wiped his brow.

"It's a warm one out here," he said.

"Good morning, Jaxon," said Carson. "We were talking to the supervisor about a former coworker of yours, Johnny Stamps, and he suggested we speak with you."

"He said you and Johnny were working together the day he left?" asked Tegan.

"Johnny? Yeah, we worked together running the bulldozers," said Jaxson.

"Did you know him well?" asked Kareem.

"Yeah, I guess. I mean, how well do you really know someone you just work with? He seemed okay. Sometimes quiet, sometimes easily worked up," replied Jaxson. "He seemed to dislike the constant expansion of homes, even though we worked here constructing them."

"How long did you work together?" asked Ty.

"I don't know. Two months? Three? He wasn't here too long," answered Jaxon.

"Do you remember anything about that last day you worked together? Asked Carson.

"We were working back in the new pre-development area. Clearing some ground for the next phase of construction. He was digging a little off from where we were supposed to be, and I called out to him that he was in the wrong area. He kept going, but soon stopped the dozer. I saw him get off and run to the front of the blade. He was down there a couple of minutes before running over to me and saying he found some bones," replied Jaxon.

"Bones? What kind of bones?" asked Carson.

"I don't know. Some kinda animal. He said it was probably old. I remember when they dug up some old bones while building Walmart several years ago. Production stopped, scientists came in, and it was a big to-do. I told him the supervisor would be pissed if he found out. Especially since he wasn't supposed to be digging over there. Best to keep it quiet. So we did. We went back to doing what we were supposed to be doing and I don't think he reported it. But I didn't see him again after that, so maybe the boss found out and fired him," said Jaxon.

"Do you remember where it was you worked that day?" asked Ty.

"Yeah, it was back on off of Via de Arboles where the upcoming Preserve at Hastings Farms section will be," said Jaxon.

"Maybe we can check it out on our way?" suggested Ty.

"Yeah, that road over there is 211th street. It will take you over there," replied Jaxson.

"Sounds good," said Carson. "Thanks for your help with this."

Carson drove down Via de Arboles and parked in a cul-de-sac at the end of the street.

"This looks like the area Jaxson was talking about," Carson said. "All the houses out here are well underway, but this section behind the cul-de-sac is still dirt. I am sure they are eager to open it up and start working."

"And the discovery of old, unknown bones would delay that work," replied Ty.

Kareem and Tegan looked over the landscape.

"Hey guys, check that out," said Tegan, pointing to a pair of tracks headed about one hundred yards beyond the road.

"You're right. It looks like bulldozer tracks," said Kareem. "And if you look around, everything else is undisturbed land, but the ground ahead is turned down."

"Turned down for what? That's the question," replied Ty.

They started walking across the dry, dusty land toward the area that showed signs of excavation.

"This had to be where Johnny was. Jaxson said he was digging where he wasn't supposed to be and these are the only tracks on an otherwise pristine piece of land," replied Carson.

Walking to the pile of dirt, it was apparent a bulldozer had been used to dig. The tracks ended next to the pile and tracks showed the vehicle appeared to have reversed and turned around before exiting via the same way it entered. The group felt around in the dirt, looking for any additional clues. Kareem was the first to find something.

"Hey guys, what's this? It looks like maybe a bone fragment?" said Kareem, passing the object to Carson.

"You're right. Looks like a metatarsal bone, and you can immediately see this was a camel, but the bone has experienced some intense weathering," replied Carson.

"We're going to have to find that address in Gilbert and try to locate Johnny Stamps," said Ty. "Say, that flash drive we found. It had the checklist of ingredients needed to reanimate the Red Ghost. Any mention of how to stop it?"

"I will have to check through the files again this evening. I noticed nothing, but I may have overlooked it," admitted Carson.

"Since we're out here," said Tegan. "I found a brewery just down the street on East Orchard Lane."

"Sign me up," said Kareem.

Moments later, the group drove down Orchard Lane, searching for the brewery.

"I don't see any businesses here," announced Carson. "Just looks like houses."

"Looking at the address, it should be right around here," said Tegan, looking at her phone, then confusedly up at the neighborhood around her.

"There are a couple of cars parked on the street up ahead," replied Ty.

Pulling behind the cars, Tegan got a look at the house beside them.

"Weird. This is the address on the web page. Should we go check it out?" she asked.

"Might as well. Maybe the homeowner knows where it is.

Likely, he or she has received similar inquiries from lost, thirsty beer-seekers. Maybe the information on the web page is wrong?"

They exited the vehicle and approached the garage. It was open and a couple of small tables were positioned in the driveway, and one was in the garage. Just then, a man exited the house and entered the garage.

"Hello. Are you looking for the brewery?" asked the man.

"Yes, well, we thought we were," replied Kareem.

"You've found it! I brew it from my garage and have a small area if you want to enjoy it here. Everything comes in sixty-four-ounce clear glass growlers, so you can take it to go or drink it here. We have a couple of choices right now," the man said.

"We might as well hang out here for a moment," said Carson, gauging the opinion of his teammates.

"We have a stout, a gingerbread porter, a regular porter, the desert dweller wheat, which is really refreshing," replied the man. "And our most popular choice is the Tangelo Ale and, of course, an IPA," he finished.

"Can't go wrong with the IPA," suggested Kareem.

"We can get a growler of the IPA and I am down to drink it with you," said Ty.

"I was thinking about that Tangelo Ale," said Tegan.

"I will share that with you," replied Carson.

When the man returned with the filled growlers and four pint glasses, Carson took a sip of the Tangelo.

"This is great. It tastes like an IPA with a subtle tangelo taste. Not too hard, like a fruited beer, but very solid. I might have to get a growler of this for the road," Carson told the man.

"The IPA is good too," replied Kareem. "I kind of place it more East Coast or Belgian? Subtle fruit and spice perfume, malt forward with a sneaky bitterness," evaluated Kareem.

"We might have to get a growler of the wheat to go," said Ty.

"The weather is wonderful and this great homebrew? I could enjoy this type of day every day," replied Kareem.

"One thing we were hoping to work in on this trip was a spring training game. Are you guys down to go tomorrow? I know we have to come up with a plan on Johnny and the Red Ghost, but there is a game tomorrow at 1:00 p.m. at the Cubs' new facility. I can get seats on the outfield lawn," reported Carson.

"I'm cool with that," replied Ty. "Who are they playing?"

"Rangers," replied Carson.

The others agreed, and Carson purchased four lawn seats on his phone as they enjoyed the rest of the Tangelo and IPA. They ordered a growler of the Desert Dweller Wheat and another Tangelo to take back to the hotel.

CHAPTER 14

HOLY COW!

Wednesday, March 23, 2016

The group walked into the Hoosier Café on Warner Road in Chandler, ready for a large brunch prior to driving to Sloan Park in Mesa.

"Nice pick on the restaurant," Carson said to Kareem as they walked in.

"The online reviews said this is a great local breakfast spot in Chandler," said Kareem. "Solid comfort food and a good staff. They have several omelets on the menu, but I can't wait to have the loaded biscuits & gravy. That's one of my favorite breakfast meals and it's been a while, so I'm excited to try it here."

Carson, Ty, and Tegan continued to look over the menus after Kareem made his selection.

"I gave that flash drive another look early this morning," said Carson as he narrowed his selection to one of the many varieties of omelets listed. "The files on the drive talked about the spells and the items necessary to bring the Red Ghost back to life. It didn't talk about how to stop it," Carson said. "But I think knowing what we know now, we need to focus on what we learned from Niles back in Quartzsite."

"He said he wasn't sure if it was just a story, but most of what he said appears to be accurate. He thought the person who bought the skull, which we know was Johnny Stamps, was a relative of the original rider of the Red Ghost. From the documents on the USB, that turned out to be he is a descendant of Hi Jolly. Using the enchantment spells, he could transfer the spirit of Hi Jolly to the skull of the original rider, William Avant," replied Ty.

"After we returned from Queen Creek yesterday, I went for a jog down Arizona Avenue," replied Tegan. "On the way back, I stopped at Tortas Ahogadas Guadalajara just about half a mile down the street."

"Did you get tacos? How were the tacos?" asked Kareem.

"Remarkable. I had two carne asada tacos. While I was there eating at one table, I saw a woman who had a cool coral and obsidian necklace that caught my eye. Her name was Jamaica Cruse, and we ended up talking about it. She works at an occult shop called Red Raven's Cauldron out in Apache Junction," Tegan continued.

"Occult shop? That sounds interesting," said Carson.

"It was, and she was really cool. After we talked for a couple of minutes, I mentioned the Red Ghost and how we were dealing with something supernatural," Tegan stated. "I presented some things we have found and what we're up against. She provided some advice based on her experience with the occult and supernatural."

"Good thinking. I didn't even consider that approach," replied Carson.

"Witchcraft with witchcraft," replied Ty.

"What did she suggest?" asked Carson.

"She said with the supernatural, the key is the head. We know that the rider's skull was one of the key elements and the symbol on the grave and the skull connected the spirit of Hi Jolly to the Red Ghost. She said if we can find the head, we can re-control the Red Ghost," reported Tegan.

"The head of the Red Ghost? Like cut it off?" asked Kareem.

"No, not the Red Ghost itself. The rider's skull. We find where Johnny Stamps has the skull. Ty, you mentioned earlier, it sounded like Sleepy Hollow. Very similar. The Red Ghost is doing the bidding of Johnny Stamps because he can't rest until the skull is returned and the bond is broken," Tegan comments.

"Returned? To where? Queen Creek? The swap meet in Quartzsite?" asked Ty.

"No, returned to the earth. When the skull is buried in hallowed ground, the rider Hi Jolly and the Red Ghost Spitfire can both rest again," revealed Tegan.

"So hallowed means holy, blessed, or highly respected. Most of the time, that can be a church or maybe a university," defined Carson.

"After the game, we should hit up that address on Greenfield Road and see what's around there. Maybe we can get lucky, find Johnny and the skull. Then we take the skull to a local cemetery or church. We could end this tonight," said Ty.

"That would be great. We fly out Saturday night, so that would give us a few days to relax and enjoy this weather and more baseball," suggested Kareem.

Following brunch, Carson drove to Sloan Park, within the large Riverview Park green space. Parking in a lot on Cubs Way, the group made the long walk to the stadium. Opened in 2014 as Cubs Park, the name changed in January 2015 to Sloan Park. It was not only the newest park in the spring training system, but with a capacity of fifteen thousand seats. It was also the largest. Given the popularity of the Chicago Cubs in Arizona, the new stadium caused Sloan Park to be a must-see during spring training.

As they continued walking toward the stadium's will call window, the design of the baseball complex impressed them. A large new hotel, the Sheraton Mesa Hotel, stood next to the stadium in an area named Wrigleyville West. The surrounding streets mirrored those in Chicago as Cubs Way changed to Waveland Avenue behind the stadium, with Sheffield Avenue running along the side. The park had great reserved seats, spacious lawn seating, a children's play area, a small citrus grove, and plenty of food trucks.

"This should be a great game," said Carson.

"Just as I imagined a spring training game would be. All the fans, and even though we aren't inside the stadium yet, the atmosphere already gets me excited for the game and for the start of the season," stated Ty.

Kareem was busy checking out Untappd on his phone.

"Guys, they have some excellent selection of craft beer here, but also they have Old Style," commented Kareem.

"I might have to go with that, just for the feeling," replied Tegan. "Old Style is Chicago's beer. That and a Chicago hot dog? Even though we're here to see the Rangers, I gotta say I love the feeling of being in Chicago here in this section of Arizona," she said.

"It's cool a team from our home state is playing, but it's not the Astros, and really the Cubs are an American classic. Growing up, I used to watch the Cubs on WGN and the Braves on TBS after school because they were on television every day. Even though they weren't great, they were on and I grew up loving them," replied Carson.

"And you gotta love Harry Caray," said Ty.

"Good ole Harry. Even though Chicagoans adopted Old Style as the local drink, Harry was a Cubs Fan and a Bud Man," replied Kareem, referring to the old Chicago commercial featuring the Cub's iconic former announcer.

"I don't think I will have a Bud in his honor," said Carson. "But an Old Style and a Chicago dog? I'm down with that."

They picked up the tickets at will call and made their way inside the stadium, walking around to the grassy area behind the left field wall.

"Wow, the grass is crowded," replied Tegan.

"With this weather and the town's love for the Cubs, this

is the best seat in the house," replied Carson. "And this seventy-three degrees, sunny weather doesn't hurt either."

Kareem unfolded a blanket that he brought and spread it across an empty section of grass. They looked around and scouted out the area from their new spot.

"Looks like the beer man is coming through this section. We just need to get the hot dogs," said Carson.

"Kareem and I will get them. You two secure the beer," suggested Tegan as she and Kareem stood and headed out to the pavilion to get the hot dogs.

Kyle Hendricks took the mound for the home-team Chicago Cubs while Derek Holland started for the Rangers. Hendricks cruised through the first four innings with scoreless baseball before giving up a couple of hard-hit balls in the fifth inning. Both pitchers went five innings, with Holland having the better performance. After the starters were out of the game, the Rangers held a 2-0 lead.

By the seventh inning stretch, the group was ready to stand up and take part in the traditional stretch that has been part of baseball since President William Howard Taft first rose from his seat to stretch in 1910 as the teams changed sides in the seventh. The middle of the inning featured a sing-along playback homage to Harry Caray's rendition of *Take Me Out to the Ball Game*, as he did throughout his time as the Cub's broadcaster. The Rangers still held a 2-0 lead.

"I'm going to check this Old Style in on Untappd with a selfie of me and the beer at this baseball game," replied Kareem.

"Thinking about tracking the Red Ghost, right by the highway over there, is the Salt River, which we experienced earlier in the trip. It runs out through where the earlier sightings and our own later run in with the Red Ghost happened. That might not be a bad spot to return to for our investigation," said Carson.

As the game resumed, the Cubs offense had little success against the Rangers' pitchers. Kyle Schwarber finished the day with two hits, and that was the largest offense for Chicago as they fell to the Rangers 5-0. For the Rangers, Hanser Alberto, Pedro Ciriaco, and Drew Stubbs had two hits apiece.

"Good game for the boys from Texas," said Carson as the group stood up and prepared to leave the stadium.

"Glad to check something off my bucket list," replied Ty.

As they walked out of the stadium and back to the car, Carson suggested since it was still late afternoon and sunny, they should head out to Gilbert and see if they could locate Johnny Stamps.

Carson drove from Riverview Park, up 101 North, to US-60 East where he took exit 185 Greenfield Road. From there, it was only a couple of miles to the intersection of Guadalupe Road. As they continued on Guadalupe, they passed a large nature reserve.

"What's that area?" asked Tegan as they drove up.

Ty pulled up his map application and reviewed the area.

"Says it's Riparian Preserve at Water Ranch," replied Ty. "Looks like there are several large ponds in there. It's a whole block long and backs up against the canal," he added.

"Maybe we should check that place out?" said Kareem. "We know the Red Ghost traveled along the canal system getting from Goldfield to the area behind Pearl's."

"Might be worth checking out," said Carson. "But first, let's pay Johnny Stamps a visit."

"What's the play when we find him?" asked Ty.

"I just want to talk to him. Find out if he's behind this and, if so, why. We're not cops. We can't really confront him. We could give the police information and they could pay him a visit, but really we need to find where the skull is and put an end to the Red Ghost," answered Carson. "And I don't know that the cops would take it seriously if we told them a guy was using a supernatural camel to terrorize the city."

Just past Escondido Place, they slowed down at a gravel driveway that had four houses branching off it.

"This looks like the spot," said Ty. "A bit of a come up from where he was staying before, if you ask me."

The second house on the left side of the driveway matched the address given to them by the supervisor at Johnny Stamps' former employer.

"Time to pay him a visit," replied Carson. "You guys want to stay in the car so it doesn't look like we are ganging up on him?"

"Sure, we'll wait here, but if he makes a run for it, we'll be the jump out squad," said Ty.

Carson approached the house. A metal chain-link fence bordered the yard, but the driveway was open. As he walked toward the house, he noticed a pool in the backyard.

Knocking on the door, he awaited a response. A man answered the door, but it was not Johnny Stamps. Ten minutes later, Carson returned to the car.

"Good news is that Johnny Stamps is living here. I spoke to the homeowner, and he confirmed he is renting out a room to Johnny. Bad news is he isn't here right now," replied Carson.

"Damn. Any idea where he is?" asked Ty.

"The man said he went out for a couple of drinks. A place called Sun Devil Liquors," answered Carson.

"Do we know where it is?" asked Tegan.

"Not too far, about ten miles from here. It's a bottle shop, but he said they have a cool basement downstairs with a bar, a lounge, and it's a pleasant spot to just chill. Johnny is supposed to play a set with his band tonight at a place called Club Red, and it's not too far from Sun Devil Liquors," replied Carson.

"Well then, let's check it out," responded Kareem.

Carson pulled into the parking lot of Sun Devil Liquors on Country Club Avenue in Mesa. Walking inside the front door, the number of bottles, including beer and liquor, impressed the group. Before looking for the entrance to the basement, they walked through the aisles admiring the many offerings.

"We might have to stock up for the trip home here," suggested Kareem.

There were several shelves with bottles and cans and a full wall of refrigerated coolers for beer ready to drink. As they were perusing the cold beers, an employee asked if they needed help. He mentioned the cellar permitted purchase and onsite consumption of cold beer.

"Well, that changes things," said Carson.

"We also have beer on the shelf and a refrigerated section downstairs if you are heading down there," the employee informed.

He pointed to the cellar entrance, and the group headed downstairs down the dark and creaky wooden staircase. When they reached the bottom, it defied expectations. They saw three people standing around a small wooden bar that at capacity could hold six people. A bartender was behind, offering samples, serving draughts, or pouring beer brought to him by the customers.

"Does Heaven have beer, you ask? Why, yes, it does," said Carson as the group walked to the bar and started looking over the menu.

"This place is totally unexpected," replied Tegan. "The upstairs is nice with a lot of hard-to-find beers and wines from around the world, but this? This has a charm that is hard to find!"

"Wow is all I can say," replied Kareem. "It's a little Narnia-like. But it isn't Narnia - it's a really cool looking bar secluded in a liquor store."

"It's a little chilly down here," added Ty. "And not just the atmosphere. Definitely noticeably cooler than you would expect a basement to be."

"A few good choices up there on the menu too," replied Ty. "I only see a couple from Arizona at the moment."

"Yes, and I am a sucker for beers on nitro, so I think I will have that Wanderlust Pan American Stout on Nitro," replied Kareem.

"I think I will look at the shelves and find something local," said Tegan. "Plus, I just want to explore this cellar."

Ty and Carson followed her while Kareem placed his order.

"This one sounds nice," said Tegan to the guys. "Undercover Cucumber Blonde Ale from Historic Brewing Company."

"Nice choice. They are up in Flagstaff. I've heard there are several good breweries up there now. Between Flagstaff, Phoenix, and Tucson, Arizona is really doing well with some great beers," Carson replied.

"I think I will pick one from Historic also," stated Ty. "This Screaming Goat sounds like something we'd probably get called on to investigate. Maybe I can tame the beast easily."

Carson continued to look at the local beer section of the cellar, eventually finding one to his liking.

"I am glad they have this on the shelf," said Carson as he removed a can of McFate Candy Bar Milk Stout from the cooler. "I heard about this one when it won the 2013 Great American Beer Festival Silver Medal. Talk about dessert: milk stout brewed with honey roasted peanuts, cacao nibs, vanilla bean, and a touch of sea salt. That sounds tremendous," he followed.

They took their cans to the bar to have them poured and rejoin Kareem, who was already sipping on his beer. Near the back wall, the cellar opened into a large, dimly lit room with several couches, chairs, and tables placed to allow customers to hang out and enjoy the atmosphere. They walked into the lounge and looked around at the customers as Mega Ran's *Infinite Lives* played. The song seemed fitting for the current investigation as it explained we know we all will die, but the goal isn't to live forever, but to create something that will. Johnny Stamps created something from the past using the legend of Hi Jolly and the fear of the Red Ghost to return to the modern world and disrupt the status quo. They were still attempting to figure out why.

"Hey, look over there in the corner," said Ty, pointing to a large accent chair where a lone man was sitting and drinking a beer from the bottle and reading over some notes.

"I think that's Johnny Stamps," replied Kareem. "Gotta be him. And three empty chairs around him. Let's go over and say hello."

Tegan took a seat at the other end of the room while Ty, Kareem, and Carson approached Johnny.

"Mind if we join you?" asked Carson.

"Plenty of seats over there, but whatever, man," Johnny said without looking up as he returned his focus to his notes.

"Nice place here. I feel like a kid in a delicious adult candy store," replied Kareem.

"Yeah, it's a cool place. If you don't mind," Johnny responded in a direct tone and pointed at the papers in front of him.

"What notes you working on?" asked Ty.

"What is this? Twenty questions? I'm in a band and I'm playing tonight. Going over the playlist. Now if you don't mind…," he repeated a little more harshly.

"Oh, playlist. That's cool. We thought they might be notes about that crazy camel running around town frightening people," replied Carson, staring at Johnny.

The sentence struck a nerve with Johnny as he stared intently at Carson. "Look, old man, I don't know what you and your buddies think you know…," he started.

"We've been to Quartzsite, to Dreamy Draw, and to Queen Creek. We've seen the files on that little flash drive you left behind when you moved out of your last house so quickly," interrupted Ty.

The comment got Johnny's attention. He gazed at the three men, putting his notes down on the table.

"Man, screw that! I'll do what I want. The Red Ghost hasn't killed anybody. He's scaring people and hoping they will stay away. It's time to take back my land and get rid of people poisoning it," Johnny explained.

"That might work for some small community on Scooby Doo, but it will not keep people away from coming to the fifth largest city in the country. And there *has* been death associated with the Red Ghost. At least one," explained Carson.

"What? That old man in Goldfield? That was an accident, and he probably had poor health anyway from eating junk food," replied Johnny.

"Or maybe the heart attack was caused by a stampeding supernatural camel in the night," replied Carson.

"The more people see the Red Ghost, the more scared they will be to come here. Then I will retake what's mine! This was my family's land, and we were prosperous. But now? Growing up around here, there are no jobs. And living on the land that should be mine. After a time, anger gets passed down from generation to generation," replied Johnny.

"What's this talk about the land?" asked Kareem.

"This entire area was supposed to have been my ancestor's, Hi Jolly. It was his, and I have the deed to prove it. They lost it for years and when my grandparents tried to claim it, the city rejected it because they didn't have the damn paper. Now I have it and can prove it should be mine, but look at it now. On the side of the reservation, there are no jobs and no opportunity. On the other side of the highway, Scottsdale has taken over, and it's nothing but houses and more houses, pollution, and no respect for the land," Johnny replied angrily.

"Look, I get it. It sucks," replied Carson.

"You get it? How? You've had everything handed to you. You might have some tough times here or there, but the system isn't designed against you. To hold you back," he replied. "I put that into my music too. That's what these notes are. I have a little hogan dwelling out near my mom's house on the Rez. Best place to clear my mind, reconnect with my ancestors. I spent a lot of time there, alone. Grew up listening to Iron Maiden. Loved the album covers. It made sense. I just like dark imagery because, you know, it's not too great around here. The music just takes you somewhere else. I write about what goes on here. The struggles, the experiences here that many people on the outside don't even know. There's a lot of frustration. Everyone here grew up poor. My music is letting out aggression and energy. It's not just me. Plenty of people are angry and frustrated, and it's depressing being here. The suicide rate is the biggest killer - comes in waves. I've lost a couple of friends over the past few years. Sometimes you don't see it, no signs. It's crazy. Growing up here is a constant struggle. No jobs, little to no opportunity. You have cultural roots with grandparents, family, and parents. Back in Hi Jolly's day, before rapid expansion, we were alright. We took care of ourselves, and we were very self-sufficient. When we had to conform to other people moving in here and taking our land, that's where everything went straight to hell for us. I'm not an activist or anything. I am aware of our history. I am proud of my ancestors. It's hard to balance that cultural heritage with living in the twenty-first century. It's a constant struggle. Cultural trauma passed down is what I play in my band. That's how we feel. Anger, aggression, growing our hair out. You gotta live fast to play fast," replied Johnny.

"And using the Red Ghost? Is that part of your dark imagery and anger?" asked Carson. "How's that going to get your land back? I don't think the city or the state is going to support that document now that you found it. It's more than a hundred years too late."

"It's embracing the dark side of our culture. Things I learned from my grandparents. Stuff you're not supposed to talk about. The dark magic, those things. We get in a completely different state of mind than who we were. To us, it relates to the culture that taught me. I have Mexican family, Navajo family, white family, and I learn from all of that. There're witches called *yin agoshi*, and they have something similar like how the corpse paint looks like. We wear the makeup on stage in my band. It's black and white and that's the reason we use it. In Western cultures, you have your good and bad. Over here, it's the same. We have our good and bad. The good, you know there are traditional ceremonies, healing ceremonies. You know you go to go see a medicine man, get healed, you know, spiritually. Then there's the opposite of that. There's people that are out there that want to hurt you and then they'll paint their face using ash and they'll get blood or whatever, wipe it on their face, and just go out and conjure up their spells and try to make the person who they're out against to suffer," Johnny said.

"So you're one of the bad? Using the Red Ghost to create suffering and revenge?" replied Carson.

"Hey, whatever, man. Over the generations, we lost connection with our own identity. Continued expansion, taking away our natural resources, invading our lands, stripping us of our culture, religion, and our true self," said Johnny.

"Dude, I get it. That happened to my ancestors, too. Brought to America forcefully. Stripped of our culture and identity. For decades, Black Americans have faced higher poverty rates, lower incomes, and higher incarceration rates than white Americans," replied Ty. "I grew up in central Illinois. A town called Peoria, where the poverty rate for Blacks was over twenty-eight percent. Compare that to just over ten percent for whites," added Ty.

"I get it too," replied Kareem. "I'm a first-generation American. My family came here from La Nalga de Ventura in Valle de Santiago in Guanajuato, Mexico. Like Ty said, incarceration rates are higher, opportunities for education and employment are lower, and there is the feeling that everything is against you. My family moved to escape poverty and violence in the area, but the opportunities were still minimal here. Pew Research conducted a study and found that right now four-in-ten Latinos say they have experienced discrimination in the past year. Like being called offensive names, being told to go back to their home country, being criticized for speaking Spanish in public, or experiencing discrimination or unfair treatment because they are Hispanic. Hate crimes are up across the United States, and crimes targeting Latinos have increased nearly eighty percent in California over the past three years," replied Kareem.

"See, that's the shit I'm talking about! You two should be with me. This part of the country used to be Mexico. Natives and Mexicans were here first, and we are told to go back. Go back to where? Where our ancestors are from doesn't exist anymore. We are where we came from. We are home," replied Johnny. "I know Mexicans and Navajo became bitter enemies. They abandoned several cities because of the Navajo attacks, but today we are fighting the same fight. Just to survive and fit into a world that tries to keep us down," said Johnny.

"There are definite stereotypes and prejudiced thinking today, even though the country is more diverse now than ever," replied Ty. "But violence isn't the way to change that. It will only make it worse."

"I know you said you're not an activist, but change starts at home and in your local community. Make sure people register to vote, volunteer, be visible, and be heard… peacefully. We have seen throughout history that large-scale change can begin with one person. It ain't easy, but it is possible," replied Kareem. "Focus on major social issues such as health care, education, and employment. Those can be the foundation for changing the outcome in your community. It requires taking small steps on a long journey."

"We are not where we need to be, but we've made some good progress," replied Carson.

"It's not enough. So you guys do you and I'll do me," replied Johnny.

"Look, we came here to talk to you and ask you to put an end to this Red Ghost," responded Carson.

"I will not tell you where he is, and I'm going to keep using hi, so whatever. He's been lying low lately, but maybe it's time for another appearance," answered Johnny.

"So far he's created some news stories and has people worried, but it has had no effect like you were hoping for, and eventually more people will get hurt or killed. This has to end," said Carson.

Johnny finished his drink, gathered his notes, and stood up.

"Speaking of ending, I have a show to put on tonight. *Gentlemen…*" Johnny concluded and headed for the exit.

Tegan stood up and joined the guys, sitting in Johnny's seat.

"That didn't look like it went as we hoped," she said.

"No, he wasn't helpful. But like I told him, I get it," replied Ty.

"So since he isn't calling the Red Ghost off and sounds like he is going to use him again soon, we have to locate the camel," said Carson.

Carson stood up and stretched as *Suture Self* from Snailmate played.

"Whatcha say we have another round, then get back to the hotel?" suggested Carson.

"I'm with it," said Ty. "Dealer's choice."

The others agreed, and Carson headed back to the refrigerated local beer section in the other room. After selecting and paying for the beers, he sat them on the table to allow everyone to select their choice from the selection: a cranberry oatmeal stout from Phoenix Brewing, Lost Highway black IPA from Mother Road, Big Blue Van fruited ale from College Street, and a Hatch Chile Gatos blonde ale infused with hatch chiles from McFate Brewing.

"Tomorrow I am going to give Dr. Williams at Marble Hills another call and see if we can borrow some thermal cameras and head lamps for a nighttime investigation," said Carson as he placed a bag on the ground and sat down to rejoin the others.

"What's in the bag?" asked Ty.

"Some beer for the road. I was checking Untappd while I was looking at the shelves and I saw they highly rated these local beers. They will make excellent beers to drink at the hotel or bring back as souvenirs. To The Wall IPA, Heatstroke American wheat ale, and My Honey Bee blonde ale from Mesquite River Brewing and a Button IPA, a couple All Souls stout, and El Jefe Vice from Button Brew House down around Tucson. I also added a six-pack of Chiltepin Red from Button House because I read it is awesome mixed with the All Souls. It's got a bit of heat to it from what I saw, so that should be a delightful mix with a smooth stout," replied Carson.

They finished the round and headed back to the hotel in Chandler to work out the deals of tomorrow night's investigation.

CHAPTER 15

NIGHT INVESTIGATION

Thursday, March 24, 2016

Sitting under a white canopy on the patio outside of a historic 1929 building in Heritage Square, the group enjoyed a late lunch and beautiful weather.

"Pizzeria Bianco has been named among the best pizza places in the country," replied Ty. "I am glad we could get in today."

"It's good we came for lunch. I read the lines for dinner can be over two, sometimes three, hours just to get in. Even at lunch, the wait was a little longer than I expected," replied Tegan.

"What do you say we get two and split them?" suggested Carson.

"We have to try the classic Margherita and that Rosa with onion, parmigiana, rosemary, and local pistachios sounds great also," replied Kareem.

"This is a magnificent spot. Not too far from the airport, and it's not too far from Roosevelt Row. I don't know if you saw anything about that online, but it sounds a lot like Austin. Some funky, eclectic stores, wonderful restaurants, and they have one of the nation's largest, self-guided neighborhood art walks called First Friday at the beginning of every month. You just walk around and check out art in different galleries and some are even in homes. It's like the central hub for art and culture in the downtown Phoenix area," stated Carson.

"That sounds sweet. Too bad we won't catch it this time around," replied Tegan.

"I've been thinking about the Red Ghost. It would make sense that Johnny would keep him close, and we know he's staying in Gilbert off Greenfield. That nature preserve we saw just across from the house would make a great place to hide the camel. We saw from the street there are a lot of tall trees and bushes, plus there are several ponds," suggested Carson.

"That's as good a place as any. We haven't heard of any sightings this week, so he's lying low, as Johnny said. I didn't see any other place around that part of town that could hide an animal that size," replied Ty.

"Riparian Preserve it is," said Kareem.

"What's the plan? We have to lay this out because Johnny knows we are on to him. I know he said he plans to use him soon, but we don't know when that might be, so we have to act. He's up and disappeared on roommates before, so we know he might decide to run again," said Ty.

"We know we don't even need Johnny and maybe we don't really even need the Red Ghost. The key to stopping him is to find the skull and break the spell by burying it in hallowed ground, right? So we find the skull and go from there," replied Carson.

"That's a brilliant plan, but we don't know where the skull is. It could be at Johnny's house. It could be anywhere. He said yesterday that he likes to spend time in a hogan and reflect. Could be there, but we don't know where that is," replied Kareem. "Finding a large camel in an urban city is one thing, but a skull? That's going to be difficult."

Carson took a sip of his water and thought about the plan of attack.

"Damn, that water is actually pretty good. I feel like I haven't had enough water here, and hydration is very important, especially in the desert. I know the Arizona heat is no joke during the summer months, but even the rest of the year being outside even for minutes at a time, the sun here will literally suck all the moisture from your body," stated Carson.

"Like they say, man cannot live on beer alone," replied Kareem as the outdoor radio played Screamin' Jay Hawkins' 1956 classic *I Put a Spell on You*, catching Carson's ear.

"Say, Tegan, that woman you met the other day at the taco shop...," started Carson.

"Jamaica Cruse?" replied Tegan.

"Yes, that's the one. Did you get her number?" Carson asked.

"No, we talked, but I didn't get her number," responded Tegan.

Carson thought again for a moment. "You said she worked at a store. An occult shop in Apache Junction?" Carson replied.

"Yes, Red Raven. That's right," she said.

"Give the business a call and see if you can connect with her again. Maybe she can join us on our investigation tonight," Carson suggested.

"Yeah, if you think it can help," she replied.

"Here's what I'm thinking. See if she can do this," he said as he scribbled a note on a paper napkin from the table and handed it to Tegan. "If she's available, let's meet her at the park at 6 p.m.," he said.

Around 5 p.m. that afternoon, Carson arrived back at the hotel where the others were waiting. He received the equipment from Dr. Williams and organized the trunk as the others met up with him in the parking lot.

"Ready to go?" asked Carson.

"Yes, let's do this," said Ty.

"Jamaica is in. I texted her the address and she will meet us there," replied Tegan.

"Good. Let's go find us a camel!" replied Carson.

Arriving at the preserve's parking lot, Carson took one of the last spots as Tegan texted with Jamaica to alert her to their arrival.

"She's already here," replied Tegan. "Oh, there she is, sitting on that short cement wall," she said, pointing to a winding curved cement wall not over three feet in height that served as a place to sit at the edge of the preserve.

Carson opened the trunk and removed two thermal cameras and five headlamps for the group, handing a lamp to each member and a camera to Ty and Kareem. As they walked toward the wall where Jamaica was waiting, he handed the other headlamp to her.

"Nice to see you again. These are my friends that I was telling you about," said Tegan.

"It's a pleasure to meet you," began Carson. "Tegan told us about your conversation regarding our investigation. It was really helpful and gave us expert direction on stopping this thing."

"The pleasure is mine. I'm glad to help. When your friend told me about what you were looking for, it intrigued me. The supernatural is something I have studied for many years and when she sent the message today about meeting up with you guys on this investigation, I was happy to do it," replied Jamaica.

"Now that we're all here, what's the plan?" asked Ty.

"I want to get another look at that camel, and Johnny said he was going to send him out again. But we also need to find the skull since that is the actual artifact that will stop his reign," said Carson. "So I think we should split up. Ty, you and I will go searching for the Red Ghost. Kareem, Tegan, and Jamaica will search for the skull."

"Sounds great, but we don't even know where to look for either," said Kareem.

"I believe the Red Ghost is here amongst these trails and

ponds," replied Carson. "And locating the skull? That's where Jamaica comes in."

"How so?" asked Ty.

"Carson had Tegan ask me to come to the park and conduct a couple of rituals. The first one is a finding-lost-objects ritual," replied Jamaica. "This is my go-to personal favorite finding-lost-objects ritual. It's never failed me yet. Usually I look for car keys, my wedding ring, or my Kindle, but it should work on the skull of The Red Ghost too," she said.

"Sounds good," replied Carson. "Do you need anything to conduct the ritual?"

"For this one, I need nothing physical," replied Jamaica. "This is an interesting park. It has an energy about it. You know there is a bit of a ghost story here too," she added.

"Really? I knew nothing about this park until we drove past yesterday," said Carson.

"The basins of Water Ranch Lake, which is the large lake here by the parking lot where many people fish, are believed to be haunted by the spirit of a woman who was killed there. Paranormal investigators have accumulated many EVP recordings of the woman's name captured near the gazebo and other locations in the park. The energy is powerful there. What do you say we conduct the ritual at the gazebo?" suggested Jamaica.

"Lead the way," replied Ty.

Standing in the gazebo overlooking Water Ranch Lake, Jamaica stood in the center while the others formed a circle around her.

"To begin, I will visualize the item that is lost. In this case, the Red Ghost's skull," she began. "Now, in my mind's eye, I will encircle the skull with a silver cord," she said.

She closed her eyes and started the ritual. Seconds later, she smiled.

"Now that I have that, I will recite a charm three times while mentally tugging the cord back toward my solar plexus and I should see the lost item being pulled back to me," she continued.

She took a deep, calming breath and recited the following charm three times:

What was lost now is found,

As my magick circles round.

Whether you are hidden far or near,

I call you now to come meet me here.

She paused and reflected on the received vision for the location of the missing skull. She felt a jolt that shook her momentarily as the visions entered her mind.

"I see an orchard, a metal silo, a Quonset hut… and the number twelve," replied Jamaica.

"I don't even know what a Quonset hut is," replied Carson, shaking his head.

"It's a corrugated galvanized steel half-round building. You've seen them. Farmers use them for hay and grain storage, livestock shelter, warehouses, and other things. Some people have adapted them for commercial use and some even have designed them as homes," replied Jamaica.

"Oh yes. We have those in Texas, but I didn't know that's what you called them. I also see nothing like that around here. I would have thought he would stash the skull somewhere close because it is valuable to him," replied Carson.

"Somewhere close, or somewhere safe," responded Ty. "We just talked to him yesterday. He knows we are on to him, and we said we were coming after the Red Ghost. We also told him we know where he lives, so keeping it at the house isn't safe right now. Maybe he put it somewhere he thinks we won't find it. Could be with someone he trusts to watch after it," suggested Ty.

"That's a good point. However, I do not know what those clues even mean. There are several trees here, but it's not an orchard. There is an observatory, but it's not a silo or one of those metal barns," replied Kareem.

Meanwhile, Tegan consulted her phone for clues.

"Guys, I searched orchards in Gilbert, and there is something about three miles from here. It's called The Farm at Agritopia. The website says it's a planned community that is a modern village surrounding eleven acres of urban farmland. They have gardens, orchards, and restaurants there. There is a community garden program, a community tool shed, and a small silo within the property, and they have metal barns housing restaurants. Inside Barnone there is a pizza place and a brewery, get this, named Twelve West, but written as Roman numeral twelve," reported Tegan.

"Orchard, silo, the number twelve. That checks all the boxes. Sounds like you guys should check out XII West and see if that's the spot," suggested Carson. "Ty and I will explore this park and search for the Red Ghost."

The group members exchanged hugs and well wishes amongst themselves and Jamaica. Carson handed Tegan the keys to the car and he and Ty started down the Riparian Preserve Trail, waving to the group as they disappeared over one of the small rolling hills.

"Good news is XII West is open until 10 p.m., so someone should be there. We can get in and have a look around. I am not sure what the connection would be to Johnny Stamps, but it doesn't hurt to look, since it's only three miles away. The boys will be fine on their own until we get back," replied Tegan as she, Jamaica, and Kareem drove out of the parking lot down Greenfield and headed toward Ray Road.

"We still have a couple of hours before sunset," said Carson. "That should give us a good chance to search this park."

"This paved sidewalk circles the lake, and there seems to be good lighting set up here. The dirt trails going around the ponds and into the wooded areas will be difficult. Still, the paths look well maintained, so we shouldn't trip on anything if we stay on the path," replied Ty.

"A lot of people fishing here. Makes me wish we had a pole. Can't wait to get back to Old Settlers Park and snag a few perch," replied Carson.

They walked down the sidewalk until they came to a dirt path that diverged to the left.

"A lot of rabbits out here. I've seen at least five so far," Ty said as they continued down the dusty path. "No camels though."

They continued walking until the trail looped back to the parking lot.

"It looks like nothing this way. Let's hit the sidewalk again and continue until we get to Pond Seven. From the map by the entrance, it looks like that continues and parts into two more dirt trails. One going around Pond Five and the other between Ponds Five and Six. Hopefully, Kareem and the girls are doing better than we are so far," replied Carson.

A few miles away, Tegan turned into one of the parking lots at Agritopia. It was a full parking lot with some people walking the trails, others in the garden, and others in the shops. Many were sitting outside at a restaurant called Joe's Farm Grill.

"That seems to be a popular place," said Kareem.

"Oh it is," replied Jamaica. "They get most of the ingredients here at the farm and heavily focus on urban gardening, local foods, and historic preservation," she said. "It's always busy, and the outside seating is awesome under nice gigantic trees and the sound of chirping birds."

"There are a couple of metal barns. Which one is the brewery in?" asked Tegan.

"It's in Barnone. They have several restaurants, from a coffee shop to a pizza place, to a vegetarian kitchen, and the brewery," replied Jamaica.

"Is that bar-none or barn-one?" asked Kareem, looking over Tegan's shoulder.

"Now that you mention it… I think it's the first one since it's all one word," she said. "Either way, the boys will be jealous they are missing investigating a brewery," laughed Tegan.

"Too bad we can't investigate the menu," replied Kareem. "Looks like the front entrance is up this way. A nice large patio. Arizona really loves its patios at bars and restaurants," he noted.

"It's certainly too hot in June, July, and August, but the rest of the year Arizona is excellent for outdoor dining and enjoying the weather and these wonderful sunsets," said Jamaica.

"Ladies," Kareem said as he held the front door open for Tegan and Jamaica.

Inside was bustling with people at the coffee shop, the brewery, and the restaurants. The group looked around in amazement at how spacious the metal barn was inside and how it provided a cool atmosphere for customers to enjoy the businesses. The brewery did not serve food, but those drinking at the bar could get food at Fire and Brimstone or the plant-based Uprooted Kitchen and bring it back to the brewery. There was room at the bar and some long tables for patrons. They could also take the beer to the restaurant dining section or out on the patio as long as they did not cross the marked borders reading No Alcohol Beyond This Point. The brewery had beer on tap, some selection of canned beer, as well as crowler and growler fills to go.

"It's going to be difficult to find what we are looking for here with these people," said Tegan.

"Right. We don't even really know what we are looking for, other than it's a skull. Did Johnny put it in something?

Did he hide it here? And is this even the right spot?" asked Kareem rhetorically.

"All good questions," replied Tegan. "Let me check in with the guys," she said, calling Carson on the cell phone.

"Go for Carson," he replied from the park.

"Hey, we are here at the brewery. We just got here, and it's crowded. We are going to walk around and see if we can somehow find anything," responded Tegan. "Any luck your way?"

"Nothing yet. Just a few rabbits, a squirrel, ducks, and a large variety of birds. More than I've ever seen in one place," replied Carson.

"But no sighting of the Red Ghost?" asked Tegan.

"Not so far," Carson stated. "But we are closing in on sundown. Maybe it will be active then. Or maybe he isn't here at all."

"Best of luck, and be safe out there," she ended.

"Thanks. Good hunting as well," Carson said.

Carson and Ty continued walking, enjoying the park, yet looking for any sign of the Red Ghost. Eventually, they stopped and took a seat at a table inside a ramada in the center of the park.

"I don't know we're gonna find anything on these dusty trails," said Ty. "We have to look for tracks, maybe signs of entering or exiting some of the brush. We have a well-maintained path and an area that receives many visitors. It would be difficult to preserve tracks or show signs of the animal. Something that big has to leave traces of itself."

"You're right. Foot traffic is declining a bit, but there are still people around. Even if he is supernatural, he's still an animal and would likely attempt to avoid people. If he's here, we need to get closer to the ponds where the ground might be wetter along the basins and show some evidence of tracks or maybe hair snagged on some brambles," replied Carson. "We've got about fifteen minutes before sunset now. Let's head over between Pond Five and Three. We haven't hit that one up for a while," Carson suggested.

They turned left at the first path, then approached Pond Four, where the path again diverged both left and right.

"These ponds are actually seven recharge basins that replicate wet/dry periods, each in different stages," said Carson. "Makes each one a different water habitat that draws different species of birds, insects, and amphibians. It's really a cool place. I would love to get a look at that observatory."

They stopped at the split in the path at the base of Pond Four to decide which way to go when they heard a rustling noise coming from inside the wetland.

"Did you hear that? Sounds like something big," said Ty as he hunkered down and tried to get a look through the brush. "Let's go through that metal gate and see if we can get a better look," he suggested.

"It looks like there is a little island just behind these bushes," said Carson. "See how the water comes in on that left side?"

They heard a huffing noise coming from the bushes, followed by a rumbling, nuzzling sound, and an increased shaking of leaves.

"I don't want to stick my face in there and get my nose bit or my face spit on," said Carson.

"He might bite you, but he will not spit on you," replied Ty. "Dromedary camels do not spit. That's Bactrians."

There was a loud cracking of branches and the sound of splashing water. Ty and Carson darted back as the Red Ghost sprang from the brushes and onto the trail where they had just been standing. The Red Ghost swung his neck toward the two intruders and turned to face them, strong warning signs of a camel annoyed by the presence of another. The skeleton rider tapped the camel on its side and pointed toward the two men. The camel stared at them and gave a loud bellow, almost a roar, and arched his head back as the sun sat behind him. His red ember eyes glowed as the beast readied for attack.

"Shit! I didn't know the skeleton was animated, too!" replied Carson.

Meanwhile, at XII West, Kareem, Tegan, and Jamaica walked around the building looking for clues, eventually finding a small space at the bar and walking up to inspect further. The brewery was actually a taproom, with the main brewing operations conducted in Mesa. Behind the bar, twelve chalkboard slats, also numbered in roman numerals, listed the draught beers available and t-shirts displayed below the menu.

"Fox on a Shelf Copper Ale, Fresh Prince of Bel Ale Belgian Ale, Shwifty Bavarian Wheat, Nelly Fonzarelly Pale Ale, Sunday Morning Saison, It's Okay Berliner Weisse… man this place has a little of everything," said Kareem. "I feel weird asking about this though. I don't even know what to say. 'Excuse me, have you recently seen the skull of a man around here?' Yeah, that doesn't have a promising ring to it," he said.

"I know what you mean. It's weird, but there are many people here. Maybe someone has seen something. If you saw a skull at a brewery, that might be something memorable, right?" asked Tegan.

"Can I get you anything?" asked a young male bartender with long black hair and tattooed arms.

"No, not right now. We're just looking the menu over," replied Tegan.

"Cool. Well, if you change your mind, I'm Cadence," he said.

"That's a cool name. Pleased to meet you," Tegan said with a smile.

"Thanks, my parents come from a musical background, so they named me something kinda lyrical. I guess it worked because I'm in a band too now," he said.

"Really? That's cool. I love live music. What's your band's name?" Tegan asked.

"It's a metal band called Shamanic Wind. We play shows around mostly the East Valley," he replied.

Tegan attempted to give Kareem an inconspicuous elbow to his side.

"That sounds awesome. I, uh, love metal," she replied.

"We're doing okay. Crowds are a little small, but we just had a show last night at Club Red in Mesa. After we play, I am pumped up for days. Say, you should come to our next show," Cadence said.

"I would love to, but I'm from out of town. My friend here and I are just in from Texas for a couple of days. We head back on Saturday," Tegan replied.

"That's too bad. Maybe you will have to visit again so you can check us out," he said optimistically.

"Yeah, maybe," she said with a smile.

A customer at the end of the bar called out to Cadence to order a drink. After excusing himself to Tegan, he walked over to the customer.

"Did you hear that?" Tegan said to Kareem. "He's in the same band as Johnny Stamps! That means we have to be on the right track. Johnny knows we are onto him and coming for the skull. After Sun Devil Liquors yesterday he probably returned home to change for the show, took the skull to the venue, and gave it to Cadence for safekeeping. He would trust his bandmate," she calculated.

"I feel a heightened energy here," said Jamaica. "It's got to be here somewhere," she said.

"Yeah, but where?" replied Tegan.

Frustrated, Kareem, Tegan, and Jamaica each turned around. Resting their back against the bar, they scanned the room. A stocky, bald man with a long beard, and both arms covered in colored arm sleeves, smiled at Kareem and extended his pint glass as in a toast.

Kareem reacted with a barely noticeable, but present recoil in response to the gesture.

"Um, no. Not my type," Kareem whispered softly to Tegan.

Kareem smiled at the man and gave a nod, but then his gaze drifted above the man's head to the back wall in the Fire & Brimstone dining area. Brown boards in various shades covered the wall. Mounted to the wall were several black shelves holding a variety of objects, plates and cups of different colors and sizes, a miniature replica of an Oscar trophy, a battery-operated Feng Shui Lucky Cat with a waving arm, a skeleton wearing a sombrero figurine, and other various tchotchkes. And on one shelf sat what appeared to be a skull.

"Hey, get a load of that. Up on the shelf. Do you think..?" asked Kareem.

"Oh, damn. It's hard to tell from here, but it looks like it is a skull of something," replied Tegan.

"The question is, how do we get it?" asked Jamaica.

"Why don't you ladies order a drink?" suggested Kareem. "The bartender is busy now, so I will walk over to the dining area. Tegan, you order a couple of drinks, and when he turns to pour them, I will stand on a chair and grab the skull," he replied.

"That just might work, but you have nothing to put it in. How are we just going to walk out with it?" asked Tegan.

"Hmm… give me your bag," asked Kareem.

"It's a purse," Tegan replied.

"Maybe it's a European carryall," he replied. "It's certainly large enough for a skull," he said as he looked inside it.

"If you guys stopped giving me shit to carry all the time, I wouldn't need such a large one," Tegan shot back. "But it will not fit in there. I have a woven, reusable shopping bag in the trunk of the rental car. Run out and get it, then you can put it in there. When we walk out, everyone will think you're an artsy friend of the environment," she stated.

Kareem gave her a hesitant stare, but dropped his resistance and turned to walk to the parking lot.

"I am an artsy friend of the environment," he said, turning back around briefly.

Tegan and Jamaica awaited his return with the bag, then turned back toward the bar as Kareem walked to the dining area. The bald man smiled at Kareem as he walked past. The women looked over the menu while waiting for Kareem to get into position.

"I know what I want. How about you? Do you drink?" Tegan asked.

"I little. Not really anything like this. If I have a beer, it's just the regular supermarket beers, ya know?" responded Jamaica.

"Berliner Weiss is my favorite style. It's a little sour, sometimes tart, depending. Maybe the Nelly would be a good choice for you? Pale ale is good, and not overly hoppy," Tegan suggested.

"That sounds fine to me," Jamaica said. "I mean, it's for distraction anyway, right?"

"Uh, yeah… for distraction," Tegan said as she looked back at Kareem.

He appeared to be ready and gave her a head nod as he stood under the shelving in the dining area. She turned back toward the bar and put a finger up, signaling the bartender.

"Change your mind about that beer?" Cadence asked with a smile.

"Yeah, since we're here, we might as well have one, right?" she said flirtingly. "When in Rome."

Cadence gave a chuckle as he approached closer.

"What can I get you ladies?"

"A Berliner Weiss for me and a pale ale for my friend?" she replied.

"Coming right up," he said, reaching down for two fresh glasses, then turning around to pour them.

Tegan spun her head and gave a nod to Karee with the extra addition of bulging eyes to clarify that go time was now. He scooted a chair over and hurriedly climbed on top, then reached up to grab the eight-pound skull from the shelf.

People in the restaurant noticed Kareem grab the skull, but none seemed to care enough to speak out. With the brewery being crowded and Cadence pouring beer for Tegan, he didn't notice Kareem abscond to the parking lot with the skull in the bag. A woman's attention gravitated to the bag as Kareem walked by, causing her to turn to her friend.

"What an artsy friend of the environment that man is," the woman said.

Outside, Kareem placed the bag in the car's trunk and returned to join his friends at the bar.

"Can I get a Shwifty?" Kareem asked when Cadence noticed his return.

He put a twenty-dollar bill on the table for all three beers and the three found a seat at the long table in the back.

"Step one, complete," Kareem confirmed. "Now what?"

"Seems we got the easy end of the deal," Tegan replied. "Step two is to bury the skull in hallowed ground. So, I guess we need to find a church around here and bury it," added Tegan.

"Not necessarily," said Jamaica. "When you texted me to come out to meet you, I wasn't sure where the skull was located, but I knew we might have to bury it in a hurry. If the Red Ghost came after us, we might not be able to get away and find a church to bury the skull. Like the Boy Scouts, a good witch is always prepared," she said.

"Oh, you're a good witch?" Kareem asked.

"Good can be subjective," she answered with a wink as she finished her beer. "Let's go to the car," she followed.

At the park, Ty and Carson were attempting to avoid the now angered camel. The Red Ghost darted at them as they dodged each attack.

"Damn, I hope the others are having better luck than we are," huffed Ty. "This thing is pissed off!"

"We should separate so he can only focus on one of us. Maybe make a run for it," suggested Carson.

"Run? If we run, it will chase us. Those things can run up to forty miles per hour in short bursts. We can't outrun it. And it apparently is happy enough crashing into the trees attempting to get us," responded Ty.

The Red Ghost ran toward Carson and attempted to bite him, and the skeleton mount attempted to grab him, but despite the excursion from the prior attacks, he evaded the attempt by enough space to avoid contact.

"Watch out for that thick area on the underbelly," yelled Ty.

"What? What area?" Carson yelled in return.

"That's called the brisket and they can pin you down and sit on you, attempting to suffocate you," Ty shouted.

"That's not the brisket I like, and I don't plan on getting that close to him," Carson yelled back.

The two men had no weapons to attack the Red Ghost with, but even if they did, they had no time as the camel kept them on the defensive throughout the attack.

"I don't know how we're going to get out of this one," Ty said.

"We can't knock the rider off because he's still strapped in like he was when he was alive," replied Carson. "It's time for Plan B, whatever that is!"

Jamaica grabbed a bag from the back of the trunk and walked off along a path into the orchards.

"Bring your shopping bag, Kareem," she said.

Tegan and Kareem caught up to her, standing under a grove of peach trees.

"I'm going to conduct this in two parts," Jamaica said. "First, I will cast a consecration spell on the object. I do this with my tools to bless them for sacred use. In this case, I will bless the skull. This will cleanse the object of past influences, then charging it with a fresh energy that corresponds to the intended magical use," she stated.

"I think clearing it of its past influences is critical," Kareem stated.

"Intent and focused concentration are the most important elements. I will begin by clearing my mind and releasing all unwanted thoughts, taking a few moments to really bring myself into the now," Jamaica continued. "Now, if you can hand me the skull," she asked of Kareem.

He reached into the bag, removing the skull of William Avant, and handed it to Jamaica. She took it and held it with both hands, then imagined a ball of white light, cleansing and purifying the light with its cleansing power. She imagined the white light flowing down her arms, flowing through her hands, and into the skull she was holding. She concentrated on removing all extraneous energies from the skull and visualized it filling with a golden yellow light.

"I cleanse and purify this sacred skull," she spoke, while continuing to visualize the skull pulsing with golden yellow light until it felt clean.

Again, she focused on the ball of white light, allowing the light to flow into the skull. This time seeing it filling with blue-white light.

"I bless and consecrate this sacred skull," she spoke, continuing to focus blue-white light into the skull for a few moments.

"He's really worked up now. It seems like he's coming at us from every direction," Carson said.

"I got my head on a swivel now!" replied an exhausted Ty as he stood and dusted himself off from escaping the latest attempt from the Red Ghost in the same ramada he and Carson previously planned their attack.

"Now for Step Two, Part B," said Jamaica. "The earth itself is sacred. We know it as our mother and it sustains us, as well as all living things. I will use natural objects here in this orchard to create a sacred space. I will bless five stones, four representing the elements by their color," she said as she reached into her bag. "Orange to represent fire," she said as she removed the first stone. "Black for earth. Blue for water. And white for air. The fifth stone, a red one, represents the Red Ghost," she said as Kareem and Tegan watched in silence.

She placed the four stones around a small perimeter large enough to hold the skull; air in the eastern quadrant, water in the west, fire in the south, and earth in the north. As she positioned the stones in their place, she recited:

"To the earth, into the ground

Here to stay, the magic's bound.

To heal the earth, and Gaia's mind,

Within this stone, the power binds.

To inspire reverence, our wounds to heal,

By my words, the magic's sealed."

She repeated the incantation over each stone as she placed it in the ground. She removed a small trowel from the bag and dug a deep enough hole to bury the skull. As she sat the skull into the earth, she placed the fifth stone in its mouth, and covered it with dirt.

At the Riparian Preserve, Ty and Carson were struggling to fend off the Red Ghost. Ty stood behind a tree, out of breath, and waiting on the Red Ghost's next attack. Carson attempted to make a run for it, but tripped over a large rock just on the side of the path. He fell to the ground and rolled over to see the Red Ghost bellowing and preparing for the last charge. The skeleton rider pointed at the downed man, ordering the Red Ghost to charge. Carson curled up in a fetal position preparing for impact, while simultaneously in another part of town, Jamaica patted down the final bit of dirt over the skull. The red aura around the camel glowed brighter from a faint hint to an intense ball of light. Carson and Ty heard a whoosh! In an instant, the charging Red Ghost was gone. The spirit of Spitfire, Hi Jolly, and William Avant were finally at rest.

Carson remained balled up, but released as the expected impact never occurred. Dumbfounded from the events of the last few minutes, Carson looked up where the Red Ghost had been, and then over at his partner to make sure he was okay. Ty continued to prop himself up against the tree and Carson laid on his back on the dusty trail, both men sweating profusely and suffering from elevated heart rates.

"Holy shit! Looks like they did it," said Ty, gasping against the tree.

"And not a moment too soon! I thought I was a goner right then," responded Ty, speaking up into the now dark, starry night.

"Can you make it back to the parking lot?" asked Ty.

Carson stared, attempting to gauge the distance to the car. He sighed.

"Yeah. Just give me a minute. I might need some new shorts," Carson said.

Carson sat up, made it to his knees, and eventually stood with a hand on his hips.

"Okay, we've got this," he said, attempting to reassure himself.

He walked over to Ty and gave him a slap on the back as they walked back to the parking lot with their arms around each other, holding one another up.

"Gets easier every time, doesn't it?" quipped Ty.

"Every fucking time," Carson answered.

The park was technically closed, leaving the parking lot empty except for the car Jamaica left earlier. A car pulled in and the headlights shone on the battered and dusty duo, now sitting on the cement short wall at the park entrance.

"C'mon boys. No time to sit around doing nothing. It's getting late," teased Tegan from the passenger window.

CHAPTER 16

THE TAP HOUSE IN THE WILDERNESS

Friday, March 25, 2016

Late morning, the crew headed back to Dreamy Draw to remove all files from the underground lab. On the way, Carson pulled into a QuikTrip and gingerly walked inside wearing a ball cap and sunglasses. He grabbed a spicy cheese taquito from the roller meat section and a store brand sweet tea from the cooler. Stepping up to the counter, he laid his items down and waited for his turn.

"That'll be $4.35," said the cashier. "Cash back?"

"No, thanks," replied Carson, handing the man a five-dollar bill.

"Cash… how old school," replied the cashier. "You look like you had a rough night."

"You could say that," replied Carson as he gathered the items and exited the front door.

Arriving back at Dreamy Draw, Carson pulled to the side to let Tegan and Kareem get out near the point where Tegan had previously emerged.

"If you don't mind, Ty and I will sit this one out," replied Carson. "There's a fifty-inch canvas duffle bag I picked up this morning at Goodwill in the trunk. Get in, grab any file, journal, folder, or notebook that isn't bolted down, and let's get back out. Think twenty minutes will cover it?" he asked.

"Getting back in shouldn't be difficult, and it's not too far to the bunker. Twenty minutes should do it," replied Tegan.

Kareem grabbed the sack, and they carefully walked down into the valley below the bicycle path and headed through the dry wash to the exit Tegan created only days ago. They entered through the busted board opening and jogged to the lab door entrance.

"Damn, this place is bigger than I expected from your description," Kareem said.

He pried the door open a little wider so they both could enter. Like Tegan's reaction on her initial visit, he gasped at the contents of the room. He saw the cell and walked over to the other door to peek in on the spaceship, still supplying a low humming noise from its damaged hull.

"You hit the filing cabinet. I want to get a closer look at the ship," he said as he walked toward the door and cautiously opened it.

Looking at the front of the saucer, he could see what appeared to be portholes. One of the portholes was broken and gave him hope he could peek inside. He also noticed the back hatch was opened. He speculated that was presumably how the military personnel removed the alien pilots. Pushing on the hood of the vehicle, he felt confident it would hold his weight. Carefully, he climbed on the front and looked inside. The control room of the craft showed severe damage, but still complete enough to confirm it was not from this world.

He removed his phone and took several photos. He noticed something on the floor of the craft that had jammed under a floor console in the vehicle's front. He wasn't sure what it was. Maybe a tool. He smashed his fist into the portal and caused the hole to grow wide enough so he could fit his arm up to the shoulder inside it. He grabbed the unknown item, removed it, and shoved it into the backpack. Scampering down the front of the craft, he turned his attention to the rear.

Below the saucer, he saw several small Ion propulsion rockets on the bottom of the ship. Turning attention back to the end of the craft, he could crawl somewhat into the back bay of the saucer. While there, he noticed two more objects similar to the one he retrieved from the front seat. Held in a mostly concealed panel, he only noticed them because a small portion of the panel had cracked off.

"You about done in there?" yelled Tegan. "It's time to go!"

Kareem took a last look around the interior of the ship and backed out of the door.

"Ready, Freddy," he said as he reentered the room and put the other found items into the duffle bag.

"Bring that bag over here," said Tegan.

She had an arm-full of folders and notebooks that she placed into the bag. Once the filing cabinet was empty, she looked around the room again, confirming there wasn't anything else to take.

"Grab a few of those bottles from the cabinet. That's where I got the space dust. Who knows what those other samples might do," Tegan said.

"I'm on it," Kareem said as he smashed the glass and grabbed as many containers as he could carry.

"C'mon, let's get out of here," she said.

They rejoined Carson and Ty in the overflow parking lot just up the street from the park entrance, and within the twenty-minute timeframe.

"Nice work, guys," Carson said as they left the park and headed back toward Chandler.

In the parking lot, a young woman wearing a navy polo shirt and hat with a StarShield logo parked in the spot vacated by Carson. She watched them drive off in the rental car. As they disappeared, she removed a cell phone from her pocket.

"Commander Williams, we have a problem," said Field Agent Muriel Washington.

"It's too bad it isn't closer to sunset," said Ty.

"Why? You have a date with another camel?" joked Carson.

"I don't care if I ever see another camel again after last night," Ty replied. "No, I saw online only a few miles from Dreamy Draw. Along the canal by Camelback, there's a bat cave. Similar to home," he said.

"Really? I had no idea," said Carson.

"This isn't really the right time of year, though. Mainly from May to October and at sunset, thousands of Mexican free-tailed bats emerge from a flood control tunnel by the canal. It's a little challenging to locate, but I think we could find it. Plus, we would see them flying around," reported Ty.

"I am excited to try the next place. A good way to wrap up our investigation this week," replied Carson.

"Where's that?" asked Tegan.

"Arizona Wilderness in Gilbert, near the Chandler border. It opened just a couple of years ago, but has already made a name for itself already," Carson reported.

"Beer and Wilderness? Sounds like our kind of place," said Kareem.

"Definitely. The brewers get inspiration for new recipes by hiking out in the wilderness, buying local organic products, and even foraging in the wild for ingredients to be included in their beer. They opened in 2013, along with about twenty-six-hundred other breweries around the world. Out of all of them, *Ratebeer.com* named Arizona Wilderness the *Best New Brewery in the World*," Carson reported.

"Best new brewery in the entire world? And we're here in the same town? Yes, it's a must visit," replied Tegan.

"They have an agricultural saison series, which interests me. I still love the stouts, but saisons are a style I also enjoy. I hope that they have some on tap. I haven't checked the menu yet, but I saw they are having an event today, so it might be busy. It's a can release day, and I don't know if we will snag one. I've read prior can releases here are very popular and draw long lines causing them to sell out in hours. They also have the beer on draught, so we can at least order that if we miss out on the cans," Carson said.

The event drew the interest of the local beer-drinking community. Even though there were parking spaces on all sides of the brewery, every space was full. Although it was smaller now, the line to pick up cans from the day's release still extended to the side of the building. Carson had to park in the lot behind the store, belonging to the extended stay hotel facility, but it also served as a satellite parking for the brewery because of its increased demand since the award announcement.

"The brewery now comprises the main dining room, a front and back patio, and a tasting room. When they first started, part of the building used to be a bagel company, but the brewery became so popular eventually they bought the bagel shop and turned it into the taproom," stated Carson.

"What's the release today?" asked Kareem.

"It's called Chocolate Bunny, a chocolate milk porter. Sounds pretty cool, and it's a splendid chance to check out a beer release in a new town," replied Carson.

"I like this setup. The signs outside are like National Forest signs, and the fence is rustic," Ty said as they walked past the line of people waiting for cans and added their name to the waitlist.

"It will only be a few minutes if you want to sit outside on the front patio," said the host. "We just have to clear a spot."

"That will be great," smiled Tegan.

Within ten minutes, the host returned to the group.

"Right this way," she said, leading them to a semi-circle shaped table with a large table consisting of a glass top and a log stump base.

A tall, slender woman, Cynamon Scott, approached and introduced herself as the group's server.

"Have you been here before?" Cynamon asked.

"No, just visiting from out of town. Headed back to Texas tomorrow, but wanted to try this place out. I hear it's all the rage," said Carson.

"It has certainly picked up the past few months," she said.

"Since winning the Best Brewery award?" asked Ty.

"Yes, that has definitely increased traffic. Since then, we've been busy every night. I've been here since almost the beginning and work as often as I can when I'm not going to school," she replied.

"What are you studying? Asked Kareem.

"Russian and Eastern European Languages and Literature at Arizona State," she replied.

"That's impressive," replied Tegan. "I'm afraid my knowledge stops at Tolstoy and Dostoyevsky," she added.

"Since you've been here since the beginning, what do you recommend?" asked Ty.

"I'm a big fan of the meatloaf sliders if you're not super hungry," she said. "There are three of them and they come with fresh jalapenos, drizzled with a wort gravy, pepper jack cheese, and served on a pretzel bun. However, they are like a shareable appetizer. No sides with that, but you can add one if you want a meal."

"Those sound great," replied Kareem. "What side would you recommend?"

"Duck fat fries," Cynamon replied. "Easily one of our favorites. If you want something a little more filling, and this might sound weird at first, but I promise it is excellent. Our peanut butter and jalapeño jelly burger. That includes white cheddar and thick-cut bacon. And I recommend getting that with the beer-battered onion rings," she replied.

"That does sound weird," Carson added, putting the menu down on the table. "But I am adventurous, so put me down for one," he said.

"Make that two," replied Ty.

"And I will also have a burger, but the apple and brie," replied Tegan.

"That is another excellent burger," Cynamon said. "Really, all the burgers here are great. The beef is a locally sourced item, and the ingredients are fresh. Even the spicy black bean burger is great," she said.

"And I guess, since it is the beer of the day, what? Four? Chocolate Bunnies?" replied Carson.

"For sure. I will bring those beers right out," Cynamon replied.

"So… Phoenix… Am I right?" Carson said to the group. "This has been some trip and investigation," he replied.

"Indeed, it has been!" said Tegan. "I've seen more than I ever thought possible."

"And, Ty, ole' buddy, I wasn't too sure either of us, or at times maybe both of us, were going to walk away last night," Carson added.

"I still feel it. All over. That was a total body workout and a couple of those charges were too close for comfort," Ty responded.

"You guys and Jamaica did a great job finding the skull of William Avant and putting him, Hi Jolly, and Spitfire to rest," said Carson.

"Yeah, we would have been completely lost without her. We wouldn't even know where to look for the skull or what to do with it if we found it," said Kareem.

"It was really fortunate running into her at Tortas Ahogadas," replied Tegan. "It's interesting how sometimes brief moments can seem minor at the time, but may have a bigger purpose later and we don't yet recognize it. She turned out to be a big part of the investigation and it was something that at first seemed to be a chance encounter about a piece of jewelry," she reflected.

"More and more, I am a believer in there are no accidents and we meet people when we need and how we need," replied Carson. "I still think back to my days at Giddy Ups and how Ty just showed up out of nowhere, and that put me on a completely different path in life. I met you guys, we started doing these investigations, and life has improved. I don't have those same feelings that were my routine. Well, sometimes, to be honest, I do, but it's rare. Not like it was. Seems like a lifetime ago, but really, it hasn't been that long," responded Carson.

Cynamon returned with four pints of the Chocolate Bunny and distributed one to each at the table. Ty took the first sip and waited for the others to try theirs.

"Wow. That's smooth, sweet, and chocolatey," Ty said.

"Look at the head on that. It just sits pretty, it's dark, and it's wonderful. This might be the best beer I've had in a while," said Kareem.

Carson just sat back with his eyes closed, reflecting on Phoenix, the Red Ghost, and this beer.

"Damn, this is incredible. It's like drinking the freaking Easter Bunny," said Carson. "A solid porter, smooth, the cocoa nibs, the Madagascar vanilla, some roastiness with some bitterness perfectly balanced out by the sweetness. Completely creamy and chocolatey. This is like heaven in a glass," replied Carson.

Cynamon returned to check on the table.

"How do you like the Bunny?"

"It's getting a solid five from me on Untappd," replied Kareem. "You guys have made a perfect beer," he added.

"Thanks, we're thrilled with that one. It's a collaboration actually with Stillwater Artisanal Ales," she replied.

"I've heard good things about them as well," said Ty.

"We have another beer that we still have on from our tapping last week. Probably won't last much longer," said Cynamon.

"What's that?" asked Tegan.

"A special edition of our American Presidential Stout," Cynamon.

"That sounds superb," replied Carson.

"Yes, it's another one of our popular beers. We usually bring it out at the beginning of the year, around President's Day. This is a barrel-aged version, aged in Old Forester and Woodford Reserve barrels. We have had a few barrel-aged versions and we use the Presidential Stout because it's so popular, and it gives people a comparison showing how the barrels change a beer they are familiar with," answered Cynamon.

"If it's available, I will take one," replied Carson.

"And one for me too," said Ty.

"Just to warn you, that one's eleven percent," Cynamon replied.

"I think I will sit this one out," said Tegan. "How about Gibraltar's Gose?" Tegan suggested.

"I can do that. And how about you?" Cynamon asked Kareem.

"Wet Beaver Wit," he replied. "Sounds interesting…"

"It's named after wilderness areas in Arizona. Wet Beaver Creek is a stream with one major tributary, Dry Beaver Creek. They come together in McGuireville, Arizona," she replied.

"It says it's a Pale Wheat Ale," Kareem said.

"And it's brewed with a heavy amount of beets," Cynamon added.

"Beets? That's unusual. I will stick with that," Kareem confirmed.

"So, one hell of a trip," replied Ty. "I love the investigations, but I always enjoy getting back to Austin."

"That's the sign that we survived it," replied Tegan.

"What d'ya say we get a group selfie here at Arizona Wilderness with this Chocolate Bunny as proof we survived another investigation?" suggested Kareem.

"We have had some tough run-ins. This week was especially scary. The prior ones were at least animals, and we knew we had a fighting chance, but this time, it was supernatural. There was no way we could have physically defeated it. Our only chance was mystically, and I didn't even know that I believed in that stuff. Animals are one thing, even hidden animals that stumble into the public eye, but ghosts?" replied Ty.

"Or aliens," added Tegan, still troubled by her time in the Dreamy Draw lab.

"Tomorrow is your chance. We will be back home getting ready for Astros games and relaxing," replied Carson.

"Or going over notes with Jourdyn and looking at the next investigation, responded Ty.

"We found all of those files and whatever Kareem brought back from the underground lair at Dreamy Draw," replied Tegan.

"Look, I know business has increased - the calls, the requests for interviews, and everything else since we began, but that's a significant sign. That means people are taking these sightings more seriously, and they see us out there and reach out. In the past, they had the same sightings but kept it to themselves because they thought their friends, family, or the public would think they were crazy. The internet and the threat of something going viral is a big enough scare that the people who report false things are actually declining more than ever before," replied Carson.

"That's true. Re-shares of videos where people say you're an idiot is something that is difficult to live down," said Ty.

"Hopefully there is some downtime once we get back, but I'm excited to see the things Tegan and Kareem brought back," said Ty.

"At least we've got tonight," said Carson.

"Who needs tomorrow?" asked Ty.

CHAPTER 17

AUSTIN CITY LIMITS

Saturday, March 26, 2016

"Before we hit the airport this afternoon," replied Carson, "there's one more spot I want to stop by again," said Carson.

"Which one is that?" asked Tegan.

"World of Beer Tempe," replied Carson. "It's on the way to the airport, and if you remember, they are supposed to have that Peach Lunacy today, which is not only hard to get, but it's pretty high ABV," said Carson.

"Fine with me," replied Kareem. "I really liked Tempe. It felt like Austin a bit to me."

"We might have to hit up VOX Table on South Lamar Boulevard tomorrow. My treat. Heard they have some good crispy frog legs," replied Carson.

"God no. Frog legs? Yuck!" replied Tegan.

"Maybe a more appetizing tidbit is the fact that I secured the WrestleMania tickets for Dallas. So let's plan next week with no monsters," replied Carson.

"At least monsters in the wilderness," said Kareem.

"Here we are," said Ty, pulling into the parking lot in downtown Tempe just outside of World of Beer. "I'm going to miss this place," he said.

"Yeah, a great way to get introduced to different styles of beer, breweries from around the world, and just beer you wouldn't otherwise encounter," said Carson.

"Let's get in here and get that Peach Lunacy. Twelve percent before the flight helps for the flight tensions," replied Tegan.

"Yes, flying used to be so fun. Now, it's more of an inconvenience and I would just as soon skip it. Maybe we need a T.I.M.E. Agency team bus?" said Carson.

"I don't think we need to go that far," replied Ty.

Walking into Word of Beer, it wasn't busy as it was still early and most of the people of Tempe, especially the college-age customers in nearby Arizona State, were saving their visit for the later night hours when the streets of Tempe came alive. As Carson ascended the three steps from the short platform at the store entrance to the main level, he smiled, seeing a familiar face.

"Vanilla Heat? You are here again?" asked Carson.

"You don't become number one by just showing up here and there," said Vanilla Heat. "You have to put in the work. I don't have many per night, but I come in frequently enough that it adds up," he continued.

"Where's the WOB Father?" asked Ty.

"Fuck, who knows? I haven't seen him in a few days. We might have to set up a search party," replied Vanilla Heat. "When do you guys head out?"

"On the way to the airport now," said Tegan. "Just time for a drink or two before we drop the car off at the airport and head back to Austin," said Tegan.

"It was great meeting you these past couple of weeks. Good luck with your future investigations. I would love to get out to Austin sometimes. I hear there are some great beers out there," said Vanilla Heat.

"Yeah, and we found some WOB's, but up by Dallas and Ft. Worth, so you won't get a point unless you drive a bit," laughed Carson.

"Then I will have to think about that!" replied Vanilla Heat with a smile that showed off his rugged good looks.

"You guys talking about the Peach Lunacy? Can I pour ya four?" asked the server.

"Make it five," said Vanilla Heat, tossing his debit card on the counter.

"You don't have that point?" asked Tegan.

"This time," Vanilla Heat said, "I'll make an exception."

"If you are ever out in Austin, I hope you look us up," replied Kareem.

"Definitely I will. Maybe grab a few beers, hunt a few monsters," Vanilla Heat said.

"You never know. I just received a text from our office manager, Jourdyn. She said that some visitors reported seeing an Ahool hanging out with the bats on Congress Street. Might be a new investigation," replied Caron.

"Ahool? That would be a substantial case," replied Vanilla Heat.

"Speaking of great, how 'bout that Peach Lunacy?" asked Tegan.

"Yeah, it's certainly a classic. I think coming out in limited quantities really builds the mystique of the beer," answered Vanilla Heat.

The group finished the beer and enjoyed talking to and shooting the breeze with the local legend, Vanilla Heat. Hanging out in Tempe and enjoying the beers, especially the local Arizona beers, was a fantastic experience.

"The Phoenix beer scene is booming. I am glad I met a few connections out here so I can keep up with my trading partners. I want to keep exploring this Phoenix market as it grows," replied Ty.

"Hey, I checked out Yelp, and if we could hit up Paletas Betty just down the road, I would appreciate it," stated Kareem.

"Heck yeah. What better way to end the trip than with wonderful handmade popsicle? Jourdyn said she would pick us up at the airport," stated Carson.

"Popsicles, I'm good with. Your idea of frog legs when we get home? Not so much," replied Tegan.

"We'll see what happens when we get back home," answered Carson.

to be continued…

BEER LIST

Arizona Wilderness Brewing Company Chocolate Bunny Chocolate Milk Porter

Arizona Wilderness Brewing Company DBA American Presidential Stout (Old Forester/Woodford Reserve Barrels) Russian Imperial Stout

Arizona Wilderness Brewing Company Gibraltar's Gose

Arizona Wilderness Brewing Company The Roosevelts American Imperial IPA

Arizona Wilderness Brewing Company Wet Beaver Witbier

Beer Research Institute 480G IPA

Beer Research Institute Belgian Tickler Belgian Dark Ale

Beer Research Institute Dark Side Till I Die American Imperial Stout

Beer Research Institute Dirty Jesus American Brown Ale

Beer Research Institute Fire Squirrel Red Ale

Beer Research Institute Sticky Morning Sex Sweet Milk Stout

Beer Research Institute Street Cred Black IPA

Beer Research Institute War Paint Red IPA

Borderlands Brewing Company Noche Dulce Vanilla Porter

Button Brew House All Souls American Stout

Button Brew House Button IPA

Button Brew House Chiltepin Red Chile Beer

Button Brew House El Jefe Vice Hefeweizen

Carlsbad Tavern Bat Brew Pale Ale

Cartel Brewery Bingo Bango Bongo IPA

Cartel Brewery Desert Pale Ale American Pale Ale

Cartel Brewery F.Y.I.T.M American Imperial IPA

Cartel Brewery The Great Save Berliner Weisse

Cartel Brewery The Real Vanilla Heat Nitro Imperial Porter

Celis White Belgian-Style Witbier

College Street Brewhouse Big Blue Van Fruit Beer

Dubina Brewing Company Fall Maple Strong Ale

Four Peaks Brewing Company Barrel Aged Sirius Black Russian Imperial Stout

Four Peaks Brewing Company Kilt Lifter Scottish-Style Amber Ale

Four Peaks Brewing Company Peach Ale Fruit and Field Ale

Friends & Allies Noisy Cricket IPA

Grand Canyon Brewing Company Scotchy Scotch Scotch Ale

Helton Brewing Company Nitro Milk Stout Sweet Milk Stout

Helton Brewing Company Northeast IPA

Helton Brewing Company Plum Saison

Helton Brewing Company Single Hopped American Pale Ale

Historic Brewing Company Barrel Aged Piehole Porter

Historic Brewing Company Screaming Goat Farmhouse Ale - Saison

Historic Brewing Company Undercover Cucumber Blonde Ale

Huss Brewing Company Koffee Kölsch

Huss Brewing Company Magic In A Barrel American Pale Ale

Huss Brewing Company Magic in the Ivy American Pale Ale

Huss Brewing Company Peanut Butter Husstler Sweet Milk Stout

Lumberyard Brewing Company Flagstaff IPA

McFate Brewing Company Coffee Milk Stout Sweet Milk Stout

McFate Brewing Company Hatch Chile Gatos Chile Beer

Mesquite River Brewing Heatstroke Wheat beer

Mesquite River Brewing My Honey Bee Blonde Ale

Mesquite River Brewing To The Wall American IPA

Miller Brewing Company Hamm's Premium Lager

Mogollon Brewing Company Wapiti Amber Ale

Mother Bunch Brewing Cherry Popper Porter

Mother Bunch Brewing Lost Highway Black IPA

Mother Road Tower Station IPA

Mudshark Brewing Company Desert Magic IPA

Mudshark Brewing Company Lunacy Belgian-Style Witbier

Mudshark Brewing Company Peach Lunacy Belgian-Style Witbier

North Mountain Brewing Nativity in Black (N.I.B.) Imperial Stout

Old World Brewery Dark Knight Porter

Owl's Orchard Brewery Stout

Owl's Orchard Brewery American IPA

Owl's Orchard Brewery Gingerbread Porter

Owl's Orchard Brewery Desert Dweller Wheat beer

Owl's Orchard Brewery Tangelo Ale Fruit Beer

Papago Brewing Company Coconut Joe Sweet Milk Stout

Papago Brewing Company Elsie's Irish Coffee Milk Stout

Papago Brewing Company Orange Blossom Wheat beer

Phoenix Ale Brewery Camelback IPA

Phoenix Ale Brewery Cranberry Oatmeal Stout

Phoenix Ale Brewery Watermelon Ale Fruit and Field Ale

Pinthouse Pizza Electric Jellyfish IPA

Prescott Brewing Company Achocolypse Porter

Prescott Brewing Company Heroes 19 American Brown Ale

Real Ale Brewing Company Commissar American Imperial Stout

Real Ale Brewing Company Phoenix Winter Ale

San Tan Brewing Devils Ale American Pale Ale

San Tan Brewing HopShock IPA

San Tan Brewing Sex Panther Double Chocolate Porter

Sleepy Dog Brewery Coco's American Imperial Stout

Sleepy Dog Brewery Feisty Chihuahua Bohemian Pilsner

Sleepy Dog Brewery Parched Pooch Hefeweizen

Sleepy Dog Brewery The Belly Rub Belgian Tripel

Sleepy Dog Brewery Wolfpack American Imperial IPA

Sonoran Brewing Company White Chocolate Ale Wheat beer

SunUp Brewing Company White Russian Imperial Coffee Stout

Superstition Meadery Tahitian Honeymoon Mead

THAT Brewery Strawberry Blonde Blonde Ale

Uncle Bear's Brewery Peanut Butter Cup Porter

Wanderlust Brewing Company Pan American Stout Nitro Imperial Stout

Wren House Brewing Company Black Caddis Porter

Wren House Brewing Company Bourbon Barrel Olmec Imperial Stout

Wren House Brewing Company Globe Miami Weiss Berliner Weisse

Wren House Brewing Company Hi Jolly Wheat beer

Wren House Brewing Company Jomax Coffee Oatmeal Stout

Wren House Brewing Company Lady Banks Gose

Wren House Brewing Company Señor Gallo Lager

Wren House Brewing Company Who Hit John American Imperial Porter

XII West Brewing Company Fox on a Shelf Copper Ale

XII West Brewing Company Fresh Prince of Bel Ale Belgian Blonde

XII West Brewing Company It's Okay Berliner Weisse

XII West Brewing Company Nelly Fonzarelly American Pale Ale

XII West Brewing Company Shwifty Bavarian Wheat

XII West Brewing Company Sunday Morning Saison

ABOUT THE AUTHOR

Mark Trollinger is a fan of cryptozoology and craft beer. He grew up in Yellow Springs, Ohio and attended the University of Rio Grande in Rio Grande, Ohio - not far from Point Pleasant, WV, thus igniting Mark's interest in cryptozoology, beginning with Mothman.

He is the author of *The Chupacabra and the Bat Rastard*, *Champ and a Bit of Sunshine*, *The Red Ghost and a Chocolate Bunny*, *The Loveland Frog and the Narrow Path*, and *Tegan Stone and the Gibson County Beast* - all books in the Texans Investigating Mysterious Entities (T.I.M.E.) cryptozoology and craft beer adventure series.

The Red Ghost and a Chocolate Bunny is the third title in the T.I.M.E. series

Mark Trollinger's

Website

Mark Trollinger's

Amazon.com Author Page

WORDS FROM THE AUTHOR

Welcome to book three in the cryptozoology and craft beer series. In the first two books, I wrote about creatures that were more well-known cryptids in the world, even with those who may only have a passing knowledge about cryptozoology. One of the challenges with popular cryptids is that because they are so well known there is a vast body of literature on them. In my attempt at writing somewhat realistic fiction I read as much research as possible and attempt to synthesis that information into my fictional story to hopefully stay true with what's already out there. One day during the 2017-2018 NFL season, my friend Tim and I were watching the games in a local bar, and he suggested that I create my own character so there wouldn't be that depth of prior information to consider.

That thought hadn't even crossed my mind before. That then became the original idea for this story, and I did create two creatures that I briefly considered for the main cryptid in this book. Then one day I stumbled upon the web page of *The Pine Barrens Institute*. It contained information about popular cryptids, but also more obscure cryptids. As I clicked through the pages one cryptid stood out, and it was actually a true story. The cryptid was the Red Ghost of Arizona – a mysterious camel with a skeleton rider strapped to its back. Suddenly I was intrigued and thought this was the creature to use. The idea of using an existing but obscure cryptid was interesting. The story could follow eyewitness accounts and it would help bring the creature back into the spotlight so it doesn't disappear. This might also spark reader interest in other lesser-known cryptids.

From the beginning, I planned to spotlight Phoenix. I left Atlanta on election night 2004 and drove in a hard rain from Atlanta to Birmingham. Originally, Phoenix was going to be a layoff move before my roommate and I moved to New Hampshire; however, that part never happened. Now I have been in Arizona for 15 years. The temperature is one of the biggest challenges living here. From May to September, it is hot, but most of the time we are in air conditioning, so it's tolerable. And don't let the cliché fool you – a dry heat is still very hot. Over the years Phoenix, I feel, has really boomed in terms of culture, restaurants, and of course craft beer. Bringing those factors into this book I think is helpful in showing what Phoenix has to offer. If you are curious about the craft beer scene in Phoenix, just look at the award winners of the 2019 Great American Beer Festival in Denver. The number of award winners continues to grow annually.

Since the release of *Champ and a Bit of Sunshine*, I set up a book signing tour. My planning phase began with a much larger undertaking of several cities across the United States and one in Mexico, but I ended up with five stops: Scottsdale, Las Vegas, Tucson, Austin, and of course San Antonio. It was a great time, and I met several cool people along the way. Thank you to everyone who came out to see me and buy a book. I do enjoy connecting with readers. My goal is to fine-tune my preparation of event planning and get back on the road again in the near future.

I want to thank Fred and Karl with Mesquite River Brewing in Scottsdale, AZ; Nathan with Bad Beat Brewing in Henderson, NV; Erika with Button Brew House in Marana, AZ; Chris and Whitney with The Brewtorium in Austin, TX; and Scott, Mekala, & Jason from Freetail Brewing in San Antonio. Thank you all for allowing me a little time and space in your breweries for my book signing stops.

Thanks to Joe Harris and Charles Verner, not only with help related to the local Texas beers, but for meeting me during my visit. Charles drove from Dallas to San Antonio, hung out with me for a while, then returned to all in the same day! Thanks to Rosalind Sterling for providing sensitivity reading services.

I have also made some cryptozoology connections during this process. Loren Coleman and I have corresponded on Twitter about my books, and one day I do hope to have a show there. We had some plans in the works, but life events got in the way. As you know, Loren is one of the most well-known cryptozoology researchers out there. I can't say enough about the International Cryptozoology Museum in Portland, ME that he runs. If you are a fan of cryptozoology, this is a must-visit location. I encourage everyone to stop by and support the museum. Help preserve these types of collections so we can learn more about the creatures that are hidden for now, but may one day step further into the light. Derek Hayes is another person who is delivering cryptozoology to you. I highly encourage you to subscribe to *Cryptid Crate*, tune into his podcast, *Monsters Among Us*, or you might catch him on television on cryptozoology or paranormal shows. I have also found an enjoyed the content on several cryptozoology sites such as the aforementioned *Pines Barren Institute*, *Cryptid*

Campfire, *Strange Little Lands* – makers of awesome cryptid dioramas, *Cryptid Comforts*, and of course an excellent combiner of cryptozoology and cocktails – the *Cryptid Bartender*.

I hope you enjoy the tale of the Red Ghost and come visit Phoenix to check out the local beers, restaurants, sporting events, and local musicians such as Marcus Weeden, Blaine Long, Snailmate, Walt Richardson, the Darts, and Mega Ran, as well as many other wonderful artists in town.

This cover of the book reflects the craft beer-inspired redesign from Nyssa Iniguez. She is a graphic design student and I have enjoyed working with her on this series.

Here we go for Round Three, and as always, ¡Viva World of Beer Tempe!

ONE NIGHT ONLY
Pensive Opossum Productions Presents
CRYPTOZOOLOGY & CRAFT BEER
BOOK SIGNING
SATURDAY
03
NOVEMBER
6 pm - 8 pm
PAPERBACKS
$15
SIGNED COPY
SPECIAL APPEARANCE BY
MARK D. TROLLINGER
AUTHOR OF:
THE CHUPACABRA AND THE BAT RASTARD
CHAMP AND A BIT OF SUNSHINE
MESQUITE RIVER BREWING CO.
13610 N SCOTTSDALE RD, # 18, SCOTTSDALE, ARIZONA 85254

Mesquite River Brewery, Scottsdale, AZ

Bad Beat Brewing, Henderson, NV

Button Brew House, Marana, AZ

The Brewtorium, Austin, TX

Freetail Brewing, San Antonio, TX

FIELD NOTES

This is the re-release of book three in the cryptozoology and craft beer series. This cover represents a lighter, chalk-like version designed by Nyssa Iniguez. I call it the craft beer-inspired cover.

The non-profit organization I selected for this book and will donate 15% of sales to support their mission is the Phoenix Indian Center. Founded in 1947, it is the oldest American Indian non-profit organization of its kind in the United States. The Native American community is a large part of Phoenix, with 22 federally recognized Native American tribes.

If you would like to donate individually, please use the QR code:

Cover

This cover has had a few alterations. Bobooks created the original cover, but then I decided the book should match the rest of the series. I turned back to Abir Hasan, who drew the original covers for books one and two. I used the Bobooks as an alternate cover, but also created my version as a third variation of the cover. I planned to sell the third cover only at book signings. Since then, Nyssa Iniguez has redesigned the cover, and is the current series artist.

Dedication

The book's dedication includes the names of family members included in prior books. Also mentioned, my friends Marsha & Ronda, with whom I have shared many traveling adventures. My good friends Tim & Aaron. We went to college together, have battled against each other in fantasy football for now thirty-three years, and they always keep it real with me. I mentioned Loren Coleman, one of the most prominent cryptozoology researchers in the world. I appreciate his help in some of the background of the cryptids in this series. Derek Hayes, not only is an excellent podcast host and makes frequent television appearances in paranormal and cryptid shows, but he helped me get my first book in his Cryptid Crate subscription service, and put me in contact with his friend at Odd 13 Brewery when I was looking for book signing events. Scott, Mekala, and Jason are from Freetail Brewing in San Antonio. Scott was the brewery's founder and was the first person to reach out to me about my book and offer to have a book signing event. Last, David Landau. He was a good man and a coworker. We unfortunately lost him to cancer prior to the original publication of this book. He was always great for a story and marketing advice. He was a talented chef, too.

Chapter 1

Goldfield is a cool area just outside of Phoenix. I enjoy visiting there, even on down to Tortilla Flat. If you haven't been to a ghost town, this is convenient if you are visiting the Phoenix area.

Chapter 2

The quinceañera in chapter two reflects my daughter, Karmina's own quinceañera. Like everything else in this series, an included event actually took place on the date detailed in the book. Her quinceañera took place on this exact date and at Pearl's Banquet Hall. Her dress was pink and black, she had a mariachi, as well as Banda La Finikera. There was no ghostly camel in the back alley, but the basin where the camel sighting occurs in the book is behind Pearl's • At the end of the chapter we see Kareem enjoying a beer at Friends & Allies Brewing Company. He searches for strange animals in Phoenix and gets multiple hits. One mentions a turtle man creature. Originally, in this book I was going to create my own cryptid. At first, it was The Salt River Centaur, which lived on the grounds near the Salt River. Then it became the Tempe Turtle Man. I knew I wanted to do the Loveland Frog next, and I felt a turtle man was too close to a frog man. He also finds mention of a winged creature chasing a poor local author. In the original publishing of *Champ and a Bit of Sunshine*, there was a short story included in the back of the book. That story was about me struggling to write the next story. After no progress, I went out for some drinks in Chandler, and after leaving the bar, a winged cryptid called the Santanimal chased after me. Later, I revised the book and removed the short story. Maybe it will reappear somewhere someday.

Chapter 3

The group briefly mentions WrestleMania 32 in Arlington. I attended the event with my son Jorge, and the timing of the chapter coincidentally fit. • Real Ale Brewing Company's Phoenix Winter Ale foreshadows the location of the investigation to come in a few chapters.

Chapter 4

Kareem mentions he loves a good rodeo. That is a tie in to book five. • The stories about the Mesa Walmart and San Tan Vista Drinking Water Treatment Plant camels are true stories. At the time I started writing this story, I was unaware of them until I started researching the story. It is another odd element of the story that fell into place. • Kareem's familiarity with tracking the prints of a camel may also be a tie in to book five.

Chapter 5

The book is called the chocolate bunny, and in chapter 5, we have a sighting: "A lone brown rabbit… ", but that's not the Chocolate Bunny we're thinking about. • The incident with the tents and the reaction, I attempted to mirror off the actual events of the original Red Ghost sightings. • You might also spot odd bolding and capitalization in this chapter. It's not an error, it's a hidden message to my daughter. The chapter falls on her birthday.

Chapter 6

My first attempt at climbing Camelback Mountain, I also only reached about the saddle. • Kareem mentioned those rock-climbing classes back in Austin. I nearly missed that as I was writing it. It came back to me at the right time. •Although unintentional, the butterflies fluttering mentioned here reminds me of the beer cellar chapter in the *Chupacabra* called Flutters in the Basement. •The Carlsbad Tavern is not only a place for the habañero burger, but it we see the bat connection to Austin.

Chapter 7

The hike up A Mountain is a great, short hike if you are in the Tempe area. The World of Beer was my favorite hangout spot in Phoenix. Thanks to my friend J.P. Watts. • Vanilla Heat is my nickname, and I was the top loyalty drinker at WOB, so I added myself to the story. I received the nickname in Jamaica, so again an unexpected connection between Hot Pot Jamaican restaurant (one of my favorites), the look of Walt Richardson, and the nickname earned on the island. • Arizona has some bad laws regarding awarding people for loyalty points, and I rarely received those loyalty prizes after WOB got in trouble a few times. • There are strange sounds and activity in the WOB building. I have heard that from many former employees. The building has now changed hands multiple times, but I would love to do a paranormal investigation there. • Marble Hills University is a fictional university. • Bobbye mentions the Turtle Man of Tempe Town Lake and a centaur on the reservation. Even though I didn't create those cryptids as I had planned, I've introduced them a few times in these early chapters, so maybe we will see them again one day. • The Real Vanilla Heat beer is a real beer that I brewed with Cartel Brewing (now the Shop) and J.P. Watts at WOB. It was only available on draft. However, I added the canning system here so I could add it to the story.

Chapter 8

Here we get into some genuine history of camels in Arizona and introducing the Red Ghost. The Eagle Creek sighting is like Chapter 1 in Goldfield. The sighting in Clifton also mirrors Chapter 5 when the team camped near the Salt River.

Chapter 9

This chapter brought in several verifiable facts about Hi Jolly, his life, death, and some background into the Camel Corps. Georgette the camel is real, and the inscriptions on the signage in the graveyard are also real.

Chapter 10

The mention of a woodcarving of the Red Ghost is not fictional. The Cowboy Artists of America have a piece on their web page dated September 30, 2016, that shows this piece. • The mention of the original 1950s Ghost Rider helps introduce the connection to how the Red Ghost came back to life. It was also my original idea for the cover. I wanted it to look like that issue of the comic with the Red Ghost leaping from the open grave, the skeletal rider on its back, and cactus in the background instead of trees. • Mizoo Hastings shot the Red Ghost in real life, and in the town of Queen Creek, there is a Hastings Farms subdivision. The two do not actually relate, but I thought it made a good tie-in to the story if they did.

Chapter 11

The lawn ornaments in Cheyenne's yard, bipedal frogs from Ohio foreshadow Book 4. We also learn about Tegan's phobia of frogs. • The appearance of a jackalope at the Wren House Brewery is real, and ties in to the ongoing joke throughout the series of Carson's and jackalopes.

Chapter 12

The accounts of Dreamy Draw are actual stories and rumors of the area and dam. There are stories of people who hear a humming sound from the dam.

Chapter 13

This is the exploration of Queen Creek and the Hastings Farm subdivision. I used to live in this area, just passed the olive mill and orchards mentioned. • The brewery mentioned in the house was real and the Tangelo IPA was excellent. They have since closed.

Chapter 14

This was a lengthy chapter where we finally got the spring training game the investigators had planned in Book 2 • Sun Devil Liquor was an impressive place, especially the downstairs where the group meets Johnny Stamps. I had a cool date there once, and another time, I felt an unknown presence tap me on the shoulder. It was hard enough that I thought it was my friend who I saw start to come down the stairs, but when I turned around, he was still on the stairs and no one was behind me.

Chapter 15

The major action in the story and a bit of witchcraft thrown in to combat the supernatural spell of the Red Ghost. • The Preserve mentioned is one of my favorite spots in town.

Chapter 16

A return to the dam to pick up files and other items will play a role in multiple books to come. • As I have already written book four, items from this chapter do come into play in that book.

Chapter 17

Another appearance from our friend Vanilla Heat on the way out of town. Why not? He's such a great guy.

Beer List

There are some Texas beers mentioned at the beginning of the book, but the focus is on Phoenix, a few from Tucson, and Flagstaff. The Phoenix beer scene is still doing well today and winning more beer festival awards.

Scenes From The Road

This is a small selection of photos from breweries that allowed me to visit and hold a book signing in 2018. I hope that I can get back to doing more events soon.

Photo Challenge

Another way I wanted to make this series interactive was to use one of those daily photo challenges, consisting of a word or phrase related to the book. Readers could post a daily photo on their Instagram page with the hashtag **#chupacabradailyphotochallenge** and we could see what other readers are posting. I will start this up in January 2023. Check out my Instagram page for details: **mark_trollinger.**

Selfie Locations

If you picked up the reissue of the *Chupacabra* or *Champ*, you are familiar with this section of mentioned selfie locations throughout the book. I recommend you take a selfie at these locations and upload to social media sites using **#chupacabraselfiechallenge** to build a community and make it more realistic. Even though only one book was about the chupacabra, it has become a mascot of the entire series.

If you missed the locations in the story, here is a list including in this book:

1. At summit of Camelback Mountain (Paradise Valley)
2. Georgette the Camel (Quartzsite, AZ)
3. Hi Jolly's grave (Quartzsite, AZ).
4. Our Lady of Guadalupe Catholic Church (Guadalupe, AZ)
5. Dreamy Draw Dam (Phoenix, AZ)
6. Beer at Baseball game (any game; bonus for spring training)
7. Arizona Wilderness (Gilbert, AZ)

Sound Booth

I spend a lot of time listening to music when I write. During the writing of this book, I spent a lot of time listening to:

Snailmate: I saw these guys first perform at a Mega Ran concert. They have a unique sound that grew on me. Now I see them live as often as I can.

Mega Ran: For me, easily the King of Phoenix in the rap genre. You may see him touring the country or appearing on wrestling shows. I highly recommend the RNDM album.

As I did with the first two books in this series, I created a Spotify playlist of songs to get you in the mood. This one is a bit of a varied mix:

Red Ghost Spotify Playlist